THE
SNAKE
GAME

THE
SNAKE
GAME

a novel by WAYNE JOHNSON

Alfred A. Knopf   New York   1990

A NOTE ON THE TYPE

This book was set in Caledonia, a face designed by W. A. Dwiggins
(1880–1956). It belongs to the family of printing types called "modern
face" by printers—a term used to mark the change in style of type
letters that occurred about 1800. Caledonia borders on the general
design of Scotch Roman, but is more freely drawn than that letter.

Composed by Creative Graphics, Inc., Allentown, Pennsylvania.
Printed and bound by Fairfield Graphics, Fairfield, Pennsylvania.
Designed by Mia Vander Els.

NOV 2 6 1990

For Pasquale,

who has no idea what he started;

and for Karen,

who helped make it possible

Niwa'wacke'abog'
We'wendji'djiwun'

A bubbling spring
Comes from the hard ground

—Ojibway song, as recorded by
  Frances Densmore

Contents

Acknowledgments

I wish to thank the following institutions and individuals for their help: The Copernicus Society of America (and James A. Michener, whose grant was a great help to me) and The Henfield Foundation, for financial support; Jane Smiley, for her enormous energy; James Alan McPherson, for his insight and direction; and Madison Smartt Bell, for his encouragement.

I would also like to acknowledge my indebtedness to Frances Densmore, whose ethnological studies on Chippewa music and custom were invaluable to me; and to Anastasia Shkilnyk, whose work *A Poison Stronger Than Love* confirmed what I had already seen.

THE
SNAKE
GAME

GAMA'GIWE'BINIGOWIN (The Snake Game)

1951 It had all started as something completely innocuous, a joke in a bar and some tough talk, and now the three men sat in the truck overlooking the school, a knee-deep pile of ducks and three shotguns in back.

"What are we waiting for?" Joe, the driver, said.

Joe's brother, Litani, straddled the floor shift, staring out the windshield.

"Don't ask me," he said.

Osada glanced down at the school, followed the road ahead to where it forked and a thin, nearly weed-covered track sloped down to a line of tall poplars. The poplars flanked the school in back; a lake stretched flat and blue for miles in front.

"Hey," Joe said. He hung his arm out the window and waved on the car behind. "Just think of it this way, Od, think of that bastard's face when we pull up front with all these ducks."

Osada shook his head.

"Come on, say something," Joe said. "You're drivin' me crazy, you old coot."

Behind them Strong Ground and Hodie stood against the car, smoking.

"Look," Joe said.

"You're not thinking," Osada said.

"About what?"

Osada didn't trust himself to say anything now. In the bar that night, all he had said was, "Sons of bitches won't let my boy alone, either," and it had all just taken off.

"What am I not thinking about?" Joe said.

Osada took a deep breath, and exhaling, shifted against Litani, and the boy pulled himself in tighter.

Joe peered through the windshield, calculating.

"I'll drive into the lot like usual, head over to the lake side, and when he's got his paws on the goods the rest happens. You tell me. Just what *could* go wrong? If someone comes out"—Joe tossed his head back—"we'll just say we're turnin' around. Dead end and all that."

The cab was quiet, the motor ticked with heat.

"I mean, look at it this way. If it wasn't me, it'd be somebody else. Tell me it isn't so," Joe said.

Osada opened the glove compartment. It was full of crumpled paper and fuses. He poked at the tangle there, thinking. It was true, what Joe said. Osada couldn't argue it.

"Joe," he said, slamming the compartment shut. "Who else?"

"What does it matter?" Joe said.

"It matters a lot."

Joe poked Litani in the side. "Get in the back of the truck," he said.

The sun broke over the hill behind them and Litani walked back to the others.

"All right," Osada said. "Now. Tell it."

Joe rubbed his chin; it made a thin scratching noise.

"It's all of us here, Od," Joe said, turning, facing Osada. "It's everybody. All us younger ones. It's the way you gotta live now," he explained, his hands widespread, imploring. "I told you that before. And it isn't just Morton buyin' either. There's a hundred places in town'll take whatever we bring in. Christ, Od—"

Osada stared up into the headliner. Water stains ran across it like spiders. Joe's voice rambled on. Osada pulled back the door handle, stepped out into the road.

"Goddammit," Joe said. He hit the dashboard with the palm of his hand. "You don't listen to a goddamn thing you don't want to, do you?"

Osada craned his head around.

"Four honks," Joe said.

Osada swung the door shut, then bent through the window, into the cab. Joe slipped back across the seat, gripped the steering wheel.

"Hey," he said, grinning.

"You make me sick," Osada said.

Od.

He was a quiet man, a husband, a father, a canoe builder before the Lund company did away with his business, the son of a canoe builder, who had in turn been the son of a canoe builder, back twelve generations to the time before the *Men-of-the-Swinging-Crosses* and the fur traders. For his age, nearly fifty winters, he was old. He had survived the pox, bitter-cold winters, and alcohol. He had survived leaky roofs, bad diet, and bad teeth. Like some tough weed, he had grown, had held his life together through two relocation projects and an ill-matched marriage, had built wooden rowboats when no one wanted canoes, and when the aluminum boats came, went to the Sawhill company, to make furniture. Couches, chairs, dressers, bed sets. This, his talented hands and his ability to endure, he attributed to his *manito*, his guardian spirit, and he carried in a pouch an eagle's feather, the claw of an eagle, and a fragment of an eagle's skull. And always, in the product, the desk, the cupboard, the claw-footed table, there was something special, and he carved into everything he made an eagle's wing where no one would see it. An eagle's wing and the trunk of a cedar.

Od. Osada. Big Cedar.

A member of the Grand Medicine Society, a Mide. A man of the Big Piney Reservation. A craftsman.

He was a man set in time between something he did not fully know, the life his father Amous, Little Bee, had cried for and had given to him as best as he could, and the life he had learned of at the reservation school. There were Jesus and Mary and Joseph, priests, incense, and incantations in a language that wasn't even the language of the whites, and there was The Great Spirit, lying quiet on the waters of the lake, the Great Silence ringing in his ears. There were the stories his teachers had told him: deer and beaver and moose without spirit, the lake without Na'mbiza, the water monster; and there was the slow mechanical turning of all things, actions, all with equal and opposite reactions. But in the end, as a boy he had spent more time out on the lakes learning the old ways, harvesting rice, fashioning birch containers for berry picking, running the trap lines in winter, and finally learning the craft of canoe making when his father, Amous, thought he was ready.

"Listen," he said to his son, Red Deer.
The boy put his ear to the ground. "What am I listening for?"
"Just listen."

Now the boy could make a snare the old way, and a deadfall, could read the lake bottom and knew where the fish would bite. He spoke a broken tongue of the old language, and went so fast with the new. He loved the old stories, and told them to other children, could tell how Hare had brought the People fire on his back, and how the original five clans—the Awaus-e, Bus-in-aus-e, Ah-ah-wauk, Noka, and Waub-ish-ash-e—had risen with the coming of the visitors from the great deep. He knew the dances, and could sing the songs.

Osada had spared nothing in the boy's education, and the others, his father, Amous, his wife, Martha Blue Feather, and Old Man Muskeg, who had given the boy his name, had helped.

It had been the way then. Osada and his brothers, Akik and Mitigwab, and their wives and children, in the winter, up on the trap lines; spring, summer, and fall, fishing, hunting, rice gathering. Around Treaty Day they had come down to be with the others, for the gun salute, the Powwow, and the payment of treaty money, but then they were off by themselves again, out in the bush.

. .

"Listen," Osada said.

And the boy put his ear to the ground. "I don't know what you want me to hear," he said.

Osada took the boy's hand and spread it, fingers outstretched, on the ground.

"Flesh and blood," he said.

It was a difficult lesson to teach the boy now, because in his heart Osada felt this new land was evil. Against all their better judgment, the people at Big Piney had taken up the government's offer for a new reserve, and had moved onto Turtle Lake.

The move had been a disaster.

No one liked the new site, the muddy lake and the weed-choked channel out of it. On Turtle Lake the light always seemed hazy, smoky, and the Department had built the houses in tight, cramped rows just up from the beach. There had been no provisions for gardens, and the reserve sat in a hollow, and when it rained the water collected in fetid-smelling pools.

An old woman, the daughter of a chief, claimed she had seen someone surfacing on the lake.

There had been some talk about it. Some said it was *Machu-Manitou* the old woman had seen, the dark spirit. Some said the old lady needed a new pair of glasses, that she had probably just seen someone in a boat out there.

Osada had laughed with the others, but they had all laughed uneasily, full of apprehension, and they had finally settled on the nearby town, Kenora, as the source of all the disturbance. So they ran a corridor of fence around the north border of the reserve, miles of barbed wire and deadfall, bolstering themselves from the outside. They built a new lodge, storage houses for rice, and deep wells, for clean water. Osada arranged for shipments of lumber from Sawhill and haggled for fair prices, a torment which was nearly beyond him. He drew up plans and estimated material costs. He worked incessantly, as though the *Windigo*, the man-eater, were at his back. The new reserve came together slowly. Disputes broke out, family conflicts, but there had been hope, and a future.

And then the roads came.

The roads brought the curious in, the greedy, the angry. The roads brought electricity, radio, the war. The roads brought frame houses, cars, outboards, alcohol. Money.

The roads wove like snakes through the reservation, broke the clan lines, cut the land apart.

But it was school that finally shattered the cycle of the old life. Where before they had moved north for the winter, had trapped beaver, mink, otter, now they stayed on the reservation so their children could attend classes. Buses took them into town now. A new law required it. The new law forced Osada and his brothers off the trap lines, forced them all off, did away with their winter income. And with the new poverty came this thing, welfare.

At first they were drunk with it, then sick.

No one went untouched.

"I saw Two-Men-Walking going in to school," Red Deer said in the yard. He laughed, then traced a zigzag on the ground. "He was walking like this." The boy spun in a circle and collapsed on the ground.

Osada reached out and held the boy's jaw.

"Don't laugh," he said.

Things happened.

"A ten-year-old guide?" the businessman said.

Osada said nothing, and the man, a scowl on his face, got into the boat with Red Deer.

"He won't steer you wrong," Osada said.

In the old boathouse Osada leveled the new floor joists, then secured them with eight-penny nails. Hours went by and it got dark, and he couldn't see to work and he waited in the mouth of the boathouse. From shore, Osada heard them laughing. It was a kind of laughter he had heard before, drunken, cajoling.

"Where's the goddamn dock?" the man shouted.

The boat drifted out of the darkness. Red Deer stood in back, balancing himself with an oar.

"Look!" he said, blinking and straining under the weight of the stringer of walleyes he held up.

Winter, up in the Big Piney Narrows, they shot a moose, and dragging it across the bay to Turtle Lake, the rack burrowed into the snow and Red Deer tired.

"Wait," he said, his hands on his knees.

The lights of Wheeler's lodge came on and they hauled the moose over the broken crust. It was a fine, red dusk, and in the lodge they drank coffee and told how they had tracked the moose. There were a handful of new men up, hunting whitetail, and Howard Wheeler told how years before the deer had come down to the lodge, to a salt lick.

"It was like shooting fish in a—"

"It's time," Osada said.

Red Deer shuddered.

"Let the boy stay," Wheeler said. "He's tuckered out and it's awfully cold out there."

Osada turned to look through the lodge windows; down past the dock the lake was one long black stretch.

"Mo'kaun," Osada said to Red Deer, sunrise; and to the others he said, "Early."

In the morning, Osada and Strong Ground, a cousin, crossed the bay to Wheeler's. In back they looked at the moose.

"Damn fine!" Strong Ground said, slapping the moose's head. "Hell of a rack!"

They went around to the front.

Osada whistled. "Howard!" he shouted.

There was a commotion inside, and they bumped through the dining hall door. The men had stacked the tables and chairs against the walls. In the center of the room, Red Deer circled on a bicycle, his face striped with lip-stick, some feathers stuck in his hair. He rolled around to the door, and when he saw Osada, he fell, tumbled off the bicycle, and the men who hadn't seen Osada and Strong Ground roared with laughter.

Strong Ground got his arm under Osada's and bent it up and back. The pain of it was incredible.

"Let go," Osada said.

He took to spending more time with Red Deer after that day, brought him over to Old Man Muskeg's. The old man told the boy stories, about Winabojo, and The People. Tragic stories, funny stories, frightening stories. The old man would talk for hours, his hands a thousand shapes—running deer, young maidens, roaring flames. And when the old man tired of talking he loved to play games—mikazin'ata'diwin, the moccasin game, or bu'gese'win, the plate game. He took a delight in these afternoon contests, and gambled shrewdly. He played each with enthusiasm. But of all the games he loved the snake game best.

Gama'giwe'binigowin.

He had a passion for it, and Osada admired his skill.

"Watch!" the old man would say, throwing the sticks up in the air, flashing.

"What's he doing?" Red Deer would ask.

"Watch," Osada would say.

The old man was crafty, and he carved his own sticks. Losers had accused him of fitting lead into their bellies, holding the sticks too long when he threw them, or rubbing magic on them. Now no one would play with Old Man Muskeg, because in his old age he had gone off a little, and sometimes took things he shouldn't.

It had been like that the first time Osada had played him, nearly twenty years before.

"For your ring," Old Man Muskeg had said.

"This?" Osada had said, pointing to his wedding ring.

Even then the old man was a talker. He talked nonstop. He talked about the flood, and the ruined rice harvest; he talked about his son, Tossed-About-the-Winds, and his problems with his wife. His hands were always moving and he noticed things around him. A bird, someone walking, anything.

"Over there," he would say.

Osada had tried to ignore him, but it put him in a nervous

mind. He had considered himself an expert at the game, had held the sticks with great confidence, only, that afternoon, he threw the sticks too high or too low, or put too much spin on them. Belly up, belly down. Four sticks, bright red tongues on the end.

"You want to play to the end?" Old Man Muskeg had asked.

It was close, but not too close, Osada leading.

"Of course, you old coot," Osada said, poking the old man with a stick.

Old Man Muskeg shrugged, then smiled, his eyes bright.

"Watch," he said.

Three tosses. Three belly up/belly down. High score.

"I win," he said.

Osada had sat there on the blanket, dumbfounded, and Old Man Muskeg had touched his knee.

"You keep the ring," he had said, then smiled again and tapped his forehead. "Only, don't forget."

And he hadn't. Now, when he played with Old Man Muskeg, he never wagered anything of value, and he watched very carefully when Red Deer was drawn into another of the old man's intentionally bad runs.

"You're cheating," Red Deer would say, his voice changing, high, low.

And the old man, his eyes wrinkling with pleasure, would say, "Tell me how?"

There was so much said then, at Old Man Muskeg's—laughter, dark jokes, talk of magic and medicine, and the power of illusion. The old man was able to talk to Red Deer in a way Osada couldn't, teased him about his cracking voice, his sudden gain in height.

But on the walk home Osada and Red Deer were always silent and they suffered at times.

"Stop watching me," Red Deer would say.

It got so he stayed at school to escape it—he left in the morning and didn't come home till evening, when they ate—and Osada didn't ask him what he did there. He carried his books in a canvas bag now, and sat in a corner reading. Martha teased him about the girls on the reserve, but he didn't listen.

"We must talk," the principal of the reserve school wrote in a letter.

On the surface, nothing bad came of it.

The boy didn't want to spend afternoons at Old Man Muskeg's anymore, but he helped Osada, could swing a hammer and use a saw. He shot a deer up in the Nin'godonen'djigun, the one-swallow-land, dressed it out and hauled it back to the house himself.

His voice no longer cracked, and he put on weight.

It might have been a good time, only, now this thing hung between them. *When will you fast?* Osada wanted to ask the boy. *When will you take your guardian?*

It was something most boys were too eager to do. Most boys had to be held back. It was something even more important than the *naming,* something that would give the boy his spirit power.

Osada waited, silent.

He waited through the winter, reasoned it was too cold, the fast too dangerous in the snow. And when spring came, there were the rains, and he waited till summer. Summer came, hot, busy, and he thought fall, the smell of burning leaves, the eagles migrating, would be a better time. And when fall came there was no more waiting because the change was fully upon Red Deer.

"Buck," Osada said, meeting Red Deer at the bus.

They walked together up the rutted, sandy road. Osada kept his hands in his pockets; his thoughts were at war. He thought of ways to say what he had to say to Red Deer, tossed off one for another, each one wrong somehow, the wrong color, the wrong sound, and he sensed now, beneath it all, his own fear.

"What is it?" Osada finally said.

Red Deer squared his shoulders, as if to speak, then stooped, squared his shoulders again, then stooped, and when he had drawn himself up a third time, he said, "I don't want to take the fast," as though he had practiced saying it for months.

. . .

The boy would not stop running. For a week he had been out on the back roads, naked but for his brown shoes and the old shorts he had gotten at school.

"Where are you going?" Osada would say.

"Out," the boy invariably shot back.

Today he was out early. Osada watched him from the big three-story house he was building off the rise on the south shore. Hanging a door frame, he tried to figure what could have steered the boy away. He thought of the businessman, that night in the boat. He thought of the thing that had happened in the lodge, and remembered the laughter. But always he came back to the school, and he puzzled at the note he had gotten but had never answered.

We must talk.

Talk about *what?* The last time he had been in to see Morton, the principal, had been over a fight a boy had started with Red Deer. The boy had been calling Red Deer names, and Red Deer had hit him a good one. Thinking about it now, it still made Osada angry. He saw himself in Morton's office, Morton sitting behind his desk, smoking, jabbing his cigarette in the air. His face had been puffed tight with self-importance, and he had treated Osada as though he were deaf, or an idiot.

"You're going to have to teach your boy to control himself," he had said, nearly shouting.

Osada eyed the door frame.

He set a pine wedge on the right side and brought the door frame even with another nail. He got on one knee and sighted up both sides. It had been a pretty crooked deal all around, he thought.

At the Bull Pen in Kenora, Osada took the letter from his pocket. He closed the booth door, but the racket outside still came through. Strong Ground watched him from a table. Osada dialed the number on the back of the letter and waited, the phone slick in his hand.

"Hello," the voice said. "Hello. Hello?"

Osada hung the phone up and the coin rattled in the machine. He lifted his beer over the crumpled directory and drank from it, then dropped in another coin.

"Hello," the voice said. "Hello. Hello?"

"Who is it?" a woman's voice said in back.

"I'm going to hang up," the man said.

"I got a letter here from you," Osada said. "About Red Deer." There was silence on the other end. Now it was Osada's turn. "Hello?" he said.

"I'm surprised you're calling," Morton said.

At the table Strong Ground and Hodie, a friend from Sawhill, were arm wrestling now. Their arms went one way and then the other.

"Why?" Osada said.

"Why? I must have written to you *ten times.*"

"I got but one letter here," Osada said. The man was making him mad and he didn't like it. "Let's not argue. You just tell me what it's about."

There was a hissing on the other end, and Osada shook the receiver.

"Look," Morton said. "I've got a school to run here and I can't waste my time on any nonsense. Your boy has been impossible to work with lately. He won't read, won't sit, won't do anything in class. . . . I had him in my office I don't know how many times but he wouldn't say a thing. I finally had to get it out of our nurse he was down there so many times."

Osada pressed the phone to his ear. The fight at the table had gotten out of hand and Hodie was shouting.

"Listen—" Morton finally said, his voice confiding. "I know this fast thing is important to you and all, but your boy thinks there's something out there, Mancho . . . *something,* and I've had the damndest time proving to him there isn't. He's terrified there's something out in the lake that's going to—"

Osada couldn't hear for all the shouting. A crowd had gathered around the table and Strong Ground had pinned Hodie's arm and now Hodie poked at him.

"I can't hear you," Osada said.

"I'm saying you can't do this."

"What can't I do?"

"Force your boy to starve himself out on that lake."

Osada felt himself stiffen. He ran the receiver along the scar on his cheek.

"You don't tell me what to do with my boy," he said.

The woman was on the other end, asking something.

"No," Morton said, "I said 'No.' " Then, to Osada, his voice driving, "Look—I just can't let this nonsense go any further," he said. "Do you understand? I've spoken with the people in the Department and—"

Osada hung the receiver up. He stood in the booth, his arms crossed over his chest, and when Strong Ground tapped his glass on the booth window, Osada slammed his fist into the booth wall.

At the table, Strong Ground and Hodie sat opposite each other, still fuming. Joe Big Otter, a reservation sharpie, raised his glass.

"We should fix that fucker's wagon," Joe said.

They all nodded. Joe took a gulp off his beer, pointed with the mug.

"You know what I think of those sons-of-bitches?" Joe said.

"You tell us, Joe," Strong Ground said.

Osada looked down into his beer. A Mide, he usually did not drink, but tonight was an exception. He tried to shut out the arguing—it was always *fighting* now—but Joe was at it again, Slick Joe, Smart Joe, and he raised his head from his beer.

"Instead of calling it the *Department of Indian Affairs and Northern Development*," Joe said, "they oughtta call it *Dead Indians Ain't No Danger*. That's what I think."

There was a puff of affirmation around the table.

Strong Ground flicked a bottle cap at Joe. "You know what you are, Joe?" he said. "You're just a goddamned genius, that's what you are."

Litani, his narrow shoulders swinging, came through the back and Joe pulled out a chair for him.

"You're too young, punk," Joe said, slapping his brother on the back and handing him a beer.

Osada caught Litani's eye and the boy looked away.

They all got another round, and Joe paid.

"On me," Joe said. He tossed the bills on the table, Osada sizing up the roll he pushed back into his pocket.

It was late now, and they had all had a few too many.

"Last call!" the bartender shouted.

"Don't get holy on us, Al," Joe shot back. "Do you want our money or not?"

"I'm closing up in fifteen," Al said.

"Just more of the same old shit," Hodie said. He picked up his glass and drained it. "If you don't get it coming you get it going."

Joe slid back from the table and stood. "Speaking of going," he said.

"Ah, the hell with you," Hodie said.

Osada watched Joe stumble into the Men's. Joe had started them off on The Department, and they had gotten back to Morton and the reserve school, and now they were stuck there like a needle on a ruined record. It was humiliating to think about it. At one time or another they had all talked to Morton—Hodie and Strong Ground had sons in school, too—had had the cigarette poked in their faces. Morton liked to pull rank, and he was always reminding them of The Law. To all of them he seemed impregnable, unapproachable, unreasonable, unsympathetic. He always brought The Department in behind him, and it seemed there was no way to fight it.

"I'll have your Treaty Money cut," he would say. "I'll have the police come in."

"I'd like to knock his goddamned teeth out," Strong Ground said, a cruel smile playing across his face. "That bastard wouldn't last five minutes with me. I'd shove one of his cigarettes right up his ass."

Litani laughed. "I'd like to see it," he said.

The look on Litani's face surprised Osada, and something sank in his chest. Litani sounded like the others now—bitter, angry, lost, and Osada thought about the time, seven years ago, when Joe's and Litani's father had been killed in a car wreck—their mother had gone long before—and he had taken Litani in, till

Joe could get things in order. Back then Litani had been quiet and shy, a watcher and thinker. He had lacked Red Deer's toughness, and Osada had worried about him, had taken special pains to help him. Osada had shown him how to make a bow-string the old way, with a snapping turtle's neck, had taken him over to Old Man Muskeg's with Red Deer. The boys had gotten along like brothers, and just when it had seemed Litani would stay for good, Joe had come for him.

"Tell Joe he's not going," Martha had said.

Osada remembered how Litani had trudged over to Joe's truck; it was something he would never forgive himself. The boy had been too fragile for Joe.

"That Morton's an asshole," Litani said now.

Osada watched him toss back his beer. He looked tough now, mean—he wasn't much older than Red Deer, five short years—but his eyes still had that hooded, hurt look.

Joe swung back to the table.

"What do you say?" he said, holding up his glass.

"Poison," Osada said. "It's all poison."

The bar closed and they each bought another six and went down to the lake. In the dark and surrounded by the reeds they stopped joking and then they drank. They huddled together for warmth, and with Strong Ground on one side and Joe on the other, Osada floated. He hadn't been drunk for a long time, and he drifted along now as if none of it had happened, the relocation and all the bad times. He could almost believe it now. On the shore it was dry and chilly but with all the good smells, water and wood smoke and tobacco. It made him think of a time he and his father had sat on shore like this, when he had been just a boy. He remembered a song his father had sung.

"Listen," Osada said. The song skipped over his tongue, grew familiar, and then he sang.

A'niwe'we,	the sound is fading away
Na'nowe'we,	it is of five sounds
Wa'naki'meniwa,	freedom

Gi'niwe'we,   the sound is fading away
Na'nowe'we,   it is of five sounds

He was hardly able to feel his mouth for drink, but the song sounded right.

"Remember that?" he said, and he sang it again.

"You shouldn't sing that," Joe said.

The moon rose bright and clear over the lake.

"You're gonna hate me—" Joe said to Osada, "but goddammit, I can't sit here no more."

Joe stood, weaving. He brushed off the back of his pants and went down the path toward the reserve. He stopped, tossed his shoulders as if shaking something from his back, then spun around and stood there, his arms at his sides. Osada couldn't have pictured anything more pitiful if he had tried.

"Come on back here, Joe," he said. "I don't know what you've done but come on back here."

Joe tried to hold himself still. He was struggling to say something.

There was a strange stillness now. Hodie was asleep, his head cradled on his arm, Litani had wandered off upshore, and Strong Ground was lying on his back, a beer balanced on his chest.

"What if I told you there was a way to get to that bastard and get him good," Joe said. "What would you say? Would you do it?"

"Come on and sit down, Joe."

"I mean it," Joe said. "What do you say?"

Osada scrambled down the hill behind the school, cut through the row of poplars. His legs felt strong, but were filled with a wiry, almost uncontrollable energy. He felt like a fool and he felt dangerous, and he watched the school now, behind the last tree in the row.

A peal of laughter lifted out through an open window.

His shoulder was wet. A wide swatch of sap ran down from a

crack where two branches had grown off the trunk at odd angles. His hands were shaking and his mind shot off in different directions. He waited for the horn, and he thought about Joe and wondered now if Joe were right after all—things were always different in daylight. He batted his hands against his thighs but the shaking wouldn't stop.

Everything seemed off now, wrong.

Before first light they had all gone out in the truck.

"Let's get the birds," Joe had said, skidding to a stop downwind of the slough.

They had crept up on the birds, and then, in one vicious spree had shot them all dead on the water, had pinned them down under pumpfire.

Osada had strode back to the truck, furious.

"You old son-of-a-bitch!" Joe had yelled after him. "How the hell did you think we'd get the birds? Call 'em down here to eat out of our hands? What the hell are you so goddamned righteous about, huh?"

A door opened in back, and a squarish woman in a white dress came out. She put her hands on her hips and looked one way and then the other. The woman sniffed at the air, seemed satisfied, then went back through the door.

Where were they? What was taking so long?

The time was endless now, and the whole mess spun in his brain, a circle of fear, humiliation, and hate. He wondered if he should have done this, come out here with Joe and the others, and he pictured that night a week ago, his crossing over. It ran like a wheel in his head. He couldn't stop it now.

"Come on, Joe," he had said, and Joe's face had lost its pitiful expression, had become something fierce.

"We'll blackmail the bastard," Joe said.

For a moment Osada had been confused. Blackmail? And then he'd remembered the roll of bills Joe pushed into his pocket, and the times he'd seen Joe in the bush, the truck bouncing along with a tarp over the bed.

"You're a poacher," Osada said.

"Wake up!" Joe had shouted.

Even now, thinking about it here, in daylight, it startled Osada. It made his heart skip, and then the rest followed. Joe had let go with it all.

"You think it'll be any different going in there to talk?" Joe had said. "It's *always* the same old shit! You think you're sorry for me, you with your sad face . . . but just *look* what they're doing to *you!*"—Joe had pointed an angry finger at him—"Look at you! You can hardly feed yourself! You work yourself half-dead and then the sons-of-bitches pay you like dirt! WAKE UP! Don't you see? It's a game! Just a goddamned game! You think they'll ever play by your rules?"

Joe had torn at the air with his fists.

"I've given you . . . Something Big! A way to play his game. And now you sit there—Sit there!—judging *me!* But I'm going to ask you something, and you'd better think about it. Who's pitiful here? Huh? Just *who's* pitiful here?"

Litani had stepped out from the trees up shore.

"For Christ's sake, Joe," Litani had said, his voice curt, angry. "Just leave him alone. Just leave him be."

Osada forced his back up the trunk of the poplar. His stomach turned. It was impossible. He struggled not to walk back up the hill. He was alternately filled with rage and self-loathing. He had to think of the thing that had driven him to this. Joe had made him see something he had been hiding from himself. While he had labored, had put his life into the things he made with not so much as a thank you or a wage he could live on, the others had taken what they could, had made better lives for themselves. The old life was dead. How could he not have seen this? What must all of them think of him now? What a fool he had been. It filled him with a deep, pitiless self-hatred, and he thought, *What I have given away!* Joe had offered him something. It ran against everything in him; "A game," Joe had said. Now he would take it back, as it had been taken from him, he thought. It was the only way.

The horn jabbed him like electricity.

Four long blasts.

He crossed the space between the row of trees and the school, then slipped through the back door and skirted the walls of the empty kitchen. He went up a hallway, then another, each long and full of echoes, and a panic seized him. Was he lost? He walked faster, felt the walls closing in on him, then recognized the office, the windows in front, and he opened the door, nodded to the woman at a typewriter.

"Family," he said, just the way Joe had told him to.

Off to the left Morton's door was open, and Osada stepped into the room and drew the door closed behind him. A haze of blue cigarette smoke hung under the ceiling. Morton looked up from his desk; he blinked, then pushed back his chair.

"Look out the window," Osada said.

The color went out of Morton's face and he spun around, raised the blinds. Joe had backed the truck up so the bed faced the office, the ducks heaped on the tailgate.

"We don't want any trouble," Osada said. "Hodie, me, and Mr. Jackson want our boys."

Morton looked out the window, then back at Osada.

"I'll call the Department," he said, bullying now. "Or better yet, the police."

"Go ahead," Osada said.

Morton tried to hold himself still. It carried into Osada and he hated the whole thing.

"Just send our boys out."

"This is insane."

"I don't have anything to say to you," Osada said.

"You can't do this," Morton said.

"What can't I do?" Osada said. It was like something had opened up in him, and he felt a tremendous energy, a desire to lean over the desk and throttle Morton. It frightened him, that he might do it, and he reached across the desk, picked up the phone.

"Here," Osada said. "Call the police."

"If anyone gets hurt—"

"You shut up," Osada said.

In a minute Morton was back with the three boys. Red Deer was the biggest of them by years. They looked frightened and they huddled together. No one said anything. They went up a short hallway to the front door. Hodie stood outside with an armload of ducks. They all went through now, Osada, Morton, and the three boys.

Across the parking lot Joe opened his door and got out of the truck.

"Hey!" he said.

Osada pointed with his chin. It was a horrible thing, but they were outside, it was nearly done.

"Get in the truck," Osada said to Red Deer.

Someone whistled. It came from behind them, and Osada turned, saw faces lining the windows. A hundred faces, white faces, Indian faces, the children there fighting for a look at what was going on in the parking lot.

"Joe!" Osada shouted.

Morton stood glaring at Joe. "Hey, Joe," he said, his hands on his hips. "How many you got?"

"Plenty," Joe said.

A squad car pulled up the drive, slid to a stop on the loose gravel; two men got out, one with a short rifle. Litani lifted a shotgun off the ducks in back and stepped off the gate.

"Joe!" he said, turning to face the squad car.

Osada felt something come up in his legs.

The officer with the rifle shot from the waist.

The shot carried Litani up and off his feet. The second shot hit him going down. The shots echoed across the lake, then rippled back, cracked like a whip.

Osada crossed the lot.

"Don't move him," someone shouted.

But Osada had already slipped his arms under Litani's back, was lifting him. He looked down into the boy's face, saw his own face there. The shots had hit him in the neck and back of his head. The boy's mouth opened, and something shook in Osada, shook him until his whole body tossed with it; it came up from his stomach, swelled in his throat, then tore out his mouth, howling.

THE
LOST
BOY

St. Paul, 1955 It is a drop of water in a pool of fear; his voice carries across the river and echoes back.

"Daaa-Neee!"

What had been concern minutes ago, is now something else, the tenor of the doctor's voice—high-pitched, a breaking strain in it—betraying him. *It isn't serious*, he tells himself, calling again, and when minutes have passed, he turns to his wife, Mary.

"He's got to be right around here," he says.

Above them, on River Road, traffic winds home as usual, an occasional blast of horn and rumble of heavier truck carrying down the steep embankment. Across the river, the lights are coming on in the high rises, the clouds over them tufts of brightly lit cotton.

Soon it will be snowing.

"What do you want to do?" the doctor says.

Mary knows he is saying it not so much out of not knowing what to do, but to take responsibility for what has happened now. And it isn't *really* his fault, anyway.

"What do *you* think?" she says.

Neal turns to his father, standing just back of him.

"What do you say, Jackie old boy, *Pops?*" he says.

It is all Neal can do to hold back the fear and anger in his voice. All afternoon Jack had criticized Neal, the boy, Mary, even the river. From the first, Jack had complained. The sandwiches weren't what they used to be; the soda was a crime at that price; Neal's son, Marty, shouldn't be wearing that silly hat.

"He's in his pioneer phase," Neal had said, bouncing Marty on his lap. "Aren't you, Danny Bee?"

But it made no difference; in the end Neal's father had passed judgment on one and all. They'd left Marty with Jack, for just a few minutes, to be by themselves, and now Marty is lost.

"Call the police," Jack says. "I think we should call the police," he says.

"Daaa-neee!" Neal calls.

Mary stoops to put her face in Jack's. He is a shortish, fine-boned man, with deep-set brown eyes, an aquiline nose, and a fussy, almost pert mouth. She can smell the cough drops on his breath, and under it something else.

"Show me where you were sitting."

"All right," Jack says.

Walking, he is planning, weighing how to go about this thing. *An error in judgment,* he thinks, crossing the field. He should not have come. But then again he hadn't known Mary would bring the boy. He doesn't like children—he was an only child himself—and he wonders at his son's having insisted on bringing the boy out here. It is a dark, damp place, the trees huge and overgrown, the nearly brown river moving sluggishly by.

"We haven't seen you in—who knows how long," Neal had said. "It'll be beautiful out. They say it might snow tonight."

He had hoped for a quiet, early evening, a ride up old River Road, a relief from his cramped apartment, only now he is caught up in it, their folly, and there is no extricating himself. They should not have left the boy with him, he thinks.

Everything was just fine until the boy.

No sooner than the two of them were down the path had the boy tugged at him so hard and started crying. Worst of all, he had lost his temper. He thinks about that now, carefully stepping up the path. Is the boy far enough along to tell?

He catches himself with his cane, hand on the muddy path.

"Up!" Neal says, pulling him to his feet.

But that's it, he thinks: the boy, run away, has fallen. Anything is possible. Children hurt themselves like that all the time.

The boy can hear them calling. He has no idea where he is, but he can hear them calling. He scrunches up his lip, pressing his palm to it. It is a familiar taste, blood, warm and salty. He's had nosebleeds. He is through crying, and in the mouth of the pipe he watches the trees, bright in the late evening sunlight, and feels the cold air blow. He is through crying and a certain determination grips him.

He will not go back.

That man had hit him. He was yelling things. As soon as his mother had gone away the man had hit him and then he had run and now he is bleeding.

He had done something wrong.

Would they punish him?

He shivers, his feet not even there. The pipe is cold, but a good place. And thinking that, the boy forces himself further up the dark pipe and the voices go away.

"Right here," Jack says, pointing to the cabin.

"Right here?" Neal asks. "What do you mean 'right here'? What the hell were you doing when he ran away?"

"I told you, *I fell.*"

"This is getting us nowhere," Mary says. "Which way did he run?"

"I didn't see," Jack says.

He is surprised at his having said it, and ashamed; he jabs at the ground with his cane, spies something and pokes through it with the nail on the end of his cane. The nail is for walking in winter, so the cane does not slip on the ice, but now, the cane up, the nail there with the paper pierced, it comes to him as a shock.

Neal eyes him strangely, or is it just *his thinking Neal is looking at him that way,* and he quickly flicks the paper off the nail and leans on the cane, the point firmly stuck in the ground, invisible.

Neal sweeps around the front of the cabin. The windows are broken and he goes through. Inside it smells of wood rot and cigarettes. He stumbles over bottles, newspapers, then is outside again.

"You say he's been gone—what? Ten minutes? He ran away just ten minutes ago?"

"Daaa-Neee!" he calls, the voice echoing back. "He's got to be right around here."

"Then why isn't he coming?" Mary says.

Starlings swoop down along the banks of the river like fast-moving smoke. Neal, Mary, and Jack search the area in widening circles, out from the cabin.

It is a strange feeling, seeing Jack stumbling along to his right. Neal has never done anything, really, with his father. It has been some twenty years since Neal's mother and Jack divorced, and it is only on occasions like this that he sees him, always some catastrophe. He thinks, disgusted with himself, here would be a way to repay Jack for his own lost boyhood.

If Marty—

But he shouldn't think that, he shouldn't think half of what he is thinking now. He is tired, bone tired, bored, raw with nervous anxiety. He feels like a fool yelling—is this really necessary?

Only charging through the grass toward the river and the old bridge, a part of him is frightened senseless.

Where the field narrows they stop. Neal brushes the sweat from his forehead. The grass tosses in waves.

"How *didn't* you see him?" he says to his father.

"I was on my back."

"He's no goddamn deer, you know. How fast can a three-year-old run in grass like this? You must have seen *something.*"

"I've told you."

"You've told me *nothing.*"

Jack turns up his collar. A strong wind is blowing up river. The clouds over the high rises have thickened, moving west like a shade over what is the last of a brilliant sunset.

"Did you hit him?" Neal says suddenly. "Did you hit my boy?"

"Neal," Mary says.

"Did you?" Neal says. He has been thinking it since he and Mary had come back up the path.

Jack sits. He is not as sharp as he once was, it was all a mistake, this outing. His mind locks up tight, and now, all he can do is sit silent, and when his son's hands are on his coat, he turns his head one way and then the other.

"No, no, no, no, no," he says.

But Neal is shaking him anyway, and the river bottom spins around him and he feels sick, Mary's voice in his ears:

"Neal, for God's sake. Stop it! Stop it, Neal!"

Neal stands away, breathing deeply. "*Ahhhch!*" he says, smacking his legs with his open hands.

"We've got to do something," Mary says.

"Just let me catch my breath, all right?"

"He might have run down—"

"He for goddamn certain *isn't* running." And turning to his father, he says, shaking his head, "You did hit him, didn't you?"

And as if it were just the two of them now, they stand, eyeing each other.

"Goddamn," Neal says.

He had hoped, somehow, things would be different. He had hoped, maybe, the pressures, the ones he had known as a boy, gone, would make way for something, anything between himself and his father.

But nothing has changed.

Now he remembers the time he had broken his arm, and things were so bad at home he had hidden in the closet. He'd hidden in the closet, behind the coats and jackets until they'd found him, his arm swollen, the bone sticking through the skin of his forearm, all of it swollen, blue streaks nearly to his shoulder.

"What the sam hell were you hiding in the closet for?" his father had shouted.

"He's hiding, Mary," Neal says. "That's what it is. He's hiding."

"What are you saying?" she says.

Neal and his father exchange glances. Jack is wearing his sorry face now. He is *really something*, Neal thinks. But he thinks of himself, too—it's one hell of a scene, he thinks.

"Daaa-Neee!" he calls.

"I'm not waiting here," Mary says. "You two can do whatever you *goddamn please*, but I'll have all of St. Paul down here if I have to."

"He's hiding, Mary," Neal says. And turning to his father, Neal puts his hand on his shoulder. "Just tell me."

"Don't confuse things," Mary says.

"Please," Neal says.

Mary holds her arms at her sides, imagines slapping Jack, a hard, solid smack across his face. But what she does is step closer, kneel in front of him, and he turns full around, away from her, and it chills her.

"*Oh my God!*" she says, and strides up the path, toward the upper road, tearing at branches.

He is colder now, shuddering.

"Daaa-Neee!" comes his mother's voice again.

It is a relief to hear it, he hasn't heard it for the longest time, only, now her voice has in it something so piercing he is pulled out from his hiding place as if on a string. His legs don't work right, and there are lights now, lots of them up the hill, and voices he does not recognize.

Up on the road, Jack sits in the squad car, head upright; like a pharaoh, Neal thinks. It is snowing heavily. Six men with flashlights comb the area. They are big flashlights, throw wide bluish-white beams in the snow, and then another squad car pulls up behind the first and they come down with the dogs.

"He doesn't like dogs," Neal says to the officer pointing the men away from the cabin.

"You want to wait till Christmas?"

The officer's retort has the impact of a blow. Mary is down with the first group of men.

"Bernie," the officer shouts. "Ed's comin' down with the dogs. The guy here's got the kid's hat." And to Neal now, seeing how he has overstepped his mark, the officer says, turning the cap in his hands, "Daniel Boone, huh? I got one of these for my kid, too. They love these damn things."

"He's a tough little kid," Neal says, "got a mind of his own."

"I got three."

"Second's on the way."

The officer whistles, surprised. "Should we bring her up?"

Neal shakes his head, "Wouldn't try it."

He is running again. Dogs, he can hear them. Jackie, the old man, had a dog. He'd tried to pet it, when it was at the dish, and it had nipped him. It had nipped him and then he had pulled on its tail and the dog had turned on him, not the same dog anymore, snarling. The dogs are closer, but he'll find another place to hide, only his legs are collapsing and the path is slippery.

Neal's legs carry him in circles with the dogs, Mary behind him, the dogs panting, the officers, blue jackets and black Sam Browne belts, ahead.

Big, heavy snowflakes turn down out of the clouds.

Everything, even this afternoon with Mary and Marty and his father, has the feel of something excruciatingly near, yet distant.

He realizes now he hasn't been like this in a long time, not since that night in Korea, when they came over the wall, and he had had to shoot, the men coming in tens and twenties, each the same, the surprised, then bewildered, then dead eyes. There had been everything in it, all he needed to know and live by, but he had done none of it.

THE SNAKE GAME

That night he had experienced fear so pure it made him see with a peculiar clarity; he hadn't experienced it again until now. Now each tree, the bark shaggy, oaks and maples, poplar, looms out at him. His legs turning under him, the blue lights cutting up the path, he is making deals with himself.

They will find his son; he will do what he knows he should do. Everything will be all right.

He believes, he believes, he believes.

The dogs tear at their leashes, howling, eager. The officer, Bernie, holds them back, but it is all excitement now, and dread, and they converge on what the dogs can smell is there by the side of the river.

He chooses this as the moment to stand.

The dogs will tear him to pieces, but there is his mother's voice, his father's, and lurching out of the grass, the silhouetted figures descending on him, he lets out a cry, charging forward, and is swallowed up into it all.

CHAMPION
OF THE
WORLD

1957 Drunk again, Joe Big Otter aims himself up the street, headed for the Bull Pen. He stops outside the Pen door to search his pockets for the money his brother Del gave him, and a brand new Chrysler pulls up to the curb, its fins in the rear like sharp wings. A slender woman in a smartly tailored tan dress slides out, and Joe stands by the parking meter waiting for her. At the meter, the woman nervously digs through her purse, and Joe leans toward her, feeling jolly.

"Hey," he says. "Hey, there."

The woman raises her head from her purse, her mouth open and her eyes staring. *Such pretty blue eyes.*

Joe smiles, his hand held over his heart.

"Will you marry me?" he says.

Looking over Joe's head, the woman waves, her arm outstretched, her hand tossing like a flag. A shoe salesman at Penny's steps out of the store, dapper, dressed in corduroy.

"Joyce," he yells. "That you?"

The woman waves again, in wide, desperate arcs.

"This is your last chance," Joe says, smiling his biggest, toothiest smile, sure the woman is verging on hysteria. "Here he goes," Joe says, and turning away with a shrug of his shoulders, he is headed up the street again, leaning into the wind, dirt swirling up off the street into his face.

Joe bumps through the door of the Bull Pen. The darkness inside is soothing. At the bar a large potbellied man polishes glasses, stacking them behind himself on a long wooden shelf.

The man glances up from the glass he is polishing, sees Joe, and shakes his head.

"No credit, Joe," he says.

"What the hell would *I* need credit for?"

The man lifts his head, reaches behind himself with the glass, and without looking at the shelf, places the glass in line with the others.

"So how's business, Al?" Joe says.

Al turns his head slowly, his mouth set tight, and points to the shelf.

"Missin' a few, huh?" Joe says.

Al dips another glass into the tub of water behind the bar. He wipes the glass with a washcloth, then dries it, banging it on the shelf.

"Had to sell most of the German glass," Al says.

Joe shakes his head. He'd like to tell Al that it's hard all over, that the rice harvest was the worst in ten years—goddamn smut—and now the bank is clammering after his boat, but telling it wouldn't do now, not when he's angling.

"So how's it with you?" Al says, his voice sarcastic. "—Just for conversation's sake."

Joe lifts a glass off the bar and turns it in his hand. "Couldn't be better," he says.

"I said no credit, Joe," Al says.

"Come on, Al. For Christ's sake, don't gimme this shit. I paid you back. Sure, it took awhile, but hell, I mean, look at it this way—"

"You call that crazy stunt of yours paying me back?"

"You got your money."

"Sure, I got my—"

"What are you bitchin' about then?"

"What am *I* bitching about?" Al reaches into the shelf and grasps a fancy, thin-waisted wineglass. "See this? Over a hundred years old."

Joe nods. He's heard it before. All the regulars have. It makes Al a bit of a dandy, his collecting antique glass, but there's something they like about it too. They can always tell how things stand with Al just by looking up at that shelf. If the shelf is crowded, it means credit; if the shelf is lacking in some way, if there is a space where a glass had been before, it means take care of yourself.

"Glass," Al says.

"Yeah, I know," Joe says.

"Fragile."

"Blah, blah, blah," Joe says.

Al tugs on the wineglass, and to Joe's surprise, all the glasses shake, the French champagne glasses, as blue and clear as water, the long-stemmed Belgian beer glasses, the Swedish crystal.

Joe smiles. "Oh, you are so clever, Al."

"If things get crazy again, I can just take the whole shelf down. Get it?"

"You tell anyone else about this feat of modern engineering?"

Al smiles and wriggles his eyebrows. "What do you think?"

Joe rubs his chin. "What if you gotta get rid of a few more? I mean, not that things would ever get that bad, but—"

"If I've got to get 'em off, all I do is use a little paint stripper." Al points to the two spaces on the shelf.

"Yeah, I saw it," Joe says.

"No credit, Joe."

"I'll drink to that," Joe says, and smiling his biggest smile, lays the last dollar of the ten he bummed off his older brother on the bar.

The door opposite Joe swings open, and a shaft of evening sunlight cuts all the way to the big red Coke machine and the shooting gallery in back.

"We're open!" Al yells.

A tall, hollow-faced man wearing a yellow hat with fishing lures on it pushes through into the Pen.

"Come on in," Joe says.

The hat feels his way to the bar, his shoulders swaying with the motion of his feet. He stoops as he walks, as though the ceiling isn't high enough.

"Dark in here," he says.

He gets a hand on the backrest of a stool, and squats down, bracing his elbows on the bar.

"Whiskey Seven," he says.

Joe nods. "How's it goin'?"

"Okay, Jack!"

Al sweeps a bottle out from under and raises it to a glass.

"Hold it," the hat says. "None of that cheap stuff."

Al stands with his fist around the bottle, his cheeks and forehead coloring.

"What do you got?" the hat says.

Al jerks his head over, looking at Joe. "You tell him, Joe," he says.

Joe rubs his chin as if in thought, Al shuffling uneasily behind the bar.

"You *really* want me to tell him?" Joe says.

The door bangs open again, and a shaft of sunlight, like a flashlight beam, catches the hat on his chair, his eyes squinting combative, but blind, like a mole's.

"We're open!" Al shouts.

But the door has already slammed shut, and the bar is dark again. Joe raises his beer, toasting Al.

"Missed a really great place," Joe says, his mind working on the hat's eyes.

"Two more!" Joe hollers, slamming Frank on the shoulder. They have moved to a booth, so they don't have to balance on the stools. Frank tosses his hat like a saucer—the copper and silver lures sparkling—over the bar, where Al catches it, glaring, and tosses it back.

"See?" Frank says. "Easy as cake. You buy."

Joe waggles two fingers over his head, and Al raises the bottle of Lewis and Clark, a smirk on his face.

"I'm listening," Joe says.

"So like I said," Frank says, "fishing has been no-shit-and-shine-ola. Too damn hot. The kids are off with their mother. Got up at five, hit all the deep spots and still no luck."

Luck.

Joe grins. He has him right.

Al sets the drinks on the table.

"I got it," Joe says. He reaches into his pocket, and pulls out an envelope.

"Wait a minute, Joe," Al says, crossing his arms over his chest.

"*I'll* get it," Frank says.

"No," Joe shoots back, a little too much edge in his voice, "really—"

His mouth pursed, Al stares down at Joe.

Frank nervously taps his glass on the tabletop. "If you two have something to settle—"

"I said no more checks, Joe," Al says.

His head cocked at an angle so he can watch the expression on Frank's face, Joe holds out the envelope. "Come on, Al," he says. "It's a *government* check, for Christ's sake. If it isn't any good, what the hell is?"

Frank pokes at the ice in his glass with a straw. When he looks up from his drink, Joe shoots back in his seat, waving the check in his hand.

"I mean," Joe says to Frank, "am I right or what?"

Frank nods, a line of muscle tight across his jaw.

"Right?" Joe says. "I mean this is the real thing, right? If Uncle Sam's money isn't—"

"Right," Frank says.

Al shakes his head, then snaps the envelope from Joe's hand. "From here on in it's no more checks. Got it?"

Joe shrugs, his eyes merry.

"Got it?" Al says.

"All right, all right," Joe says. "Just cash the fucking thing, okay?"

Al shakes his head and turns to the bar.

"And—Hey, Al!" Joe yells. "Bring us a couple more with the change!"

Joe taps his foot on the floor, uneasy. Al is taking too long at the bar. A couple of old, stoop-shouldered guys and a young Indian woman with a nose like an owl's beak have come in and Al is serving them. Joe traces figure eights on the tabletop with his finger, leaving beer bubbles on the formica.

"You know any good spots?" Frank says.

"I know lots of places. It's in my blood," Joe says, surprising himself in saying it. For a second he pictures himself out in his boat—maybe he can keep it yet somehow—and saddens thinking how he'll miss duck hunting this fall. He reaches for his glass, but sees it is empty. "You need a guide?"

"No," Frank says. "I mean," he says, "we're probably going to take off tomorrow."

Joe nods. He smiles, for Frank. All lies.

Al raps his knuckles on the table.

"Here you go, Joe," he says, holding out the bills. "Don't ask me to do it again."

Joe plucks the bills from Al's hand, thumbing them like cards. They are new bills, stiff and bright green, and Joe bends to count them.

"—thirty-five, thirty-six . . ."

Al turns from the table, slipping back to the bar, and Joe raises his head.

"Hey, where's our drinks?" he says.

Al jerks his head toward the door. Back of the window and the neon Grain Belt sign, Trudy, a stout, heavy-chested Ojibway girl, bends low over a table with a tray of drinks.

Joe counts the last of the bills. "—forty-four, forty-five."

Frank's eyes sweep across the bar.

"Forty-five," Joe says.

Trudy slides the tray onto the table.

"Two whiskey waters," she says, her voice bright and cheery.

Joe smiles, staring into the booth divider behind Frank.

Trudy tosses her shoulders.

"My, aren't we friendly tonight," she says. In a huff she turns to Frank, confiding. "I don't see this character in who-knows-how-long," she says, "and all he can do is sit there like a stone. Hey, Joe," she says, winking at Frank, "you going to shoot up Al's glass tonight? Just for old times'—"

"Cut it out, Trudy," Joe says. Usually Al fronts Joe a hundred dollars, and now Joe isn't sure Al is behind him.

"Well, now . . . aren't we—"

"What the hell is wrong with everybody around here?" Joe says. "Al is just—"

Trudy's eyes harden, threaten like fists. She balances the tray at her hip.

"You going to pay for those drinks, Joe?" she says.

Joe shakes his head, his mouth pursed. He slips one of the new bills into Trudy's apron pocket.

"That's for the tip, too," he says, then adds, "and tell that *French bastard* I'm onto him. Okay?"

"It's late," Frank says, scratching at the back of his head again.

"Call 'em and tell 'em you're having a grand time," Joe says. "We are having a grand time, aren't we?"

Frank holds up his glass. He smiles drunkenly, his mouth lop-sided now. He looks like a service boy grown old, his hair closely cropped, his face clownish but homesick.

"I'll bet it's the first time you've been away from your old lady in months," Joe says. "Am I right?"

Frank swirls the ice in his glass. "You don't know the half of it."

"Like hell," Joe says.

"Jesus," Frank says, "why do you think I'm in here?"

Joe shrugs his shoulders. "Got tired of talking to the fish?"

"Cause of *her*, that's why," Frank says.

"She makes you mad, huh?"

Frank hits the table with his fist. "Does she make me mad! She's been bitching all day about having to use a goddamned outhouse—as though it's a crime or something!"

Frank catches Joe's eye as if they share something in outhouses, then embarrassed, he tugs at his Adam's apple.

"I spend a goddamned fortune getting the whole kit-andcaboodle up here and then all they do is bitch. 'It's cold, honey,' 'How come there isn't a refrigerator in our cabin?' 'I can't, Frank—not with the children in the next room!' "

Joe shakes his head and clucks sadly. "I'll bet you haven't had any—"

The glass tilts in Frank's hand, his eyes hooded, wary.

Sensing the time, Joe lowers his voice, leaning across the table. "Hell, it's all the same between men, right? I mean, look up there—" Joe points to the bar, to the Indian woman with the beak. She laughs with the man beside her, her lips curled and teasing.

"Come on," Joe says, leaning across the table. "Just a little truth, huh? Wouldn't you like to get into that? A little squaw pussy?"

A grin crawls up Frank's face.

"Am I right?" Joe says.

Frank shakes his head.

"I mean, do you see the tits on her?"

Frank smiles. "Kind of wide in the rear," he says. "But you got 'er right—she's a real honey."

"Go up and say something."

"Are you kidding?"

"Would I kid you?" Joe says.

Up front the door opens. A friend of Joe's, Hole-in-the-Day, a huge, moon-faced Indian, stumbles into the bar, a smaller, mean-looking Indian behind him. There are no tables open now, the men are so tightly packed in, and Hole-in-the-Day, looking for a place to sit, spots Joe in the booth. He lumbers across the bar, his wide-spaced eyes blinking in his chubby face.

Joe springs out from the booth.

"Hey, Hodie!" he says, jubilantly. "Want you to meet a friend of mine here," he says. "Frank, Hodie."

"Frank," Frank says, offering his hand.

Hole-in-the-Day nods, then slides in next to Frank, his gut puckering up against the table.

Someone has dropped a few nickels into the jukebox and the speakers crackle, a mournful voice singing.

"We were just talking about big-lungs over there," Joe nearly shouts over the music.

Hole-in-the-Day turns to look. "What about her?" he says.

Joe jabs his thumb at Frank. "Casanova here has the hots."

"You looking for a fight?" Hole-in-the-Day says.

Joe pinches Hole-in-the-Day under the table. He finally takes Joe's stare as a sign that he should leave, and scoots across the seat, and Joe catches his arm.

"Hey! You want to shoot some ducks?" Joe says.

Lifting the steel legs of the shooting gallery, Joe grunts as though he has ruptured himself.

"Careful," Al calls out over the men at the bar.

Just some painted tin, five fist-sized wooden ducks, and a little hardware, the gallery is not heavy, but Joe, opposite Hole-in-the-Day, strains as though it weighs a ton.

"Goddammit, can you help a little, Frank?" Joe says.

He cranes his head around and is surprised to see Frank standing behind him, his arms crossed over his chest. Joe had thought Frank might slip out while they were moving the gallery, and now his eagerness to help is unsettling, and Joe feels a knot forming in his stomach.

"Here?" Frank says, reaching under the front.

They slide the gallery out from behind the Coke machine. All the hardware—the motor, chain, and electrical rigging—is in the back, and for a second the gallery balances to one side, almost tipping. Al butts through his customers.

"Hey! I said 'Watch it'!" he shouts.

Joe, smiling, salutes Al. He stoops to plug the machine in, and when the board lights up, orange and red and blue, the battered ducks bobbing along, the bar takes on a new cheer. The lights streak over the ceiling and into the mirror behind the bar, and refracted through Al's glass, the beams shoot off in all directions.

Joe pushes through the men waiting for drinks, sliding sideways up to the bar.

"Okay," Joe says, teasing, "where's the gun, Al?"

Al drops a handful of ice cubes into a blender jar, sets the blender going—it roars and crackles—then turns his back to Joe, cleaning glasses with his towel.

"Hey, Al," Joe says.

On Joe's right, a big hulk squatting on a stool raises his head.

"Can't you see he's busy?" the hulk says.

Joe slides an elbow onto the bar.

His shoulders squared, Al jerks the glasses out of the tub under the bar and wrenches them around in the towel.

This is what Joe has been dreading.

For nearly an hour, since Al faked cashing the check, Joe has worried that Al won't hold up his end of the deal this time.

"Never again," Al had said last year after the mess with the skinners.

It pains Joe to think about it, but with Al's back to him this way, and the cash in his pocket, he does. Last year, when the paper company laid the skinners off, they had come to the Bull Pen to drink steady and hard, and the gambling over the gallery had gotten out of hand. Joe had raked in a bundle for Al. It was a sixty/forty arrangement, forty going to Joe, and when it was all over, Joe had put Al's share down the crack in the booth seat and had gone up to the bar for a few drinks.

Al was whistling.

"Well, there's your vacation," Joe had said.

Al slid a thick glass down the counter and filled it with his best whiskey. He poked Joe in the shoulder.

"So, how's it feel to be robbing your own this time?" he said.

Joe remembers having blinked.

"Thanks, Al," he had said.

He crossed the bar to the gallery and picked up the rifle.

"Turn it on!" he said.

Al reached for the switch, the pump puttered, and then in one burst of corks from the gun, Joe knocked nearly every glass from Al's shelf, popping the skinners in their booths until they pinned him to the floor. It had taken Joe some time to come up with the money to cover the damage he had done, but even then, Al would never forgive him for what he had destroyed.

"Hey," Joe says. "Hey, Al."

Al hangs the towel from his belt, turning to switch off the blender.

"For Christ's sakes, Al," Joe says, "don't be such a son-of-a-bitch. Gimme the gun."

Al, his eyes on Joe, pours the daiquiri from the blender jar and sets it on Trudy's tray. He reaches under the shelf of glasses, then has the rifle out.

Joe is nearly ecstatic. "How about some ammo?"

"No funny stuff this time, Joe," Al says.

Joe holds a hand up, three fingers, scout's honor.

"I mean it," Al says.

Around the gallery the men huddle close, jostling each other to see better. Joe's shirt is heavy with sweat and Frank has bought another round of drinks.

Hole-in-the-Day slaps Joe on the back. "Come on, Joe. Give 'im hell."

The gallery whirs and chugs, and the door in front bangs open and shut. More customers.

Al whirls, spins, dances behind the bar.

Frank tips his glass back, the ice rattling against his teeth, and taking the gun from Joe, presses it to his shoulder and fires. A duck pops over, and Frank raises his glass again.

"Another round," he shouts.

Al bangs a sale home on the register.

"The same," Frank shouts.

Al nods curtly from behind the register, his face pinched and angry, and Joe feels the knot in his stomach tighten. He has never shot even with anyone, and Frank is bigger than he is, and these drinks, which he cannot refuse, are making his hands numb.

"Gimme a handicap, for Christ's sake," Joe says when the drinks come. "I had a few before you came in."

Frank shrugs. He tosses down one drink, and grinning at Joe like a kid who has just crushed a frog under his shoe, tosses down the second. "You happy?" he says.

. .

The air is thick with smoke and the gallery lights cut brightly colored swords around the room. The semicircle of men has deepened, half guides, half fishermen and hunters.

"This is it," Hole-in-the-Day shouts.

Frank levels the gun, there is a hush, and when the cork ricochets off a duck's head, there is a hollering from the guides, a guttural blast.

Joe wipes his hands on his pants. He can't stop the sweating, and his heart jumps like a rabbit in his chest.

Hole-in-the-Day slams him on the back. "Pick up the money, Joe," he says.

On the table, Frank's hat sits upside down, filled with bills. Joe had thought to just lose, and pull out easy, but now Frank has somehow missed two shots, leaving him one up. Joe does not want to touch the hat, but when he does, he hears what he knew was coming.

"One more," Frank says.

Holding the hat, Joe would like to go out the door—he suspects now *he* is being had—but the ring of men is so deep that pushing through them with the money is unthinkable. Hole-in-the-Day slams Joe on the shoulder again.

"I'll back ya!" he says.

Frank has a book of traveler's checks out. He signs a check with a flourish, and on the table slaps his hand over it.

"I'll stand you another hundred," he says.

The hat tugged tight to his stomach, Joe feels as though he is being chased in a nightmare, unable to run, and before Joe can stop him, Hole-in-the-Day has his hand out, and they're putting more money in the hat.

"You can do it," Hole-in-the-Day says.

Frank counts the money, then sets the hat back on the table. The dirty green bills bulge out of it like some horrible salad.

"You ready?" Frank says.

Hole-in-the-Day shoves the rifle into Joe's arms, and Joe stands there with it. He stares up into his friend's big, uncomprehending eyes, reminded of the time his father had given him a broom for his birthday.

"Sure," he hears Hole-in-the-Day say, "sure he's ready."

The wall of hot, sweating men press in toward the gallery. Frank squeezes off his last shot. The cork ricochets off the head of a duck, and Frank stomps his foot on the floor.

"Goddamn!" he says. But still he is elated.

Even if Joe knocks down all five ducks now, he can still only tie the game.

"Another round," Frank hollers.

Joe takes the rifle. The ducks grind in circles, their bills turned up as if they are laughing at him. He follows one, hands shaking, then another, holding his breath. He squeezes off a shot, and a duck pops over and the guides cheer.

"Go ahead, take your time," Hole-in-the-Day says.

In Joe's hands, the rifle stock is greasy, and he can't seem to get a good grip on it. His whole body points the gun, and he squeezes off another shot, the cork careening, the duck barely going over. The game is clear to Joe now—he has been had, and for some very big money—and aiming the gun, he struggles to hold back his panic. He had got this one wrong, or part of him, and somewhere he had lost the game a long time ago.

"It's no use," Joe says, handing Hole-in-the-Day the rifle. "I gotta get something to eat."

Frank, riding Joe, pushes now. "Don't take all night, goddammit," he says.

At the bar, Joe watches the door open. Cool air drafts in, smelling of freedom. Al sets up three whiskey-waters, his hands hammering at the glasses.

"Al," Joe says.

"Don't fucking talk to me," Al says.

He shakes a jigger, then reaches for a gimlet glass on the shelf. The beer glasses on the shelf rattle, and in that second, a thought rears up in Joe's brain like an explosion:

Glass!

Rows of glasses—blue glass, green glass, the Belgian glasses with the eagles on them. Cheap glasses, clear glasses, thick glasses. Beer glasses.

"What the fuck are you looking at?" Al says, slapping a washcloth on the bar in front of Joe.

"Look, Al—"

"Don't fucking talk to me, Joe," Al says, bracing his arms against the bar. "I've had it."

Joe leans over the bar.

"How'd you like a vacation, Al?" Joe says. "Would you like that? Hawaii, or someplace like that?"

Al shakes gin into a glass.

"How'd you like to be dead?" he says, looking up from the bottle, his lips drawn back from his teeth in a smile.

"I just wanted you to think about it," Joe says.

"Oh, believe me, Joe," Al says, "I will."

Joe slides back through the crowd to the gallery, scheming. Frank waits with a beer in his hand.

"Have another beer," Frank says.

The rifle tight across his chest, Hole-in-the-Day stands like a cigar-store Indian beside the table, as though he is guarding the hat.

"Gimme that," Joe says, taking the rifle.

He shoulders the rifle and leads the first blue and red duck, the head looking mean now, and squeezing off the shot the duck pops over. He exaggerates the shaking of his hands and stumbles a little, and Hole-in-the-Day pushes him upright.

"Come on, Joe," he says.

Joe braces himself against the table.

"Hey!" Frank says.

"Sorry," Joe says, backing away.

But he catches it, the twitch in the corner of Frank's mouth, and he steadies himself, leads the fourth duck, the lights spinning bolts of raw color, and fires, knocking over the duck.

Joe settles down for the fifth. He's got to make this look right. Too sloppy and no one will back him, too sharp and Frank won't go for it. He follows a duck around the track, raising the rifle, and bumping forward, fires. The cork spits across the range, grazes a duck's head, and the duck, wavering, rattles up and around the track.

"Goddamn-son-of-a-bitch!" Hole-in-the-Day bellows, the guides rumbling behind him, the fishermen excited, whooping.

Joe stands with the rifle, his shoulders rounded.

"Turn the goddamned thing off!" Al yells from the bar. "Turn it off, Joe!"

Frank reaches for the hat, grinning triumphantly, and Joe catches him by the wrist.

"It was fair and square," Frank says.

Joe fixes his eyes on the hat. Crumpled bills curl over the sweatband.

"Fair and square my ass!" Joe says.

There is a rumble from the Indians in the bar, and Hole-in-the-Day crosses his arms over his chest. The deer hunters and fishermen pull tight into themselves, counting heads. A few slip out the front door.

"You're some kind of sharpshooter, aren't you?" Joe says.

Frank shrugs his shoulders, smiling, pleased with himself.

"Bet you were in *Ko-ree-uh!*"

"So what if I was?" Frank says.

Joe looks back into the clot of men, then at Frank.

"So," he says, "you think you'll just screw some drunk Indian out his welfare check? Is that it?"

Frank's eyes flicker, then narrow.

"That's bullshit and you know it," Frank says.

He pulls at the hat, but Hole-in-the-Day leans toward him.

"You tough enough for one more, *fly boy?*" Joe says.

"*Marines,*" Frank says. "Let's get it straight, *Chief.*"

"All right, Mr. *Mo-reen,*" Joe says.

They stand, holding the hat, Frank with his free hand twitching at his side. Behind them the rifle pump wheezes.

"Double or nothing, Mr. *Mo-reen,*" Joe says. "And to make it interesting, let's make it three glasses off the shelf there." He points at Al's antique glass. "Champion of the World."

Frank cranes his head around, scans the shelf of glasses. Al slides a glass onto the shelf, and Joe thrills with it.

"You are full of shit, you know that?" Frank says, shoving the hat into Joe's stomach. "I'd like to see you try it."

Joe holds the hat up, and Al raises his head from the drink he is pouring.

"What the hell is going on?" Al yells. "I said, 'The Game's Over!' "

Joe puts his hand to his ear as though he can't hear, the music twanging and pounding. Al reaches under the bar and switches off the music.

"I said, 'Shut it down!' Joe!" Al's voice booms.

The men on the stools, Trudy, her tray at her side, and the regulars in front, have all turned to watch.

"Three of your glasses, Al," Joe says, standing as straight as he can. "Double or nothing, Champion of the World."

Al braces his arms against the bar. His forehead is cut with lines and his mouth is arched.

"Come on, Al," Joe says. "Stake me, Al. Double or nothing."

Against the west wall of the bar the men stand packed against each other, shabby-looking, a fool's army. Al has turned the gallery off, and now only the pump chugs. The light is gray with smoke, and it gives the bar the look of a cave.

"Tails," Joe says.

The coin turns, flashing, and Al catches it in his palm.

"Heads," Al says.

Frank steps up to the orange extension cord Al has laid on the floor. The glass on the shelf shines, dusty, naked.

"Off the shelf," Joe says.

"Shut up," Frank jabs.

He toes the line, peering down the barrel of the rifle. His tongue pushes his cheek out, his eyes hard fixed on the shelf. Joe cannot stand to watch. He raises his head to the ceiling, following the long, forked crack in the plaster. There is the Thut! of the gun, and the sound of breaking glass, another Thut! and another glass breaking, and then Joe is on the ceiling, the crack there widening like a canyon to swallow him. He sees himself old, tired, burned-out, *alone*. In his aloneness he feels like crying out—what he has believed for some time is true now, his life is already gone and he is left here somehow, empty—and he squeezes his hands into fists, the blood rushing to his head, and in the hollow there he prays, he prays *Please*, and when he hears the third Thut! He feels himself falling away, abandoned, until a hollow crystal ringing, a pure yellow sound like a bell in a boxing match, catches him.

Frank scowls, breathing hard, his nostrils flaired.

"Your shot," Hole-in-the-Day says, handing Joe the rifle.

Joe caresses the stock with his hand.

"Come on," Frank says.

Hole-in-the-Day turns to look at Frank, his brows bulging, and Frank stares back, then turns away, his mouth set in a hard, sharp line.

Joe shoulders the rifle.

The thin, champagne glasses on the end of the shelf glimmer like water. He feels he is flying high and away from it all, his spirit buoyed up on impossible hope. He sights down the black barrel, and slowly squeezes the trigger.

Thut!

A cork spits out of the gun. A glass slams back off the shelf and falling, shatters on the floor.

Joe draws his hand across his forehead, then puts the rifle back to his shoulder.

The rifle pops again, and another glass shatters.

Joe pulls the rifle tight to his shoulder, his eyes searching the length of the shelf.

Somehow, the glasses all look the same now—did Al move that glass when he came in? The glasses turn like a kaleidoscope, bright colors and fine-edged shapes, and it makes Joe feel sick. He closes his eyes and the feeling of spinning gets worse. *Just this once, and I'll change*, he promises.

Joe opens his eyes and sights down the barrel. The bead on the barrel floats over the glasses. A tall, narrow glass on the left catches his eye. He breathes deeply, the rifle stock warm in his hands. *All right*, he thinks.

He slowly squeezes the trigger, the gun pops, and the cork rockets away, hits the lip of the glass, and the glass, to Joe's amazement, swoops in circles on its base as if waltzing.

. . .

Headed up the street, the wind spinning eddies of dirt around door fronts, for the umpteenth time Joe listens to the purest sound he can remember—the shattering of the third glass—and feels his soul swell. His car is up and back of the bank, and he passes first Culla's Tavern, then The Huddle, thinking how he will have his boat all fall. He thinks of the ducks, the rice, and even after the way Al had treated him, and Frank, too—Al staring, and Frank shouting obscenities—he no longer feels alone. He's paid up, and then some. He pushes his hand into his pocket and squeezes the thick roll of dough. The flashing bar signs on the street, yellow and blue and green, remind Joe of a carnival, and he smiles to himself, and raises his arms over his head, his fists clenched, and shouts. He passes the Penny's clothing outlet, and looks through his reflection in the window to the boots displayed on dark carpet strips. He'll get a pair of Red Wing boots, that's what he'll do. And a new knife, a Kay-Bar, not that Japanese shit he's had lately. He strolls up the block, ripe with possibility, and passing the last bar before the bank, looks in the open door. Just one for celebration, he thinks.

Just one. Really.

He climbs the steps, then is over the threshold, and nods at Duffy, the bartender. Only the late ones are out now, drooping over their drinks. A woman to Joe's right sucks the last of her drink off her ice cubes.

"No credit, Joe," Duffy says.

Joe smiles and pulls two crumpled bills from his pocket.

"A beer, Duffy," he says out of habit, and then thinking, adds, "make that two beers, and two of whatever Beautiful here is drinking."

The woman beside him turns, and with her hand pulls back her hair. Her face is heavily rouged, her eyes not entirely inviting. But she smiles, and Joe feels it bubbling up in him already.

"Hey," he says, nudging the woman with his elbow. "Hey, will you marry me?" he says.

THORNAPPLES

1958 She was a woman nearly forty, big waisted, and cross-eyed. Once beautiful, she had been so sought after she had taken for a husband a man nearly sixteen years her senior, a man who, at the time, had been a builder in an old profession, boats, a man respected, even revered; and now, in her bed, she was waiting for another man.

Through the west window, she could make out the hood of Joe's truck in the dark, like an animal's snout turned toward the cabin. A match flared, Joe's face illuminated, well-intentioned but sad under a stiff black hat.

Then another.

Martha felt some wild voice rise in her throat, her legs threatening to carry her to the cabin door. And when she could stand it no longer, she picked up her quilting. Already, the truck there in the dark, she had scoured the cabin, had, on her hands and knees, rubbed beeswax into the pine floor, and she was tired beyond endurance now.

She jabbed a series of holes through the tough buckskin, the prick of the thornapple spur waking her.

Work. Work would save her, the nuns at the off-reserve school had said.

"See how Martha works?" Sister Agnes had said.

It made Martha groan to think of it now. At every occasion possible, Sister Agnes had recounted the visit of Jesus, how Mary had squandered herself in idle talk and vanity.

"Martha worked while Mary played," Sister Agnes told the class.

It was a story she never tired of. Sister Agnes's bitter old eyes would sparkle at the recounting of that night. How Martha, devout, and in right spirit, had served Jesus in that poor household.

"Your talent is work," Sister Agnes had told Martha after class on more than a few occasions. "You were named for it."

She'd said it with a certain inexhaustible relish, one Martha had not understood at the time. Sister Agnes had had the face of a pig, upturned, squinting eyes, wore tiny steel-rimmed—"gold is vanity"—glasses. She'd had a wide-bridged nose, skin as rough as walnut rind, and only now, all these years later, could Martha see what Sister Agnes's chastisement had been all about.

Martha had been sought after. Sister Agnes was loved only by Jesus. It put Sister Agnes in a rage, the boys eyeing Martha in class, courting her. Joe had helped her to see that.

Martha poked with the spur, broke it, chose another from the handful on the quilt.

Joe was another of these things in her life. A thornapple. In the spring they bloomed, bright pink and white blossoms, smelled sweet, bees hovering over them; not long after, the haws, like tiny crimson apples, came out, inviting, but bitter, inedible. Only the thorns were good for anything.

Martha raised herself off the bed, peered out the window. Anytime now. He had promised.

But what was a promise to Joe? He was a wheeler-dealer, a fancy-man, a drinker—everything the nuns had taught her to hate early on. But he smelled nice, too, and could make her laugh (he could make *anyone* laugh), and he was smart—he had a way of seeing into things. She could talk to him, when he wasn't off on one of his binges. But there was always this about him:

She didn't love him—or was it *she didn't love him the way he loved her?*

She felt like waving to him through the window, but forced her head down by the light, working the spur through the skin, fixing the seed beads—iridescent blue and gold and red—to the buckskin. She tried not to think about Joe, but that was impossible now. The first time, a little over six years ago, she had met him at the cabin door, a loaded gun at her shoulder.

"Get out of our yard," she'd said.

Months later, in town, he'd run into her again. He followed her around Halbert's grocery. She was down to money for lard and flour. He was watching her, took note of everything she did. Now, nights he left things outside the door. A huge slab of bacon. A can of pecans. An expensive serge blanket. At first, years ago, Martha had thought he left these things out of guilt over his part in the reserve shooting, when everything had gone sour. The tribal council had met, discussed the shooting, and had pronounced it the fault of the deputies who had fired on Joe's brother. But secretly, the finger of blame, needing some object, had swung in Martha's husband's direction, and not long after, Martha found a juggler's medicine bones in their cornmeal. While her husband was in town getting supplies, someone wired an owl to the hood of his truck. The owl had been wired down by the grill so that not until the truck was moving along at a good speed did the owl bang up onto the windshield—the worst omen possible.

And now, that is how Martha thinks of him, as though he were dead. She cannot speak his name, because to do so brings him back, and she cannot bear it. At first she had ached so badly for him she thought she would die herself. She broke out in rashes, had fevers, fainted. Her son, Red Deer, took it in a different way. Silent, he ran in circles around the reserve. He was the image of his father, tall, rawboned, and to look at him made Martha ache, and so they did nothing together. Martha, to take her mind off it, did what Sister Agnes had said she should do: work. It was her God-given strength, Sister Agnes had said.

So she worked. There was no electricity on the reserve, and

she even worked at night, by candle, and to bury the greatest sorrow, she quilted, as her mother had, using the sharp spurs of the thornapple. She cut her hands badly doing it—her fingers were not callused as her mother's had been. She sewed fancy leggings, leggings so intricate and fine her hands bled for the work. Nightly she bent low over the beadwork, even used porcupine quill, dying them in a bucket over the stove, always pushing herself further back into her past, until she could go no further.

Her husband had gone so as not to bring the sickness on them all: jugglers, medicine men gone bad, had poisoned their food, he'd said. But this was worse than any poison.

And where was the gift in this? Sister Agnes had said the gifts of the spirit always came with pain. "You'll know," she'd said to Martha, as if pronouncing her fate. "A worker like you will know."

Then Buck had gone to be with his father.

Alone, she worked all the harder. She worked all day, then late into the morning, leggings, a jacket, moccasins, snapping the barbs from the thornapple branches behind the cabin, working them through the buckskin, a trail of blood around the stitches. She cured the hide the old way, with the brains, and she felt something go in her when she crushed the skulls. She had to do this exactly. Okitchita, a sorceress, had told her so. When her prayers had failed she visited Okitchita. Make him leggings in the old way, Okitchita had said. Quill, seed beads; the barb of the thornapple. Cure the skin with brain. So she had done all that, half-believing, more hoping, working into the night, a furious intention in her hands. But something else had come of it. When she was done, she'd held the leggings and shirt up, looking into the mirror over the sideboard, and what she saw there drove her to her knees:

Her right eye, in the strain of the poor light, had crossed, as if something holding it in her head had broken.

Outside the cabin, lights came on. The headlights cast bright squares on the wall behind her. The lights were blinding. Martha swung her legs around, sat on the edge of the bed, listening for the *ca-wunk!* of the truck door, the sound of Joe's feet on the gravel, but he was not coming in.

Other than that first night, when she'd drunk herself blind, she'd refused him. She had the boy to think about, she'd said. Bear, her cousin's boy. You'll upset the boy, she said. I can't have you coming in now.

Martha shook her head, stabbed with the spur. That Joe hadn't noticed the resemblance all these years—what now? Six years— or hadn't mentioned it, was a source of amazement to her. Men. But now, maybe now she would have to do it: last week a social worker had come by. The social worker said the diet was no good, and where was money for school? Clothes? Where was the boy's father?

No one would take Bear away from her, Martha thought. But she could see it had come to this: She needed something, anything, soon, and she hoped it was not this, what Joe was offering her. Something had to happen.

Joe lit another cigarette. The bright end bobbed tantalizing in the dark. Martha worked the quill into her hand. She would not go out to him.

Is this what Sister Agnes had meant?

Sister Agnes had been married once. She'd said to the class one day, "Love is cruel." And at that she had swept down on Martha and slapped the candy from her mouth.

Love with her husband had been nothing like that. He had had big, big arms, warm breath, a gentle touch. He had treated her with decorum, with tenderness.

But love with Joe?

She breathed deeply; the candle fluttered beside her. The wood in the stove snapped. A cold sweat covered her legs.

She would go out to him. She would lie to him. That one night, she would say, it was just that. She wouldn't tell him about the boy, Bear. She hadn't and she wouldn't. She thought this now, preparing herself, but when Joe started the truck, revved it as if to back out the drive, she felt her heart race. And just as she felt it, Joe shut the motor down. He was playing with her, she thought, and she felt small, defenseless, almost wishing him into the house to be done with it.

At first it had been shameful. She remembers how she felt, the others' eyes on her. Curious, incredulous, condemning. "Does she really think anyone believes that?" a woman whispered to another behind the magazine rack at Halbert's.

She had gotten so heavy at the time.

"My cousin's boy," she'd told them. And only Okitchita, who'd delivered the boy, knew.

Martha turned from one side to the other, angry one moment, nearly in tears the next, stabbing at the buckskin with the thorn-apple spur. She shouldn't have sent Bear away, she thought. Not even for this one night. She hadn't wanted Bear to get caught between them, her and Joe. He'd hit her once, and hard. Sister Agnes had been right, she thought, and in thinking it, the cabin squeezed in on her, suffocating, there in it the smell of smoke, an afterscent of bacon. Joe was in the cabin already. What difference did it make now? She tried to force herself out of bed, but finally she sat, her back squared against the wall behind her so as to face what was coming through the door. She would say, No, she thought. She would tell him, another six months, only, now she realized she could not let him go, either. The social worker would be back. He'd already threatened they'd take Bear away.

There was the *ca-wunk!* of the truck, then Joe's footsteps on the gravel drive, gritty, balanced, forceful. He opened the door, slowly, head erect, his eyes inquisitive, a determined look on his face.

A chill autumn breeze whirled through the cabin.

Martha cupped her hand around the candle. It frightened her, what Joe might think: in times past, when a man came for a wife, the girl sat up for him like this, a candle in hand. If she would have him, she blew the candle out and pulled back the quilt.

They looked at each other, Joe's clothes torn from work at the mill, his rough hands hanging at his sides.

He took a step closer, reached for her.

And at that moment, Martha's breath caught in her throat— no sound came—and as if she had known she would all along, she drew the candle to her face and put out the flame.

SEEING
WILD
BILL

1961 While Bill Miller went on about the valves, and how they controlled the flow of blood, and how the heart didn't *really* feel, Martin reached into the cooler behind the table for another hot dog. He moved slowly, hoping Bill wouldn't notice, his eyes on the curious, brown face in the high grass up the hill.

"It's the subject closest to my heart," Bill said, in a high, facetious voice.

The other boys laughed.

Martin tossed his head and laughed, too, dropping the hot dog under the picnic table. For the last hour Martin had waited for the Indian boy to come down from behind the hill, had stashed food away for him, only now that it didn't seem he would, Martin was beginning to feel foolish.

"Who wants more?" Bill asked.

Steve, towheaded and large bellied, flung his arm over his head.

"How about you, Danny Boy?" Bill said. "You aren't eating too much."

"I'm not hungry," he said.

"You sure now?" Bill said, winking. "You better think about it because they'll be gone before you can say *Jack Robinson.*"

Martin bent over the table. With his plastic fork he made a pattern of holes in his paper plate.

"Hey," Bill said. "I'm talking to you."

Martin nodded, working the fork around and through the paper. He didn't want another hot dog, he thought. And he didn't want to have to listen to Bill. He couldn't figure out what was wrong with Steve and Vern, why they were always fighting, and thinking about the rest of it, he didn't like being called Danny Boy.

"Danny Boy," Bill had said, just once, and Steve and Vern had picked up on it.

It was a source of embarrassment to Martin, how the name had been pinned on him like a sign. It had been his father's name for him, *Danny Bee,* for the longest time, only it had become *Danny Boy,* and he didn't like it, especially coming from other people.

"I'll bet my dad's winnin' all the money up there," Steve said.

Vern snorted. "Like heck," he said. "Your dad couldn't play his way out of a paper bag."

Martin looked up from his plate. There was nothing up on the hill now, and Steve had got his arm around Vern's neck in a half nelson.

"All your dad does is look at girls' doohickeys all day," Vern teased.

Steve gave a not-so-friendly tug on Vern's neck.

"All right, you two," Bill said.

The boys tumbled off the table and onto the ground. Bill poked Martin with his elbow.

"Hey," he said.

Martin jabbed at the plate with his fork. It was a pretty even match. Steve was bigger but Vern was faster.

"You going to be a party pooper?" Bill said.

Martin shrugged. What was he supposed to do now? Jump on top of them and act like the whole idea was just thrilling? None of it was thrilling. Steve was always talking about what he would do when *he* was a doctor like his father, and Vern, Vern always wanted to argue—over anything. Vern's father was a lawyer, and Vern was always saying, *Let the defendant speak*, and *Council wishes a word with his client.* He smiled a lot and said witty things he had gotten from *Mad* magazine: *Is it raining? No, it's a funeral. Where are my flowers?* Martin didn't know what to make of it. When he was with Steve and Vern he felt he had to be somebody else, and everything felt unreal. It was even worse because Martin would never be what his father was, a doctor, an angry, brooding man, and Martin didn't feel like acting like his father or saying the things his father said. It was a game he didn't understand or fit into.

"What're you doin' with your plate?" Vern said, back at the table.

Martin held the plate up. He could see Steve and Vern through the holes.

"Making a spaghetti strainer," Martin said.

Vern shook his head. Steve rolled his eyes.

"God you say some dumb things," Steve said.

Martin did not listen to the rest of it. He worked the fork around the paper plate in fancy swirls and sweeps. He wished the Indian boy would come down, hoped he would come down, but now Martin knew he wouldn't—it was a *Firemen's Ball* night, and he was probably across the bay to Osada's with the other Indians now. In the lodge the men would drink and play cards, and Martin would have to stay up all night with Steve and Vern. It was all the worse since Bill had drawn the bad straw.

Martin had heard Bill in the lodge after breakfast. Martin had gone back for his jacket, and standing outside the lodge he had heard the men laugh.

"Ah, Jesus H. Christ," Bill had said, "I knew I'd get stuck with keeping those little peckerwoods up all night."

Out in the boat, Martin had asked his father about Bill. He couldn't understand Bill's over-friendliness, his funny way of talking without saying anything.

"Don't pay too much attention to Bill," Martin's father said. "He's always mad."

"But why did he say that?" Martin asked.

"He's just got to spout off. He isn't too happy, you know."
Martin's father shook his head. "His younger brother, Charlie,
got all the attention, and then he married Delores. Remember
her?"

Delores had had a high, tittery laugh, and she never stopped
talking. She painted her nails a bright, blood red; her hands
shook, and she was always smacking her tongue on the roof of
her mouth as if her mouth were dry. She'd scared Martin—he'd
never met anyone like her.

"He's had a pretty rough time, so he takes it out on everybody.
You understand?"

Martin had said he did.

Now, out of the corner of his eye, Martin watched Bill pull at
his long nose. He took a pipe tamper out of his breast pocket and
fiddled with his pipe, then held a match over the bowl. He made
eager sucking noises, his lips puckering around the pipe stem.

"What do you say, Danny Boy? More beans?" Bill said.

A swirl of blue smoke hung between them. Martin smiled for
Bill, a flat, over-the-teeth smile, and when Bill held the ladle of
baked beans over Martin's plate, Martin shook his head.

"You gotta eat, Danny Boy, or else guys like Steve and Vern'll
pass you up. You got to keep up with the Joneses. Right, boys?"

Steve puffed his chest out like a fancy bird.

"I'll bet I could lift you over my head and throw you in the
lake," he said.

Martin stared dully across the table at him. It seemed odd to
Martin how these things repeated themselves. Last week, during
recess at school, one of the Hale Brothers had gotten him around
the neck, and when he had felt himself being choked, he had
fallen to his knees, taking the bigger boy with him. On the as-
phalt was a jagged piece of cement, and Martin, seizing the op-
portunity, picked up the cement and smacked the bigger boy
square in the forehead. It all seemed a matter of what you were
willing to do to protect yourself, and when the principal bawled
Martin out and sent him home, he felt confused. After all, really,
what had *he* done wrong?

"Come on, Danny Boy," Steve said.

Bill winked again. "Okay, tough guy," he said. "You want a hot dog?"

"Sure," Steve said.

Bill turned away from the table and dug into the ice in the cooler. The brown face came up over the grass again, the eyes searching, curious. Martin had seen the boy on the docks earlier, an Ojibway. The boy's father was a guide, and in the afternoon, out fishing on the lake, Martin's father sitting up from Osada in the boat, Martin had made a big mistake. He knew Osada was the boy's father, and he knew that the men would be having the *ball* and that someone, like the year before, would throw a little picnic and they would sleep in their bags at the end of the island and have a campfire and tell stories.

"What's your son's name?" Martin had asked Osada.

Osada had turned to the front of the boat. The motor was puttering and there was a questioning look on his face. He pointed to Martin with his chin.

"What's your son's name?"

Osada's eyes wrinkled in the corners. Martin liked his face. His skin was a reddish color like brick and his eyes were a warm brown.

"Bear," Osada said. "My wife's boy."

Martin fidgeted in the bow, jigged his rod back and forth. He watched his father's face. His back was hunched and he seemed to be thinking about something.

Martin slid closer to Osada.

"Do you think Bear would want to—"

"Let's try across the bay," Martin's father had said, turning to face Martin, his eyes threatening. "It should be better across the bay, don't you think?" he had said.

"I don't know what the hell happened," Bill said, his mouth an angry line. "We had plenty of hot dogs here. All the damn dogs you could ever want. How many did you eat, Steve?"

Steve grinned. "Six!" he said.

"How about you, Martin?"

"Four," Martin lied.

THE SNAKE GAME

. .

On the rock shelf at the end of the island they built a second fire and rolled out their sleeping bags on a stretch of moss. Bill was lecturing again.

"And so you see," he said, "that's how the Russians got into space first. With that dog."

The fire crackled. Vern kicked at a stone. Martin looked up and behind him for Bear. He hadn't seen him in some time and he felt disappointed but somehow relieved, too.

Bill struck a match, sucked at his pipe.

Martin didn't like the smell of Bill's tobacco.

"So they sent her up like that?"

"Like what?" Bill said.

"They knew they weren't going to bring her down."

"She just ran out of air," Bill said. "That's all."

The boys looked into the fire. They all breathed deeply. Martin watched them. They weren't so bad after all, he thought, they're just hiding.

"That seems kinda mean to me," Martin said. "Just think about it. . . . First they seal you up in this capsule and poke all these wires and things into you, and then *woooosh!* you're squashed, and you can't see anything, and then the air starts to—"

"That's enough, Danny Boy," Bill said. He slapped Martin on the back, sucking on his pipe, squeezing Martin's neck. "You've got to see it differently. It was an experiment. They probably got the dog from a kennel. It wasn't anybody's *dog*. You see now? You just have to look at things the way they really are, use the old scientific method."

Martin nodded. Agreeing with Bill was the only way to shut him up.

"Do you see now? It was just an animal for an experiment."

Martin poked at the ground with a stick.

"Yeah, Danny," Vern said. "It was just a dumb dog."

"A real dumb dog," Steve said.

"A dead dog," Martin said.

They all laughed.

. .

The boys lay on their sleeping bags telling stories. The sun had gone down and the mosquitos were biting and between stories they sprayed themselves with repellent. Bill sat by the fire, drinking from a tin cup. He had an amber bottle at his side and he smoked his pipe and sipped at the cup.

Steve was telling about a movie he'd seen.

He'd started out in a loud voice, telling about the invisible monster, but as it had gotten dark his voice had quieted, and now the three of them huddled together as if to hear better.

"That was a dumb movie," Vern finally said. "There's no such thing as an invisible monster."

Bill raised the cup to his mouth. He drained the cup and poured himself another.

"What do you mean?" Steve said.

"Quiet up there!" Bill shouted. "You're makin' enough noise to wake the dead!"

Martin rolled off his sleeping bag.

"I gotta go pee," he said.

Up the hill, by the table, the coals were settling into a white ash. Martin thought to pee on the fire, then remembered Bear. He stood by a tree and did his business. When he turned to go back down the path, he jumped.

Bear stood behind the table. His eyes watched, like Osada's. He looked bigger in the dark, and Martin couldn't think of anything to say.

They stood like that for a long time.

Martin went to the table and reached under the leg where he had dropped the hot dogs.

"I saved you some," Martin said, holding out the hot dogs. "I mean, I know they've been on the ground but we could wash 'em off in the lake."

"Fire'll take care of that," Bear said.

He gathered twigs off the ground, tossed them onto the coals, then took what was left of the firewood the boys had gathered earlier and set it on the kindling. He blew on the coals and the kindling burst into flame. Martin shifted on his feet. He knew Bill and the others would be expecting him back soon, and he worried. He wanted to tell Bear he had to go, but now that they were by the fire and they had the hot dogs, he couldn't.

Bear broke a green branch from a tree, a long branch, then broke a second. He took a knife from his pocket and expertly snapped it open. He skinned the sticks and sharpened them.

Steve's laughter rose up from the end of the island.

Bear slid the hot dogs onto the sticks and handed one to Martin. Martin was hungry now, but felt queasy with fear. He wondered if Bill would be mad if he found them by the fire. Martin had seen Bill explode before, over something a guide had said.

"Can I see your knife?" Martin said.

Martin opened the knife. The blade had been sharpened down to the width of his little finger. Up toward the handle end there was a small sun.

"Japanese," Bear said.

"Is that bad?"

"It won't hold an edge."

Martin ran the blade across his thumbnail. A small curl of nail came up under it.

"Looks pretty sharp to me."

The fire crackled. The hot dog skins bubbled up and darkened.

"Your dad at the *ball?*" Bear said.

Martin nodded and Bear laughed.

"What's so funny?" Martin said.

Bear looked into the fire. "Are they still telling you that stuff?"

Martin felt the blood rise in his face.

"They don't call it a *ball* for nothing, you know."

Martin looked across the fire at Bear. He'd never questioned what was going on at the lodge. Now all kinds of things went through his head—what *were* they doing up there?

Bear pointed into the fire.

"Your hot dog's burning," he said.

Martin pulled his hot dog from the fire. It was black on the outside.

"Eat it," Bear said.

The meat was hot and spicy. Martin tugged it off the stick

with his teeth. He watched Bear. Bear bit off the skin and nibbled at the pink meat under it. He had his mouth full, was about to say something, when he stiffened and swallowed hard.

A flashlight beam swung across the path in a broad sweep, then stopped on the table. Bear blinked in the light.

"What are you doing up here?" Bill said. His speech was slurred and he stepped forward, aiming the light into Martin's eyes.

"Get the hell down with the other boys, Danny," Bill said.

Martin thought to raise his arm over his face, but it was as if Bill would do something bad.

The powerful beam of light made a circle of the table.

"Son-of-a-bitch," Bill said. "Danny, I want you to get up, right now—that's right, stand up—I want you to go down that path and I want you to sit on your sleeping bag. Is that perfectly clear?"

Martin did not move.

"Move, Danny."

Martin set his stick on the table. He still had Bear's knife. A rough hand grasped the back of his shirt and he was torn from the table.

"What's wrong! Are you deaf?"

Bill swung around. Bear stood in the light like a deer in the headlights of a car.

"Did you steal these?" Bill said.

Bear blinked, his arms at his sides.

"I said, 'Did you steal these?' "

Bear did not move.

"Sure you did, when we were off getting firewood you went into our cooler and stole these, didn't you? You couldn't just come up to the table and ask for them. You had to steal them."

Bill swung the light around.

"I thought I told you to get the hell down there with the others," Bill said.

Martin stared into the light. It made his eyes go all red inside.

"What the hell is wrong with you?"

Martin shook his head. He struggled to say what he had to.

But then Bill was poking him in the chest with his finger. The finger was like an iron rod.

"Don't you lie to me, Danny," he said.

Martin shook his head.

"You see that?" The beam of light swung around and caught Bear in the face again. "Look real close, because what you see is what you get. You aren't even ashamed, are you?"

Bear stared into the light.

"I said, Look!" Bill said. He grabbed Martin by his neck. "There's a thief. And a liar, too."

Bill swung Martin around and heaved him down the path. Martin stumbled onto his knees, then got to his feet. He saw Bear up by the table, and when Bill got close to him, Bear shook the hot dog off his stick and held it out.

Bill stepped closer and Bear lunged at him.

"Your father's going to hear about this," Bill said, backing away.

Bear held the stick out until Bill was well down the path.

Bill swung the light around.

"What the hell are you looking at, Danny Boy?" he said.

Martin stared up at Bill. With the light in his eyes he was as good as blind.

WHAT HAPPENED TO RED DEER

1962 Red Deer turned the ball in his hand.

They were yelling in the bleachers now. "Chief! Go home, Chief!"

The ball fit in his palm like a stone. He caught the stitching with his nails and raised his eyes to the catcher. The catcher thrust two fingers at the ground.

A slider.

Red Deer nodded, coiled himself back, leg raised, stretching, and hurled the ball. The ball went low, looked like a gutter ball, then rose and smacked into the catcher's mitt. The umpire jerked his hand over his head, thumb up, and the batter shook his head.

"Out!" the umpire shouted.

There was a chorus of booing from the bleachers.

Red Deer watched them out of the corner of his eye.

Since the start of the game they had jeered, and when the game had gone into a tenth inning, they began yelling "Chief! Go home, Chief!"

He had ridden on the crest of it, letting it carry him through the game. But something was happening now and he didn't know what it was. It was as if something were dissolving in him, dissolving and going flat.

Darius, the coach, walked to the mound from the dugout.

"How's your arm holding up?" he said.

"Okay," Red Deer offered.

"We'll have her licked if you can hang in there."

Red Deer pulled the bill of his cap down.

"Don't mind those sons-of-bitches. They're just a bunch of drunks. You're pitching like a pro. Just get back in there and kill 'em." Darius slapped Red Deer on the back, then strode past third, up toward the bleachers.

"What the hell are you waiting for, Chief?" the loudest of the drunks yelled.

A batter stepped up to the plate. He practiced his swing, dipping in mid-stroke and pulling up. He tapped the bat on his shoes and positioned himself. The umpire and catcher squatted; the catcher pointed to the ground with his index finger. Knuckle. Red Deer turned the ball in his hand, found the stitching with his nails again, drew back like the hammer of a gun and hurled the ball. The ball went straight and fast, right down the pipe. The batter uncoiled, the bat scooped down into the ball, there was a loud crack, and the ball went high, up and back into the bleachers, a foul.

"Whoooa, Chief!" the drunks yelled.

Red Deer turned to face the bleachers.

He could see the men who were doing the yelling. They were wearing white shirts and colored ties, and they had brought women with them. Attractive women, who laughed and pushed and when the men yelled laughed into their hands.

"Go home, Chief!" the biggest yelled, standing, a beer in his fist. The woman at his side laughed, pulling at his pants leg.

Red Deer shook his head. He turned to the other side of the field. There his father, Osada, sat with the boy, Bear. A few rows up from them a knot of men from the reservation stood. Red Deer had not asked them to come, and when he had run out onto the playing field, he had been startled to see them. Joe Big Otter had waved and Red Deer had felt something in him sad and old and hurtful.

"Hey! Chief! You missing the Lone Ranger?" There was a cackle of laughter.

The men from the reservation glared across the field.

Red Deer turned the ball in his hand.

He wished the ball were a stone.

He took the sign from the catcher, eyed the batter, drew his body and arm back, and hurled the ball again. The batter swung around, connected, and then it was all moving, Red Deer carried across the field, the ball sizzling by his head, his mitt out, the hard break of the ball against his hand, then opening the mitt and lobbing the ball to first, the baseman reaching, throwing to third, the runner coming on hard, then sliding, the umpire charging, the ball, the baseman, the runner, and the umpire all converging there. In the dust you couldn't see at all.

"Safe!" the umpire yelled, spreading his arms wide at his waist. "Safe!"

An organ broke into a frenzy of scales and the scoreboard flashed. Bottom of the tenth. Six to five, visitors' lead.

Red Deer swung back to the mound.

"Go home, Chief!" the drunks yelled.

The shortstop caught him on the way. The man on third kicked the base, watching the two men.

"Two outs. Anything goes home, okay?"

Red Deer nodded.

"Just give 'em some of the old Buck stuff," the shortstop said. He spit through his teeth and slapped Red Deer on the back.

"Buck!" he said.

But Red Deer was staring off over the bleachers.

In grade school, when they ran the races on the playground, he never pushed himself and still he could beat them all, even the straining, grunting boys who couldn't stand to lose to an Indian.

It wasn't a hard thing to do.

He loved to run, and he ran to school and back home again and wherever else it was he went. Somehow rather than tiring him, as it did the others, it set him free. He loved the feel of the ground under his feet, the trees flashing by, the pumping of his lungs, the pain he pushed through into a solid rhythm that carried him away from everything. If he wanted he would change the rhythm, his legs working harder, the ground beating up with more power, but always the ground carried him, and he was surprised, when one day at school a man watched him run the circumference of the football field, a watch in his hand.

The man stopped Red Deer back of the goalposts, his face swollen with excitement, his thumb held down on the watch. "Wait! Stop there!" he said.

Red Deer had looked back to see where the others were. They weren't around the field yet.

"I can't believe it," the man said.

Red Deer's teacher came over. "Didn't I tell you he was fast?" he said. "Didn't I tell you?"

"Is that as fast as you can run?"

"No," Red Deer said.

"How old are you?"

"Fifteen."

The man held out his hand. "I just can't believe it," he said. "Jim Thorpe couldn't have done that at your age."

The others ran by, breathing hard, and Red Deer stepped into the stream of bodies. Halfway around the field he looked back. The two men were still talking, the man with the watch gesturing with his hands.

Red Deer heaved the ball down the baseline to the catcher.

"No!" the shortstop yelled. "Goddammit! Throw it around the horn."

Red Deer turned to face the shortstop.

"Haven't you ever played baseball?" The shortstop pointed to the second baseman with his mitt and shook his head. "What the hell is he doing out here?"

Red Deer shrugged his shoulders. They had him on first, and he didn't know what plays to make. He didn't like standing around so much, and they were always yelling at him.

"Hey! Chief!" Joe Fossen, the catcher, yelled. He threw the ball and Red Deer caught it, tossed it to second, and then it went around again.

It was the first time anyone on the team had called him "Chief." It was the first time *anyone* had called him "Chief."

He wasn't sure he liked it.

But he wasn't sure he liked playing baseball, either.

They had called him down to the principal's office not long after the man with the watch had been on the field, and Red Deer had wondered what they had singled him out for now. After the business with his father and the shooting, it seemed the teachers were afraid of him, or afraid that something would happen to them if they had anything to do with him. And the other Indians didn't know what to make of him, either—he was too big for his age, and there was still a general bad feeling on the reservation about the incident. He had gained notoriety without wanting it in any way.

In the office the principal, a short, bald-headed man behind a desk, had asked Red Deer to sit.

"Well, we've got it all fixed," he said.

"Did I do something?" Red Deer said. His heart was pounding. He felt uncomfortable and crossed his legs and uncrossed them, pressing his feet into the floor so his toes curled under.

"We thought you'd want to play baseball," the man said. He adjusted his glasses and leaned back in his chair.

Red Deer crossed his legs again.

"Joe Bradley's going to be driving up to Kenora just about every day. We thought you'd like to be playing on the team."

Outside the room a typewriter was snapping.

Red Deer didn't know what to say, so he stood. The principal stood with him.

"So what do you think?" he said.

Red Deer pushed his hands into his pockets and looked over the man's shoulder, through the window. The wind was blowing and the poplars in the schoolyard swayed.

"Okay," he said. "Sure."

The ball came around the horn again.

"Hey! Chief!" Sampson, the shortstop, yelled. "For Christ's sake don't just stand there!"

Red Deer caught the ball and carefully set it beside the base bag. He covered the distance between first and shortstop and there Joe Sampson stood, his fists tight at his sides. Red Deer hadn't realized how big Joe was until he got right up to him; he was the only boy on the team that could stand head to head with Red Deer.

"Hey!" the coach yelled.

"Don't call me that," Red Deer said.

"Make me," the boy said. He leaned toward Red Deer, so close Red Deer could smell his breath.

The coach headed across the field, then was running.

"Make me, *Chief!*" the boy said.

It made Red Deer think of his father, Osada, and how the men he had been a guide for had called him "Chief." Sometimes, when Red Deer had been out in the boat with him, he could see Osada was enraged when it happened, and other times he didn't seem to care at all. Sometimes, with the men who had had a sense of humor, he even seemed to like it.

"Break it up!" the coach yelled. He was nearly across the field now.

"Tonto," the boy said.

The word worked like a key in Red Deer's brain, and then as with a stone he hammered at the boy's face, and even when the boy was on the ground and bleeding Red Deer couldn't stop hitting him.

They called him "Buck" after that, and they were all a little afraid of him. He got bigger, his shoulders broadening, his legs getting longer. The boy he had beaten didn't come back; his jaw had been broken and one of his eyes damaged. No one said anything about it, but Red Deer felt bad.

Somehow they all seemed to feel bad.

They drank a good deal and had girlfriends and every now and then as they got older a boy would disappear from the team.

"Where's Freddie?" Red Deer asked one afternoon at practice. Freddie had become a friend of his, though a silent one.

"Didn't you hear?"

"No."

"He's not playing anymore. They got him down at the super-market in Fort Frances."

"What the hell's he doing down there?"

"Gettin' married, I guess," the boy said, a wry grin on his face.

It puzzled Red Deer. And not long after, when he was down in Fort Frances to see Osada, he stopped by the new supermarket to see if Freddie was there. It really was super. Huge. A long, low, cinder-block building with a giant red-and-blue sign in front. Red Deer stepped through the doors and it was cold inside and smelled of floor wax, like when they had had dances at the old school. The lights were bluish and buzzed and there were three women in yellow dresses at the registers.

"Is there a Fred Levine who works here?"

The women looked at him suspiciously.

"You mean a young guy? Eighteen or so?" the biggest said, tossing her head back.

A door opened off to one side and Freddie came out. He was wearing a green apron and had his hair slicked back.

"Hey! Freddie!" Red Deer said.

Freddie's eye puckered and his eyebrows drew down and then he smiled, too broadly.

"Come on back," he said.

Red Deer went up the aisle. There were all kinds of beans on the shelves, beans he had never even heard of.

"How's it goin'?" Freddie said.

He seemed nervous and stood on one leg and then on the other.

"How's the team? I heard you guys wupped shit out of Fond du Lac."

"Nine to three," Red Deer said.

"I heard you were pitchin', too. Is that right?"

Red Deer nodded. Something was wrong. Freddie was the one guy who'd gotten the others to lay off the "Chief" stuff, and they had been friends in the way a pitcher and first baseman can be friends if they are both good at it.

"So what's this all about, Freddie?" Red Deer said. He was so tall now his head was even with the top shelf.

Freddie looked up the aisle one way and down it the other.

"You heard, didn't you?" he said.

"You're getting married."

"That's it," he said.

Red Deer braced himself against the aisle divider. "So what about all that other stuff? Chicago and that school down there?"

"I'm just makin' some money now. See? Then I can go later."

He dusted the shelf Red Deer leaned on, rearranging the cans.

"So," Red Deer said.

The girls laughed up at the registers.

Freddie carefully straightened the cans, his hands shaking. He reminded Red Deer of a squirrel caught in a snare, his eyes wild.

"You don't have to get married, you know," Red Deer said.

Freddie looked up the aisle again and back.

"Look, I gotta go, Buck. I can't just stand around here talking. . . ."

A heavyset man with shiny black shoes stepped around the end of the aisle.

"Can I help you?" he said.

"Just a minute," Freddie said.

"Freddie," the man said.

Freddie's face had reddened. "Just let me explain," he said. "It's not what you think . . ."

"It's okay," Red Deer said. Though it was not okay.

"Hang on. Just wait a—"

The manager was coming up the aisle now. Red Deer could not stand to see Freddie this way.

"See you around, Freddie," he said.

He didn't toss up the tuft of Freddie's hair the way he always had, and walking across the parking lot in the bright sun, the new gravel sharp under his feet, Red Deer felt a hollow in his chest.

It seemed to Red Deer that they were all liars. And he had become a liar, too, though he lied in a different way. He said nothing, or as little as possible. It wasn't that there wasn't anything to say, but to say it would have torn up the fabric of all the lies and Red Deer knew none of them would stand for it. So he pretended he didn't feel the discomfort of the whites around him, or the hatred and bad feeling of the other Indians. It got so the only place he could escape the lies was playing baseball, and for that reason he came to love the game. On the field the ball moved, and they played. He could walk out onto the field, the mitt snug on his hand, and win or lose, he would pitch his best and whether his teammates hated him or not, they needed him up there on the mound. Slider. Curveball. Grease ball. Knuckleball. Fast pitch. He could get his fingers on the fine stitching of the ball and it fit into his palm like a planet. Or a shooting star. It was all a game and he saw the line he wanted the ball to take, up to and past the batter. He got to know the boys on the other teams, how they batted, how they ran.

There seemed to be no end to it. It happened so fast he could only do a little at a time, test what his hand could do to the line. But he came along fast, and people knew him.

"Let him have it, Buck!" they'd yell from the stands. "Give it to 'im, Buck!"

But after the games he went home. If he was near the reservation he stayed at his mother's, even though he didn't like his stepfather. He liked playing with the boy, though. Bear was like a little animal, only smarter, and faster, and they'd tumble in the dirt in the yard and the boy loved to play catch. On hot summer afternoons they listened to Minnesota Twins games on the radio, drinking root beer—Red Deer would buy cases of it—and when the Hamm's commercials came on, sung as though by Indians, with a drum pounding in the background, Red Deer and Bear would burst out laughing.

It was on one of those afternoons that Red Deer and his stepfather, Joe Big Otter, got to fighting. They were sitting outside the house, drinking under the shade of an umbrella Joe had bought at the supermarket in Fort Frances.

"You see a guy there with slicked-back hair?" Red Deer said. "Big nose?"

"No," Joe said.

Red Deer looked up into the umbrella. The umbrella had been on sale. On it Huey, Louie, and Dewey marched with sand buckets, pink, yellow, and candy blue.

The Twins were on the radio.

"I want to hear a story," Bear said.

"Shhhh," Martha said. She reached under Bear's armpit and tickled him.

"What kind of story do you want to hear?" Red Deer said.

"I want to hear a story about cowboys," the boy said.

It made Red Deer sad to hear him say this, and he looked up into the umbrella again and took a sip of his beer.

"Why don't you tell him the one about Litani?" Joe said.

Litani had been shot in the altercation with the marshals, when Osada had gotten the men to take their boys out of the new school. Litani had been Joe's younger brother.

Red Deer did not answer. It was hot and he could tell nothing good would come of this. He noticed how whoever it was who had drawn the ducks for the umbrella had put smiles on their bills. They looked funny holding the pails.

"Tell him that one," Joe Big Otter said. "There's a *cowboy* story."

Red Deer looked across the table. Joe smiled. Martha put her hand on Joe's forearm, gripped him around the wrist.

"You see," Joe said, his drunken eyes on the boy, "there was this proud man—"

"Shut up," Red Deer said.

"He should hear it," Joe said.

"Not the way you're telling it," Red Deer said. He set his beer on the table. He was hoping this would just pass.

Martha pulled at the bottle in Joe's hand. "You've had enough," she said.

"Don't," he said.

"You've had too much. Let go."

"Tell it," Joe said.

Red Deer looked away. He didn't want to tell Bear the story, and he didn't want Joe to tell it either.

"Coward," Joe said.

"Not as big a coward as you with your bottle," Red Deer replied.

Joe stood. The boy's eyes widened. The boy could not understand what they were saying, and when they began to yell, he crawled under the table.

Joe punched Red Deer in the mouth and then Red Deer had Joe by his ponytail and slammed his face into the picnic table. Blood ran down Joe's nose and Red Deer, trying to pull away, got hit in the mouth again. He tried to pin Joe down but Joe was hollering now.

"Your goddamned cowboy—"

Red Deer hit him in the mouth. He felt the teeth give way under his knuckles. Martha's eyes were wide and Joe stumbled back from the table. Martha held her hand to her mouth, and Joe ran inside. Bear was crying under the table. Then Joe swung by the kitchen window with his rifle, and Red Deer was over the garden fence, out across the field, and he didn't stop running until he was miles out of the reservation.

He didn't tell them where he was staying. He'd made himself a lean-to down by the fish hatchery, and at night he'd swim and catch brown trout, and bake them in the hillside behind the lean-to. He knew he couldn't do this very long, but he also knew something would come up. They were playing a game down in Fort Frances, against a Toronto team, and some big-name scouts were supposed to be there.

"They're waiting for you," the coach had said.

The morning of the game with Toronto Red Deer got up early. He swam in the clean, bitter cold water, then knocked down the lean-to. The fishery people were getting wise to him anyway, and he'd have to find someplace else. He walked into town, spent his last dollar on a plate of eggs and hash browns and coffee. At two he met the others at the school, and then everything was all right.

The basement was cool, and they suited up, the others snapping each other with their towels and joking.

"Hey! Buckeroo!" one of the boys said, thumping him on the back.

Red Deer took his uniform from his locker, set his clothes out as he always did. He dressed quickly, his hands sure, finally pulling the laces of his tennis shoes tight. He reached into his locker for his cleats and swung them over his shoulder. If he could keep it out of his mind, he thought, everything would be fine.

The game went terribly. The new first baseman was slow, and Red Deer wished Freddie were there. He missed him now, though it didn't occur to him why. He pitched badly, and he watched the scouts in the bleachers. The two men wore wide-brimmed hats and pointed, nodded, and scribbled on notepads.

It seemed it was all coming to a grinding end.

They forced their way through a miserable third inning and headed for the dugout.

"What the hell is wrong with you?" the coach said.

Everyone else in the dugout looked the other way. "Huh? What's going on?"

Red Deer stared out across the field. Meyers was up to bat. He swung in short choppy strokes.

"Are you listening to me?" the coach said.

"I don't know," Red Deer said.

The coach slapped his hand on his knee. "Well, you goddamned well better know. Do you have any idea how important this game is?" He lowered his voice. "It's your goddamned baby. They didn't come out here to see Hodges."

Beside him Hodges poked at his mitt.

Red Deer felt badly that he had heard. He wasn't a good first baseman and he knew it.

There was a crack of a bat, and everyone in the dugout stood. Red Deer sat on the bench.

"Get up," the coach yelled, but Red Deer wasn't about to. Not like that.

On the mound again he couldn't force the ball down the line, and the game had all gone away somewhere. He was tired, dirty, and hungry. He had lost something, and a deep sadness was setting in. It wasn't this damn game, he thought. It was Bear. He'd lost Bear, and he figured he'd lost his mother, too, only now he could see he'd never really had her, and maybe that hurt the worst.

A big kid named Donnelly got up to bat, kicking his cleats into the dirt like a rooster. They were leading nine/five into the sixth inning and now their batters were all getting cocky.

"Come on, Chief, throw me a fast one," he said.

Red Deer looked into the stands, then at the boy.

"Come on, Chief," he said.

Red Deer tightened his grip on the ball.

"Put her right here, Chief," the boy said, tapping the base with his bat.

Red Deer found the stitches on the ball, gripped it in his hand. He got a kind of tunnel vision, and when Steadman, the catcher, signaled for him to throw a curve, he shook his head. He knew what to do with this one. He settled onto his legs, stretched as if to break himself, and when he threw the ball it hissed out of his hand, went low, then broke into the catcher's mitt with a dusty thud. The batter's mouth dropped open.

"Stcccrikc!" thc umpirc callcd.

Red Deer caught the ball, tossed it around the horn.

No one said anything.

When it was over, and they had won by two runs, Red Deer dropped the ball on the mound and walked to the dugout.

"Jesus Christ!" the coach said. "That was really something."

Red Deer wiped his face with a towel. He never wanted to play another game like that. He had wanted to kill the boy Donnelly, and had prodded himself along with him, remembering his face and what he had said. And when the boy was up to bat again, and he sensed something dangerous in Red Deer, Red Deer imagined him saying the things he had said over again.

He wasn't happy now—he was drained, and felt ugly.

The two scouts came down to the dugout.

"Hell of a game you pitched."

Red Deer nodded.

They had turned the lights off on the field and now the dugout was dark but for the light coming in from the parking lot. The bigger man's glasses shone in the dark.

"Anything you'd like to say?"

All he wanted now was to be alone.

"I've pitched better," he said. It was what he was supposed to say. And it was true, only now he wished they would leave.

"We'll be getting in touch," the bigger of the two men said.

Red Deer watched them cross the parking lot to the car. The lights came on, and the car crackled out of the lot with the others, dust billowing behind them. Red Deer settled down onto the dirt floor, the cement cool against his sides, the dugout just long enough to hold him. It was all he wanted now.

The rest was easy. It was like falling. A small league team picked him up as a relief pitcher, and then he was playing, and had some jack in his pocket. He traveled a lot, and he forgot about what had happened. He learned to forget a lot of things, and he learned how to fight too.

"Hey, Chief," someone would say.

It was like a button they pushed.

He learned to hit first, and hit hard, and it wasn't until later that he got into fights with men bigger than he was. He had his nose broken three times and lost a tooth, a canine, so when he smiled it gave him the look of someone who would take the caps off beer bottles with his teeth for fun.

And on the mound he felt it get bigger in him, like a stone, and he held on to it tighter. He learned to focus it, and he thought of it as being like a train or a bulldozer. All he had to think of was that boy, and it started again.

"Chief," he'd think to himself.

He got to love it, and it was precious.

He found it had all kinds of uses.

On nights when things were going badly, when he felt a slagging in his desire to throw the ball, he could pump himself up with it. It got to be such a thing with him he was afraid he would lose it, and then he nursed it when he wasn't on the field, and soon after he was thrown in jail for nearly killing a man in a bar.

"Don't mess with him," they said.

Red Deer thought it was funny. He was just playing the game. But something had happened, and one night, when he came in from a drunk, he had looked in the mirror in the bathroom of his hotel room and had seen somebody he didn't know staring out at him—a big, fierce-looking Indian with a crooked nose and hard eyes. It scared him so badly that he covered all the mirrors in his room with towels and lay on his bed, his arms pulled tight over his chest.

The morning after, Harvey, his first baseman, had spoken to him in the dugout. It was a hot day at the end of August and Red Deer was tying the laces of his cleats.

His hands shook on the laces.

"You'd better slow down on the sauce," Harvey said.

It occurred to Red Deer to knock Harvey's teeth out, but the look on his face was so concerned that he laughed instead.

"Nothing that doesn't grease the old joints," Red Deer said.

Harvey brushed the dirt off his glove. He shook his head. "I'll tell you something," he said. "Just between the two of us."

Red Deer busied himself with his shoes. He didn't want to hear it.

"I got an ulcer the size of a half-dollar in my gut," Harvey said, "and if it gets any worse they say they're gonna have to cut some out and sew me up. Now, I thought that was pretty funny, until they said it might kill me, see." He put his face down by Red Deer's. "Do you see what I'm saying?"

Red Deer grunted, double-tying his laces, pulling on them. He could hardly control his hands now.

"Hey, do you hear what—"

"Shut up, Harve," Red Deer said. There was a buzzing in his brain. He shot to his feet and grabbed Harvey by his shirt and twisted it. "Shut up before I knock out your teeth."

The season ended well enough, and Red Deer got himself a job in a meat-packing plant in Ohio, where he had played his last game. He hated the noises and smells at first. He hated the gray walls and the fluorescent lights. He hated his foreman and he hated Vinny, the boy he worked with.

But as with everything else, he learned to shut it out.

"Don't you just love it?" Vinny said. They were cutting the heads off pigs. A fine line of blood squirted up Vinny's rubber smock while he cut with the saw.

Vinny smiled.

He had a few teeth missing, and Red Deer saw himself in the mirror for a second.

"Cut that shit out, Vinny," he said.

But then it was baseball season again, the job and the winter shucked off. He took the train down to Tampa and the tryouts started. The weather was warm and there were birds all over and it was hard to pitch at first.

But it always happened.

"Chief," someone said. "Tonto."

And he was throwing hot again. His arm swollen and hard. He built it up slowly, added Vinny to it, but there were so many now it didn't matter. He didn't even have to think of any specific one, it just came to him in a knotted, hard bundle. A bundle he would spit out his arm and over the bag.

"Jesus," they said. "He throws a real killer-ball."

He was throwing like that in his fifth pickup game. Hurling himself into it, when a scout for the Cleveland Aces spotted him. He'd never been hotter, and like that, a month later he was in Chicago for an exhibition game against the Cubs, and somehow, someone had found out on the reservation and there they were, Osada and Bear, and Joe Big Otter and his friends.

The lights burned.

A brown bottle sailed up over the netting, turning end over end, flashing, and landed on the field. One of the men in the white shirts and colored ties stood.

"Chief! Go home, Chief!" he shouted.

A bat boy ran out to the bottle.

Darius marched to the mound from the dugout, and the umpires came up from the bases.

"What the hell is going on?" Darius said.

Red Deer glanced up into the lights. Everything seemed so bright now, the field an electric green.

"We got a goddamned game goin' on here. You can't just stand the fuck out here and pick your nose. What the hell is wrong with you? Are you on the sauce or what?"

Red Deer kicked at the mound with his cleats.

"Answer me!"

"I don't know," Red Deer said.

"I'm going to put our relief in if you don't get your ass in gear."

Red Deer turned to Darius, looked down into his eyes.

Darius could tell something was wrong.

"I'm not on the sauce," Red Deer lied.

But it didn't matter now. There was no stopping what was opening. It was just a matter of finishing now. He had to finish it.

"I got it," Red Deer said.

"Well, you better have it," Darius said.

He crossed the field to the dugout and climbed down.

Red Deer pushed his mitt on his hand. He remembered what the man with the watch had said:

"Jim Thorpe couldn't have done that at your age."

Red Deer positioned himself on the mound. Now they had done it to him, too.

"Come on, goddammit!" Darius yelled from the dugout.

"Chief! Hey, you! You old lady, Chief!" the men in the stands yelled.

Red Deer felt the anger flare in him.

The batter was holding his hands up and looking into the sky.

The catcher gave him the sign again, and Red Deer jabbed himself with his anger. Now it hardly moved him at all. It was alternately terrifying, and a relief. And when the anger came again, he gripped the ball, stared down the pipe, got his nails on the stitching of the ball, and heaved the ball down the line as hard as he could. The ball floated, dipped, then slammed into the catcher's mitt and the batter coiled around.

"Steeeeerike!" the umpire called.

The crowd roared.

The tribesmen stood, and when the others took their seats again, they remained standing. Someone started the others banging their feet on the stands, and the booming got louder, a harsh, crushing banging.

With the tribesmen standing, Red Deer could not see Osada, and he wondered whether he was sitting back there or if he had gone.

"Go home, Chief!" the drunk yelled.

Red Deer felt the ball in his hand.

The batter swung around, practicing. He stepped up to the plate, and the catcher gave Red Deer two fingers. It pushed out of him now, and he saw the batter grinning there. "Come on, Chief," the batter was saying. "Come on, Chief."

Red Deer gripped the ball, a stone.

In a flash that burned him, Red Deer saw that he might really do it this time. He saw the ball, hurling down the pipe, no curve, no spin, just hurling, the batter's skull shattering. He could kill him now, and he could call it an accident. It had come to this. And he knew, with absolute certainty, when he stepped onto the mound that he was going to kill the batter. He was going to throw the ball through the side of his head. He would crush him with his hatred, and it would be gone, he would be free maybe, and when he got the signal from the catcher the batter said it again, and Red Deer felt everything in him screaming toward that pitch, the crowd roaring, the blood in his head pounding, and sharper than ever, he saw the line the ball would take, the point where the ball would contact the batter's head, above and back of the ear—it was like tunnel vision, and there was only in front of him the ear and the hair over the man's temple, the ball in his hand, the tremendous power that moved his limbs like iron, threatening to burst him, the crowd roaring like steam and the mound pushing up beneath him. He drew his arm back, then farther, the weight of his rage there compressed, and in an explosion the ball arced around, hard, heavy, and as it shot from his hand, Red Deer caught the stitching with his thumb, and the ball, as though it were on a track, swung wide across the field and smacked square into the batter's startled face.

The umpire burst out from behind the catcher.

The field came alive, the crowd roaring, and Darius scrambled from the dugout. The batter kicked on the ground, and the umpire tried to hold him down.

Red Deer turned his back to it, and tugging at his mitt, walked to the mound. He stared up into the bleachers, at the big man with the bright blue tie, the one who had started it all. The man raised his fist, opened his mouth to shout. Something settled home in Red Deer's chest, found bottom, and he held his eyes on the big man until he turned away. He remembered his father's scream when Litani had been shot, and what the officers had said after the commotion died down.

"It was a *terrible mistake*. We're sorry," the man Harris had said.

Red Deer drew back the bill of his cap. Without the cover for his eyes the stadium lights were blinding.

They were coming up behind him now, he could hear their feet on the dry grass.

He remembered his father's face, how when he had screamed it was as though something had shattered in him, and when the noise had stopped and his mouth had closed, something had gone away.

"Buck!" Darius said.

Red Deer turned to face him. He puffed along, swinging his arms, two press men behind him with cameras.

Darius reached out, grasped Red Deer's forearm. "Buck," he said. "Buck, just tell them—"

Red Deer bent low, and as if to confide in Darius, pulled him closer. He could smell the oil in Darius' hair, his aftershave.

"Buck, you gotta—"

"Let go," Red Deer said, his voice quiet and sure as death now. "Let go of my arm, Darie," he said.

WHAT DANNY DOESN'T KNOW

1964 To Dr. Sorenson, the laughter echoing off the lake is as maddening as the mosquitoes dancing across his face. He patched the screens on all sides of the cabin, in the dead heat of the afternoon today, careful not to miss even the smallest of holes, but now he realizes there must be other places, too, a crack in a window frame, or gap at the bottom of the front or back door, where the mosquitoes crawl in. It's just little holes like this, he thinks, that let the unpleasant things in.

The doctor lies on his back, sheets draped around his calves, his wife's arm slung across his chest. It is hot, and her arm warms his chest so that sweat runs to his armpit, where it makes his T-shirt cling.

There is a far-off splashing, then more laughter.

"You'd think they'd have gotten off the lake by now," the doctor says, staring at the wall beyond his feet.

The room is tiny, barely large enough for a bed and dresser, and even then, the bed is really too small for more than one person. The doctor's eyes wander across the gray wall, then fix on a discoloration in the corner. Above it there is a dark spot in the ceiling tiles. The roof leaks, and the doctor knows that soon he will have to reshingle it.

For a second he jerks awake.

"What is it, Neal?" his wife says.

He tries to recall if he has forgotten to write a prescription for a patient's meds, but his thinking is slow, dulled somehow. No, he thinks, rolling onto his side, thumping his head onto his pillow, he didn't forget.

Into the wall, he says, "If they don't knock it off soon I'm going to go out there and fix their little party."

"Just let it go this time, all right? Neal?" his wife says, resting her hand on his shoulder.

The doctor rolls onto his stomach, and raising himself on his elbows, looks over the headboard into the porch. His son, Danny, is perched on a chair by the lakeside windows, his face pressed to a screen.

"Danny," the doctor says, "what did I ask you to do?"

Danny turns from the window, but says nothing.

Across the road a stereo is blaring, the music strangely like carnival music, raucous, tinny.

Danny can feel where the screen has cut little squares into his forehead. With his head turned, he looks out the window by screwing his eyes to one side. Down shore, in front of the Nelsons' cabin, two older boys and two girls swim near a rickety diving dock. The smaller of the two girls, a blonde, titters playfully, a bit drunk, and the round-headed fat boy cannonballs into the lake, his butt whapping the water.

"Jesus, Al," his friend says, a sneer in his voice, "that was one hell of a dive."

The blond girl levers herself out of the water, her arms braced against the dock in a wide V, and Danny feels a swelling in his chest. In the weak light from the Nelsons' cabin, he can see the girl isn't wearing her swimsuit. Her breasts swing freely as she walks to the diving board, her nipples like big Hersheys Kisses.

From the water Al whistles. "Whew! Those are dangerous, Jody."

"I'll say that again," the smaller boy says. He dog-paddles, his head barely above the water, a smile on his face like an actor's on a TV commercial, one showing hamburgers or milk shakes.

Dr. Sorenson watches the mosquitoes crawling on the screen around his son's face.

"Danny, what did I say?"

"Do I have to?" Danny says, shooting back from the window, his eyes shadowed so the doctor can't see in what direction he is looking. The way Danny snapped his head back makes Dr. Sorenson wonder what he is watching.

"Danny . . ."

"Neal, don't make a big thing out of this," the doctor's wife says, turning on her side so she can see out the door.

Dr. Sorenson reaches under the bed for the clock, turns it so he can read the luminous green figures on its face, then sets it back on the floor.

"Mary, it's almost two o'clock," Neal says, swinging his legs off the bed.

"It isn't his fault, Neal," Mary says. "Those kids next door would keep anybody awake." She tugs Neal toward her, so he lies on his back with his feet on the floor, and turns to look into the porch. "*Please*, Danny," she says, "go to bed." Then she pushes the door home and locks it.

She runs her finger down Neal's chest, playfully zigzagging. "Why don't you forget about it for a while, Neal," she says.

Neal laughs softly.

Mary runs her finger down his chest again, pulling up the elastic on his briefs. His body is stiff, and his breathing is shallow. For some time he has been like this, hard and distant. At first it was his work, but now something else has come between them, and Mary no longer knows whether it is Neal or his work she resents. It seems when they talk now, it is always an argument, a confrontation.

"Neal," she says, "are you awake?"

He nods, shifting onto his side, away from her.

Mary wants to ask him what he's thinking, but doesn't want to risk being drawn into an argument. She presses her breasts into his back, and he slides away. Mary is not excited, but sometimes this can bring Neal back to her.

"Make love to me," she says, touching him then.

But lately, when Neal is distant, or angry, especially at Danny, for reasons she can never understand—a spanking for a running faucet, the belt for leaving a light on or dirtying his school clothes—she uses this to keep him from hurting Danny, and she knows Neal suspects as much. It has become a kind of tool, and for that reason, Mary no longer enjoys it.

Neal feels Mary's breasts against his back. He isn't sure what he wants to do. Pull away, or be drawn in. He is aroused, wants to swell inside her, move, with that aching, slick motion, and he wants to be alone, too.

Mary tugs on his shirt, then his hands are on her breasts, and in the same way they have done this a thousand times, they begin. He wants to suggest something new, something he read in a magazine, but to do that he would either have to lie, or tell her where he'd gotten the idea. He imagines her scorn, and quickens his movement, so as not to lose his erection, and *there*, too, would be more friction. So he thinks of the young receptionist they've hired at the clinic, Vicki—(both *i*'s, in her script, dotted with *oh*'s)—and imagines Vicki's legs parted beneath him, her young breasts in his hands, and he nearly whispers "Vicki," but catches himself, stops the wrong fluttering of his tongue, then clearly says, "Mary."

Mary cradles Neal's head against her own. Now, even when he uses his mouth, she is not responsive. He is too fast, too hard, and there is no passion in it. Now it is only with herself that she is responsive. During the day, when she is home alone and Danny is off to grade school, she does this thing herself, to release the frustration she feels. She tells herself this will make her more responsive to Neal, but she feels perverse somehow, like she is hiding some dark secret, and her own touch never satisfies her.

It is affection she craves.

"Neal," she says.

Neal moves faster. Mary knows he will come in a moment and a terrible sadness fills her. She misses the kissing, and the way Neal would watch her brush her hair at night, and she rises to meet Neal, without any real excitement, remembering how she had pleased him, how he was nearly insatiable for her.

"I could just eat you all up," he said once.

"Not so fast, Neal," Mary says, holding his hips. She feels the warm thrust of him inside her, and for a moment responds, but is drawn back into herself again. She remembers how when they first met Neal would call her from work to say he couldn't wait to get home from the office, and later, frantic with their desire, they'd do it on the living room floor—there was the scent of wool and sweat and sea wrack on his mouth—or in the backseat of the new Chrysler, where everything smelled of leather, saddle soap, and cigarettes.

And here, on this bed, at the lake.

Summers cicadas buzzed, and the air was rich with the smell of lake, and rush, and pine. Fall, everything smelled of damp earth, decaying pine needles, camphor, and from far across the lake came the sporadic whine of saws. Winter they never visited the cabin, but in May they opened the windows, and their bodies puckered with the near chill as they made love on this bed, the sun warming the old blanket they wrapped themselves in.

Here, at the lake.

The bed creaks with the doctor's motion.

"Stop, Neal," Mary says.

He jerks his head from her, pulls his arms away and slides off to the side nearest the door. Mary wishes Neal would ask her why she wanted to stop. Danny, she would say. Danny will hear us.

But they are back into it now.

Dr. Sorenson jerks the sheet over the bed, and after minutes of glowering at the ceiling, opens the door a crack. Danny is still at the window.

"I thought I told you to go to bed?" he says.

Danny turns his head from the window, angled so he looks in the direction of neither the bedroom nor the lake.

"Danny!"

The doctor hates it when Danny is like this, and watching, something sinks deep into his chest. Dr. Sorenson wants Danny to be stronger than he is, at least strong enough to shake hands without looking at the ground. But Danny is shy, and when he isn't, he's a smart aleck, a wiseacre, a clown. Danny is bullied by bigger, stronger boys, and Neal worries about him.

One afternoon, years ago, Danny came home with a bruised eye and dirty streaks down his nose and neck.

"Who did this?" Neal said, feeling as if his eyes would pop for all the pressure behind them.

"Nobody."

"Don't lie, Danny," he said, wanting to help.

But Danny had cried then, thumping his fists on his thighs while Mary held him.

This crying is something Neal is afraid of.

"You gotta hit back, Danny!" he'd said.

And Danny had, with a piece of cement, and the following day the principal, Harold Jacobson, called to set up an appointment for a meeting of the two boys' parents. After that mess Neal decided he'd give Danny some fighting lessons, but the thought of taking a jab at Danny, to teach him how to protect himself, was finally too uncomfortable. Already Danny looks at the ground when Neal talks to him.

Mary rests her hand on Neal's shoulder. "Just let him be," she says. She wonders why Danny is making things so difficult by staying at the window. She reaches over Neal's head and grasps the door.

Danny watches the door close and turns back to the lake. The blond girl scampers onto the dock. She is nearly as drunk now as Danny's dad was that night at the wedding reception. Reeling drunk. The boys in the water, their heads like black bobbers, sing out, "boom ba-ba, boom ba-ba," as the girl walks to the end of the diving board.

Then the big fat girl bounds across the dock, her heavy breasts and thighs shaking like Jello-O. She tackles Jody with a knee-buckling slap, and they both tumble headfirst into the lake.

"Atta girl, Rox," Al, the fat boy, drawls, clawing onto the dock, his hairy belly hanging to his thighs in folds. He clutches a beer bottle in one hand, raises it to his mouth and throws his head back.

When the blond girl climbs onto the dock again, Danny realizes he is stiff, and touches himself. It feels good, watching and touching himself. Just to see what happens.

He hopes his mother keeps his father away.

Mary takes Neal in her mouth. She thinks this is the way to take the pressure off. She can't quite get her breath, and the hair on her mouth sickens her. She draws back, disengages from him, and strokes him with her hand.

"How is this?" she says.

Neal pulls her hand away.

"Show me," she says, reaching for him again.

"Stop it!"

"What is *wrong*, Neal?"

Neal shakes Mary away. God! he thinks, it can't always be like this. It isn't supposed to be like this. He's done what he was supposed to do.

But it isn't enough just to do it.

None of it is enough.

And now, even the simplest things get him roaring mad.

"I'm sorry, Neal," Mary says, a touch of anger in her voice. She lies on her back, wanting to touch him, just put her arm around his waist, wanting to say, "Let's stop this, Neal." But she pulls away too, hoping Danny has gone away from the window, back to bed. She is nearest the door now, and she opens it, just enough to see what Danny has done.

Danny has never seen breasts before, not like this, but here it is, right in front of him, this girl with the big round breasts and mysterious dark spot between her legs. Something slick has come out of him, and when he rubs himself, he gets a scary, tingly, burning sensation, one that is almost unbearable, especially when the blond girl stands on the dock. He almost can't stop rubbing himself.

Maybe this is what they do.

The bedroom door clicks behind him, and he stands with his hands at his sides, aching to touch that place again, but afraid and feeling sick to his stomach. He hopes his father doesn't get up, but, there is the creaking of the bed again, and heavy, bare-footed steps on the porch floor.

Danny is sure his father will grip his shoulder and hurt him. He waits.

The air is still, but for the record player's blasting and the occasional splash and laughter at Nelsons'. The dock is an ice-white diamond on the black lake. Dr. Sorenson can't understand what Danny finds so interesting in these drunk kids. And then, a girl, her hair hanging in dark strands over her shoulders, raises herself onto the dock, and Dr. Sorenson's pulse quickens.

At the end of the diving board the girl balances, her muscular thighs poised to carry her up and into the water.

Mary was like this.

Tan, muscular from tennis.

Looking at her made him want to eat her. Just anywhere, swallow all of her, and be full.

Neal knows what Danny has been doing. He wants to tell Danny that touching himself is right, and normal, but there is a twisted, sick feeling in the words he finds, and he can find no others but the dry, lifeless ones he uses with his patients.

Mary flicks on the lamp by the bed. With the light coming from below, there are dark hollows under her eyes and her hair is matted over her shoulders. Neal and Danny jerk back from the window.

"Neal, what is it? Is something wrong?"

Neal shakes his head, too quickly, too certain.

"Why don't you just go over there and tell them to quiet down? Otherwise you'll be up all night."

"Turn off the light, will you?" the doctor says. "It's blinding." The lamp goes out, and Neal stands behind Danny, touches Danny's shoulder.

At his father's touch, a jolt charges through Danny. He can't understand why, right now, his father wants to be friendly, and it scares him more than does the yelling and hitting.

Mary stands in the bedroom doorway tying her robe. "If you aren't going to do it, Neal, I will."

"I'll do it," Neal snaps back.

"That's all right."

"Why don't you go back to bed?"

"Is there something wrong?"

Danny looks up at his father.

"Nothing's wrong. Go back to bed," Neal says.

Neal shuffles on his pants, kicking his feet out the legs. In a rush he is out the door, crossing the lawn to the Nelsons', and Mary stands with Danny at the window. Danny wonders at the puzzled look on his mother's face. She looks old tonight, and tired more than he has ever seen her.

The feeling Danny has is like that at a game, when there is an upset, and you wait for your team to win, or lose. He wants this feeling to go away, but it is growing instead.

He has only seen his mother and father like this once before, at a pool on the way down to Florida, a big, aqua-colored pool at Howard Johnson's. His father played volleyball with some college kids, and there was this girl he splashed a lot, and the whole trip after was one angry silence.

Danny feels like crying.

Mary laughs, pointing for Danny to watch. On his toes, Neal steps around the front of the Nelsons' cabin to the record player, his mallard print shirt ballooning around his chest.

As Neal removes the tonearm from the turntable, a naked girl runs drunkenly across the diving dock on the lake, her breasts bouncing obscenely.

Skin. White dock.

The girl skids to a halt in the middle of the dock, her eyes blindly trained on the cabin.

"What happened to the record player?" she says. "Al, is that you?"

"I'm down here," comes a voice from the water.

Facing the dock, Neal holds the tonearm. He looks like something has just been torn from his arms. He turns and sheepishly stares across the lawn, into the cabin, and Mary recognizes that look, the little-boy smile, the "late at the office look."

Danny watches his mother's face. It is like Bobby Peterson's, when he leaned over to pick up his croquet ball and Patty Zmolek hit him in the face with a mallet.

"People are trying to get some sleep around here!" Danny's

father yells, his voice high and desperate. He holds a fist up, but there is nothing behind it, and Danny aches for his father, and is ashamed.

Danny's mother's eyes are pressed together, like little sparks will come shooting out of them.

"Go to bed, Danny," she says.

Danny is sweating now, a cold, shivering sweat. He slides into his roll-away bed, pulling the covers up to his chin. He wonders if dying is like this.

The front door slams, and Neal steps around the roll-away bed to the window.

Car doors slam, and the boys, as they drive away, talk loudly.

"Needs a good fat lip," Al drawls.

"I'd have shown the bastard," says the little one.

The burble of the car's exhaust fades, and then there is only the wind tossing the pines, the rattling of the storm windows, and the sharp buzz of crickets.

"Is he asleep?" Neal says.

Danny lies still. He can feel it coming, and he pulls his knees up under his chin. He watches through a tiny hole between the blankets. It reminds Danny of the blind he sat in with his father, waiting for a deer to come along.

"Mary," his father says. He raises his hand, and before it rests on her shoulder, she tosses her head back and steps away from the window.

In the dark her eyes are like shiny marbles.

"Don't touch me," she says, her voice so hard Danny feels it tear through the cabin like a gunshot.

ACT
OF
LOVE

1966 I remember turning the axe in my hands and *thinking*. The phone was ringing off the hook. And then, clear as a trumpet, I heard Netta say, *Answer it, Dusty.*

I went around back and into the kitchen. I'd gotten up a sweat splitting cord and could hardly hold the phone.

"Yes?" I said.

"It's Tomato," Tomato said.

I looked at the clock—it was half past one. A chill runs up my back; early-morning calls usually mean one thing. "What's wrong," I said.

"Nothing's wrong."

"Nothing."

"Well, not exactly, but—"

I had my hand on Netta's desk in the dark. I was starting to get a little mad. Tomato's about ten years younger than me—I was forty-five then—and I could just see him, tugging on his Adam's apple, the phone pressed to his ear. He'd only had the resort a few years and we were still getting used to each other. At times we didn't get along well.

"Don't gimme any gas this time of night," I said. "What the hell do you want? What is it? Somebody dead? You got a mess over there with the bloods?"

"No," he said.

"So what's the big mystery?"

"We've got a late fly-in."

I listened to the high-pitched hum on the phone. "I don't get it," I said.

"They want to be out on the lake by six."

"So, you're trying to tell me no one else'll go out with them?"

"No, that isn't it."

"So what the hell *is?*"

This Tomato considered. It was a good long time he took and I could tell was trying to decide which version to give me. The lie came back in the form of flattery.

"They said they wanted the *absolute* best," Tomato said, smooth as honey. It really took my breath away.

"That's a crock," I said, hanging up.

Around five I woke and made coffee. It was my routine to wake at five or a little after—to make a fire and coffee and read—only since Netta had died I'd slept later, so as to spend as little time as possible awake in the cabin. My cabin is quite small, just a bedroom and kitchen and loft, and back then it was filled with Netta: the chair she bought at some rummage sale in the bedroom, a cheap painting of sad-looking willows over the refrigerator, moccasins (hand beaded) on the wall of the loft, appliquéd leggings hanging from a hook behind the door. None of this had I been able to move or rearrange in any way. Some mornings, early on, I would reach out to that old chair and feel Netta's arm, just as it had always been, beside mine, and then other mornings, I *wouldn't* feel it and it scared me just as much. But that morning, the birds were out and the sky was blue as the glass in old power insulators, deep and watery-looking, and I was happy not to have to spend the morning alone.

I got my gear together, poured myself a thermos, and rowed my boat over to the lodge. It was quiet on shore, but I could see smoke coming out of the chimney and I figured they were having breakfast. I brought the biggest of the new boats around front and gassed her up and went for a long time tying leaders and filling minnow buckets and all the stuff the kids hated doing. I had hated all that too, only now, with Netta gone, and thinking about my boy, and Hodie, when I couldn't help it—this was the only time my hands were sure, and it felt good, the ritual of the knots, and I thought if there was a kid along I'd show him how to tie a bowline.

Slick as can be, I'd say. *You take this end, wrap it around your waist—That's right!—make a loop, and then with the free end, you make like it's a rabbit and go up the hole, around the rope—That's the one—and back down the hole—There's a dog behind you, see!—real fast.*

Sheep shank? You bet, it's easy.

An hour later I was still waiting. I had run through all the knots, had the boat cleaned (something I let the kids do now) and the gear stashed, and was feeling my stomach grinding away. The sun was up by then and I drew my cap down over my eyes in the back. It was getting hot. I never have liked waiting, and I still don't like it now, but then it was very hard. I was accustomed to filling every waking minute with something, tidying the cabin, chopping wood, carving—I even did the *Toronto Star* crosswords, and I have never liked crossword puzzles. But there I was in the back of that hot boat, moored to the dock and bobbing around doing absolutely nothing.

Don't lose your temper now, Netta teased.

I bolted up in the boat, looked up shore and back. I felt something grab me under the ribs, and when I got control of that feeling, the lodge door slammed again and out came Tomato with the guests.

I will never forget the figure the three of them cut: Tomato, red faced and broad across the gut, striding along, full of purpose. And behind, the dark, fast-moving, clean-shaven figure, his hands swinging briskly at his sides. And the boy. The boy wove back and forth behind the two men, his eyes darting from side to side. At first I thought it was a boy who'd been staying with one of the guides, playing a trick on me, but as they came out of the shade of the poplars his head caught the sun and his hair shone all coppery like a new penny. The boy gave away nothing, and when the men came forward, he cocked his head to one side, watching me. I couldn't help smiling, and stepped up onto the dock.

"Well, you're up bright and early," Tomato said.

I smiled.

Tomato motioned to his left and the boy's father had his hand out.

"Dr. Sorenson," Tomato said.

"Neal Sorenson," the boy's father said.

I shook his hand.

"Dusty," I said.

He had a quick, aggressive grip, and I made a mental note to myself not to let him make my day miserable.

"Well, what do we have here?" I said, looking down at the boy.

The boy stuck his tongue in his cheek.

"Marty," the doctor said.

The boy put out his hand. He looked at me out of the corner of his eye. There was something in his look that made me stop. His eyes were wide set, and he had bright, blue-green irises and big, dilated-looking pupils.

"Well," I said, squeezing the boy's hand. "You all set to go fishing?"

I am a quiet man, not prone to gossip or small talk, but in the boats I am quite different. In the boats talk is a kind of commodity, something the guest has paid for, and it behooves you to know what the lake is about. I have it backwards and forwards, as I see it, first from my parents and the bloods I schooled with, and then from books. I can tell you there is a tremendous amount you will never know from those books, how it is to find your way through a labyrinth of lakes, over a thousand all interconnected, and if not by water then by something as thin and tenuous as a portage; how the back of a musky glows metallic green in dawn light; how graceful the flight of an egret is, its wings spread wide like fingers of white air; how when it gets dark the loons call like madmen, or lost lovers, or like all the hurt inside you, and if you're out on the lake long enough you will some night stand on the edge of a dock and laugh crazily with them. There are the geographical details, the lake is nearly seventy miles north-south, though as I've said it isn't *one* lake at all, and forty east-west. I can show you where the Hudson Bay fur traders first had their post, and where Wijaugojib, the first council of the Pillager Clan to the Minnesota Senate, died, shot through the head in broad daylight by no one knows who. I can tell you how the land changed hands in the early teens and twenties, and how the bloods were sent away. I can take you down to the Morson straights, where they still harvest rice.

But all of this will tell you nothing about the spirit of the place, the feel of it, if you do not listen with your heart, and out on the lake, the doctor seemed to hear nothing. He was preoccupied, crashing through his tackle box, organizing lures, jabbing at his son. The doctor had big hands, and they were filled with a stiff energy, and I kept my mouth shut. It seemed as if he were waiting for something, and now and then he checked his watch, then cast again, and when it was late in the afternoon, and we should have been thinking about going in, he turned to me and I knew from the look on his face that this was it.

"Take us east," he said.

My heart gave a little kick in my chest. "Over toward Big Piney?" I asked.

The doctor's eyes flickered like a camera shutter. Open-shut. But I had caught it, and thought for a second of excuses, reasons to go back.

The boy tossed his lure out.

"Reel in, Marty," the doctor said. "We're pulling up anchor."

On the way over to Big Piney, I pointed out the old campsites to the boy—Threefoot, The Bear in the Moon, Old Woman's Fire. The boy came back and sat by me, the doctor in the bow, the boat faster then, planing more cleanly. The air was heavy, layered down on the water, hot pockets, then cold, the scent of lake and duckweed strong in it. Not far from Big Piney, the doctor pointed off north, toward a narrow channel, and we went up it, into Knife Lake.

Knife Lake is a clean and deep and good fishing lake, but I knew for sure, then, that the doctor was not thinking about fishing. I wondered, with some fear, if he were a policeman or investigator, and thinking about it with the boy along, it made me a little angry, too.

"East shore," he shouted over the outboard.

I brought the boat around and we coasted into the reeds.

"We'll fish here," the doctor said, turning his back to me.

I cut the motor.

We had our gear out, and the fish were biting. Walleyes and hammerheads, small northerns not much bigger than your forearm. I was so busy baiting the boy's lures and filling the live net that it came as a shock to me when we drifted out of the reeds and the Sportsman's Inn, as bright and yellow as gold in the evening sun, rose up out of the trash around it, burned in part, the windows broken and jagged.

"Hey, look at that," the doctor said.

He made a point of looking surprised, and he put his hand on the boy's back. The boy looked uneasy. I could see it wasn't the old place on shore, it was his father's hand on his back, and it made me sad to see it. But I was thinking about other things then, and as is always my policy with guests, I let things play out.

"Let's go explore it," the doctor said to his boy. I pulled the boat up to shore, set the anchor in and sat on the bow. The Sportsman's dock had rotted away long ago, and all that remained of the gravel path up to the stoop was a bald spot halfway. The whole two-story affair was leaning off to one side, held up by the basswood around it, and on the cracked cement stoop was a shower of bright glass.

The doctor, ducking his head, went through the door first, the boy behind him, and I looked long and hard, thinking to turn my back on it, the broken windows and the charred roof, but sometimes it is good to look at what you have done when you have paid some price to make peace with yourself.

I looked. What I saw was this:

A winter day, the snow drifted to the windows, the Hamm's sign over the bar, neon blue. I smelled cigarette smoke and heard voices and the crack of balls on the pool table, saw my buddy, Hodie, in a booth by himself, a beer in his hand. It was a nice way to remember it. Like a Norman Rockwell painting, one in which none of the inevitable things in life have crept in. But, of course, they had, and soon I was there in the boat, miserable, with nowhere to go.

Where to begin, I do not even know.

I'll start with Hodie.

Hodie and I met in high school. There weren't many Chippewa in school then—most of them were working out on the trap lines or were down on the iron range—and they pretty much kept to themselves, and the same was true of Hodie. He ate by himself, studied, when he did, by himself, and was first out the door when the afternoon bell rang. He wasn't the kind of guy that would inspire how's-the-weather talk is what I'm saying. He was big, and carried himself very slowly and deliberately, though when he was angered, as he was when he'd been hit on the field playing football, he would burst into a frenzy and there was no stopping him, and that made you think twice about being chatty. I don't think I would have ever gotten to know him, really, if it hadn't been for a dance I went to one crummy, rainy Halloween night.

I was sitting out another rotation, watching the others turning and bumping and flirting under the orange and black crepe-paper streamers, when Hodie slipped around the row of boys on the floor waiting their turn. He sat down a chair from me and two couples came in from the other direction and I was sandwiched between. The girls giggled, and Hodie and I looked at each other, then down the row. We were in the middle of the Depression then, and we were all wearing the closest thing to rags, and there was Tim Bolan in a brand-new, store-bought suit and tie, his shoes all black and shiny, and sitting with him was Bob Mullally, a white cardigan draped over his shoulders. Their families were in timber, and they looked the place over, snotty-as-you-please. The girls I had never seen before, but they were dressed like dolls, and soon they were playing the names game.

"Do you know Joe Stoppard?" the big-bosomed blonde said.

"Sure," Bob said, though I could tell he didn't.

They went at it for the longest time, and it got so they nearly cheered when they found another name in common. *Oh, sure, of course I know her, do you know so and so. . . .* It went on forever. I was looking off across the gymnasium floor, all the couples pinching and grabbing, and in the middle of a peal of high, tittery laughter, I saw Hodie lean over toward me. He cupped his hand around my ear, and this is what he said:

"Do you know Smiley Shitbag?"

And fishing with him out on the lake the week after, he was quiet, but waiting for that moment to let loose on me with another joke. It got to be a regular thing, our fishing together, and he was always pulling my leg, teasing me.

"Dusty," he said one fall afternoon, "why don't you quit that Eliot High bullshit and work out on the lake. Melman's got an opening. He's expanding."

I knew from Hodie that Melman was a hard-ass, ran a pretty tight operation, no frills; the last time I had heard anything about him he had fired four bloods. So I took it as a joke, but it wasn't funny.

"You can do better," I said.

He looked hurt, then, blinking, said, "I'm not funning you, Dusty."

I don't know.

Things were happening then that nobody could have set right, whole families run under and the Chippewa fighting for what was left of their land. There was a whole bunch caught right in the middle, and I think that was the hardest, and Hodie was one of them. He was what they got to calling "in-betweens" —somebody who'd lived out in the wild until the new school bills came, and had to move permanent onto the reserve. It was like he didn't know which way to go, left or right, up or down.

You could see there was something turning over and over in his head, but he'd never tell what. I felt like putting a hand on him to stop it. He was spinning around so bad in there he was like a broken compass, one that always end up on south.

"You ever thought about killin' yourself?" he said one afternoon.

We were walking pheasants outside Kenora, in a cornfield.

"No," I said, which wasn't true. I didn't know what to say. We were just kids still and I didn't take it too serious, and then he holds his gun up and looks down the barrel. My heart went right up in my throat.

"What are you doing?" I said.

"Lookin' at the swirls in the barrel," he said. "Everything just goes around and around and around."

I felt like I was taking root there in that cornfield I was so frozen. I tried to think of something funny to say. It seemed like the right thing to do.

"What goes around comes around," I said, but the way it came out didn't seem funny at all, my voice quavering so bad I hardly got it out. It was one of those moments. I thought he might just take me with him if it went that way.

He looked at me, eyes blinking, and set his gun down. He did that a few times, glanced over, and then he was rolling on his side and kicking his feet, and every time I tried to pull him up so he could sit, he'd kick his feet, laughing so hard he couldn't get up.

I couldn't figure it.

Was it really that funny, or was it that awful?

Of course, there was the usual stuff—he could navigate the lakes without a map, and he knew how to use the sun and the stars. He knew where the fish were and when, and what baits to use. He could read weather signs that were altogether invisible to me (a dampness between the thumb and forefinger when rubbed, a shininess on birch leaves, the texture of the surface of the lake) rain, hot weather, a thunderstorm—what you could say about any guide who was first rate. But under it all was what he'd learned in the bush, and he secretly courted eagles and believed men could, and did, turn into animals at night, owls and bats and snakes. You'd see him staring into the lake, and he'd tell you a story.

"There's a whole world just under here," he'd say, poking an oar into the water.

I guess the thing I remember best is the time I got pneumonia. I shouldn't even bother to say it was one of the worst winters ever, but it was. Bitter cold and heavy snow. Hodie and me found a big drift under a tree, a ten-footer, and jumped in head-first from quite a ways up. It makes me shudder to think about it now, but that's what we did—climbed the hell up that pine and dove in, hollering and laughing. We went at it all afternoon; we were still in school then and the roads into town looked like pictures I'd seen of the Atlantic, one endless stretch of drifts. Around midnight I woke up and couldn't breathe, and by morning they had the doctor in and he said I was about as good as gone—I could tell by the look on my father's face. I was in a fever and couldn't hold my eyes still.

"What'd he say?" I asked.

"He said you'd be all done and healed by tomorrow."

One minute I was drenched in sweat, and the next I was shivering like I'd toss off my arms and legs it was so bad. Everything got real quiet, and my mother was crying outside in the kitchen. I heard sleigh bells, and in comes Hodie with Amous, a medicine man.

"Get out," my old man says. He was a Catholic and pretty set in his ways. They argued some and then I could feel arms under me and then we were outside, in the sleigh. I saw a lot of things I'd never seen before that night: My father standing in a hole in the ice yards off shore, naked. Amous floating around my head in a haze of rainbow-colored smoke. Hodie dancing and singing, all fur and hair. At the end of it, Amous blew a whistle—a high, piercing one—and snapped his hand down, and it was as if I had been shot through the head, all the sickness in me escaping like steam out that hole.

And that's what they call it, *shooting the medicine.*

I believe in all that now—*spirit medicine,* and that trees can and do talk—though I still don't know much about it. I didn't have much of a chance, I guess. Back then, when I was up and around, Hodie didn't say anything, and neither did I. But we had a funny kind of connection after. I could tell when he was around—when any of them were around—and I got to thinking about it the same way as people who see halos and such. It's there, that's all. And that's how it was with Hodie and me, like I had half a foot into something I didn't really have a clue about.

And into this picture of Hodie and me, now add Netta.

Netta, *my Netta*.

Netta I met in the middle of it, on a day Hodie and I had been out duck hunting. I remember it was one of those yellow September afternoons, when the ground warms beneath your feet, and the sky has that paler, moving-into-the-winter look. I remember Melman pacing down on the docks when we came in. His daughter was flying up from Chicago, where she lived with her mother, and he went from boat to boat, never satisfied with the gear or the anchor rope or whatever. We worked on the boats for a long time, and then Melman went up the steps and into the lodge.

"Jesus, I'm glad that's over," I said.

Hodie pointed at the lodge with his chin. In a high, nasal voice, imitating the Old Man, he said, "My daughter is coming up from Chicago."

"She'll probably have fish eyes," I said.

"Chip off the old block," Hodie said.

I laughed. The Old Man had a face no woman would ever want—bulgy eyes, a lantern jaw, and ears like Bing Crosby's.

I don't think anyone actually *saw* her come in. The old man sent Hodie and me over to Wheeler's Point for supplies, and by the time we got back they were all in the lodge dining room.

"What's up?" I said, and to Osada, one of the older guides, "*Hoka Hey!*" My teasing Osada—greeting him in Sioux—produced some warning looks. I sat down beside Strong Ground and Hodie sat across from me. Hodie made a fish-eyes face, and at that moment the Old Man stepped into the dining room with his daughter.

"This is Netta," he said, only I think now that is what he must have said.

There are many ways of relating how one first saw the beloved, accepted and often used ways—stars in the eyes, love at first sight, heart palpitations and all that—but I am not going to use any of those ways here. They are all grossly inaccurate and at times silly, for kids. Back then I was somewhere in between—I was twenty-six, had been on the lake ten years, and had nearly drowned a time or two, like all the others, and had hardened in the cold of the deer-hunting seasons, sometimes forty below or worse.

But this is what I saw:

A slender, dark-eyed girl, her face lit up with excitement and adventure and the promise of something new. A face like that September day. She was beautiful.

Marionette Lynn Melman.

"Netta for short," she told me later, teasing.

I guess I should have seen her for the trouble she was, but I wasn't seeing much of anything then, just that face and all the rest, her birdlike, nervous hands and her shy but coy way of standing, her head down so she looked up at you through her eyelashes. I couldn't figure it. She was a strange mixture of personality traits. She was sharp, a bright girl, with a good sense of humor, and very easygoing, but when she wanted something, or you crossed her, she was meaner than the Old Man himself. She had a brooding quality about her, and sometimes she just wanted to be alone and she would fish by herself, later on, anyway, a day at a stretch. She collected things—bones, strangely colored rocks, arrowheads. She had brought her books with her, and coming up to the dock evenings I could see her head propped up in the window, a book held high in her hands.

I liked a good story myself, and one night after dinner I asked her what she was reading.

"*Wuthering Heights*," she said. "How did you know I was reading?"

I felt my face heat and instead of replying—about how I had seen her in the window—I asked her if she had ever heard how the lake got its mosquitoes.

"Mosquitoes?" she asked.

It was a short-lived moment of relief, because then I found myself caught in the telling of the story. I acted the part of the giant who ate the village tribesmen, hunching my back and arms, then acted the part of the braves who caught the giant and chopped him to bits, throwing the pieces in the fire. I felt like a fool. Netta did not smile or laugh. Her eyes narrowed and she watched me with a strange intensity, her arms crossed over her chest.

"The ashes, see, turned into mosquitoes." I reached out and pinched her arm. "Like that." I couldn't believe I had pinched her. I was expecting her to slap my face, run for the Old Man, or cry.

"Who told you that?" she said.

"Hodie." I could see she was looking at me differently. She was looking right into my eyes.

"Tell me another one," she said.

An island is a strange place for someone who is running from himself, and I think that is exactly what Netta was doing, though I didn't know that then. She never talked about Chicago, or her mother, but something bad had happened. Something she thought about a lot, got lost in and looked broken over, but she would never tell me what it was (and never did, even when we were married). She reminded me of Hodie that way, a whole life buried but in no way dead.

She would paint her nails red in the morning, and by night they would be another color.

"Do you like my hair?" she would ask, and if I said yes, she would change it, and if I said no she wouldn't.

She ordered things from catalogs, had tens of them shipped up. She would waltz around the island in beautiful dresses and silk scarves, never once the same, and she sent each and every one of them back. Merchandise refund, no questions asked.

"Does this look like me?" she'd ask.

"Yes," I'd say, but two weeks later she'd have something entirely different on, jodhpurs, where before it had been pointed red shoes. It was strange, if not just outright ridiculous, the things she wore. You'd see her floating up the paths at night, like some spirit, her skirt billowing like a sail.

"Dusty," she would say. "Tea?"

It was as though she took me places I had never been. London, or Paris, or just downtown Chicago. I'd get to thinking of her as Melman's daughter, and then she'd show up wearing some wide-shouldered, low-cut blouse, and all I could do was hope she would go before I broke down, I ached so bad to touch her.

She'd flirt with most everybody, I guess. And it made me pretty mad. I figured for a time she was the most big-headed, spoiled child I had ever known, and it really set me against her until one evening we were out on the lake together, just me and Netta.

We had our lines in the water but weren't really fishing. I was looking at her and thinking how pretty she was, those dark eyes and hair, and out of the blue she says,

"You know, Dusty, you don't know the first thing about me. Do you?"

It really surprised me. I was hurt. I shrugged my shoulders.

"Did you ever think to ask?" she said.

I shook my head. I wanted to say *all the time*, but couldn't, so just sat there miserable.

"Nobody . . ." she said, and then she was crying.

I hugged her and she rocked back and forth, and it all sunk down in, awful. We sat there like that for a long time, and then she turned her head up and kissed me. It felt like something I'd been waiting for, something that just finished what was already there.

"Tell me I'm beautiful," she said.

"Netta," I said.

"Just tell me I'm beautiful," she said, hugging me so hard it squeezed all the air right out.

It has always seemed a curious thing to me how much death there is in life, and years ago I thought about it quite a bit. But all these years on the lake have taught me some things, and these things have augered into me as sure as beetles into a big spruce.

THE SNAKE GAME

They don't kill the tree, but the bark takes on a funny, mottled look, and I suppose my thinking is a bit like that now. I suppose after all these years I shouldn't be shocked at the rest of it, but I am, only, now, the shock is buffered by distance and doesn't set me off in a rage or sorrow like it used to. Thinking about what happened, it all seems so unnecessary now, just one thing happening after another. The days Netta and me, and Hodie, went fishing, I'd seen just like that. Netta and me, and Hodie.

As I saw it, everything just went along.

Netta came up summers, six, seven years, and then she was expecting and we got married. We built the cabin and Netta filled it with her things. She was in a nesting mood, and then the boy came. He was a fat, happy baby; he learned to walk early and he was into everything, my lures, Netta's collection of moths and rocks and whatever off the lake. We named him Jackie, after an uncle of mine, and when he was old enough, Hodie took him to powwows and brought him carvings and beaded moccasins. I wanted my son to have a chance to see the lake for the magic thing it is, for the breath and life in it, and Hodie was always willing, even eager. He ate dinner with us now and then, joking as always, making us laugh. But as the years went by Hodie and I became more distant, and Netta more extreme in her moods. She was all over me one minute, threatening, and the next she was making eyes at me across the table. Jackie got bigger by degrees, and one night, watching him as he ate, something went through my brain. It was like a puff of breath in my face, just enough to make me blink.

That was after Christmas, the snow drifting to the roofs in places, and we were all stuck in the lodge, playing cards and such. On the coldest night Jackie got fussy, and Netta bundled him up till he looked like a brown marshmallow and took him out back. He was eight then, and he insisted on doing what we all did, wanted to grow right into it, and—as Netta told me later—he insisted on chopping wood with Netta, using the hatchet we had for kindling.

Melman and Strong Ground were at the table, and I was reading over by the fireplace.

I remember the pitch of the screams, first my son's, a high, startled wail, and then Netta's long, tearing shriek. It was as if I had been skewered, right to the chair I was in, and then I was out of the lodge, carrying my boy in, my stomach in my throat for seeing what he had done to his hand. There was no way to take him into town, and I knew we would have to do the best we could.

"Take him upstairs," Melman said.

"Jackie," I said, holding him to the bed. "Don't look."

But as soon as I would release my grip on him he would turn, his eyes wide, and he would scream again. I gave him some whiskey, and then while I held him Melman ran the gut leaders up his palm with a big leather needle. He was bleeding so badly you couldn't see anything. When Melman was through with the sewing I let up a bit, and I was surprised to see Netta there beside me, her mouth working as though she were talking to herself.

"What?" I said, but she just shook her head and looked up into the ceiling, her hands clasped together over her heart.

Around midnight Jackie took on a fever, and we gave him aspirin, then everything we had, ladies'-time-of-the-month-remedies, some pain killers. He would wake screaming and I would have to hold him down. I was desperate.

"Go get Hodie," I said.

Netta gave me a queer, surprised look, then took off across the room and down the stairs. Jackie was sleeping and I went to the window. Nothing seemed to make sense that night. I stood there for the longest time, and then there was a light out on the lake. It was a lantern, and then I saw it was Netta, and when she got to the shore on the other side of the bay, the light went out in Hodie's cabin and he came out to meet her. I turned and looked at Jackie, his dark, sharp features.

My God! I thought.

It is easy to think *if only*, and I'm sure many people's lives are ruined that way. I had my time with it: If only I hadn't frozen up with rage; If only I hadn't blamed Jackie's death on them; If only I hadn't shown that I knew. For the longest time I played that winter over in my head, each time something different saving us in the end. I imagined how things would have been if I had said something, if Hodie had left, if, even, Netta had left. I imagined what would have happened had Melman seen Hodie in his grandson—maybe Netta and me would have moved to Chicago, or maybe Melman would have sent Hodie off to who knows where. I imagined having more courage, or more determination, or more—*something*. But always, it was that extra something that wasn't there then, and perhaps wouldn't even be there now.

I tried not to think about it. Years went by. Melman turned bitter and moved down to Chicago, and Richard "Tomato" Burke bought the lodge, and there were changes all around. We put a new roof on the dining hall, got rid of the last of the wooden boats, and bought new motors, Mercurys. We got a generator from Detroit, a big diesel, and wired the cabins. Some of the old guides left, and we got a new bunch. They didn't know which end was up, and it was hard working with them.

I worked till I dropped.

But in all that time, I never once went to the east side of the lake.

"Find somebody else to take 'em over there," I'd say, no questions asked. So it was strange sitting in the boat, waiting for the doctor and his boy. After a time I raised my head to peer up into what was left of the Sportsman's. The roof had rotted away, the shingles green scabs in some places, and where the fire had burned through to the rafters gulls had made nests. The doctor, careful, his hands out for balance, swept across the upstairs window and I saw Hodie there.

He turned, looked out the window. A chill shot up my spine and into my head.

"It's gettin' awful goddamn late!" I shouted.

The doctor turned to face me. *Had they been in that room?* He craned his head around, said something, and then the boy was running down the path to the boat. I thought of my boy, Jackie, and wondered why I had let this happen, why I had come up this way again. The boy got in and we sat there, the loons calling from across the lake, warbling like mad. I lit a cigarette and watched the last of the sun slip behind the far shore.

I thought about how Jackie had died.

That night, Hodie had come back with Netta. He brought his medicine bag and set up a sweat teepee downstairs; he had a blaze going in the fireplace, so hot the flames licked out into the room and the rocks under the iron grid cracked. I pushed my hands into my pockets, my head spinning. I fought impulses to break somebody's head open or to just walk out onto the lake to freeze. Melman and the others went into the back and then it was just the three of us, Hodie, Netta, and me, and Jackie. Hodie danced circles around the teepee; at first his voice was nearly a whisper, and then it broke through, made sounds I'd never heard, bold, pleading. It was as if I was seeing him for the first time.

He was a father, too, after all.

But the fever held, and just before dawn Jackie died. We looked at each other. No one knew what to do. What could we do?

I was thinking about that when the doctor came down the path, back to the boat.

"Hell of a mess," he said.

I nodded. The boy was looking off across the lake.

"What happened up there?" the doctor said.

For a second I thought I might hit him, but then a quiet took hold.

"How come all you people ever want to hear about is the bad things?" I said. "Tell me, why is that?"

The doctor shook his head, another look of surprise.

"You know damn well why you wanted to come up here, don't you," I said. "And I'll bet you told the boy all about it." I looked at the boy and his face colored. The doctor cleared his throat. I looked him square on. "What you probably heard was some god-damn Indian was screwing some guy's wife on the side, and when the guy found out, all hell broke loose, right? Am I right? Just

some big, stupid Indian, and some—that's right, look away—
and you have the gall to take me up here."

The doctor looked at me, his face not so friendly. "That woman
the Indian killed—"

"It was an accident," I said.

"That isn't what I heard."

I was sick of it. Except with the police, I had never talked
about it with anyone, ever.

"So what *did* you hear?" I said.

The doctor squinted. "What's it to you, anyway?"

"Who said *I'd* know?"

"Tomato said you'd know."

"Tomato."

"I'm writing a book."

"That gives you the right to drag me the hell out here where
you got no business—"

"Look, it's no secret. Everybody up here knows about it."

"What do they know?" I said.

The doctor shifted in the bow. It was dark now and it was
hard to see him.

"I think we should head back," he said.

Somehow that struck me as funny. I laughed. "We'll just head
back now, is that it?"

I could see the doctor staring at me in the dark.

"Tell me," I said. "I really want to hear."

The doctor shook his head. I gave the boy my jacket. It was
getting cold.

"We're not going anywhere," I said.

"Look," the doctor said, threatening, "if it comes down to—"

"Sure," I said, patting the sheath on my belt, "and I could put
this fillet knife right through your neck."

"Is that a threat?"

"Only if yours is."

I could see the doctor was furious. He shifted on his seat. I
was sorry the boy had to be a part of it.

"So what the hell's wrong with you, anyway?" the doctor said.

"There isn't anything wrong with you?" I said. "You get me

out of bed, don't show up for hours, and then you drag me all the way up here under the pretense of fishing, only to stick your nose—"

"Christ," he said. "All we're talking about here is a drunk who killed somebody a few years ago and then shot himself. It's in the papers every day."

And it struck me then, how amazing it is, that we can forgive nearly anything in the people we love, can see *their* actions in the context of how things happened, but in our own lives we are cursed, trapped in ourselves, all the failings we cannot even admit to ourselves buried, even hidden, but deforming us, the way a house can turn crooked on its foundation. I had done one horrible thing, and had lived with it since. After Jackie died, I had gone to Netta, and in my bitterness and loss, I had lied.

"Netta," I'd said. "Hodie told me. He told me *everything* right from the beginning."

I got some satisfaction, seeing her face swell, the color high in her cheeks. I felt powerful, vindicated, but by the time she took off across the lake in my greatcoat I was regretting what I'd done.

"And all of it over a medicine bag," the doctor said.

It startled me.

"What?" I said.

"He killed her because something about a medicine bag. Isn't that what happened?"

I laughed. Deep bitter laughter.

The moon had risen and the Sportsman's was bathed in silver light. I looked up at the wreck.

"Wasn't it?" the doctor said.

I didn't so much as shake my head. I wasn't about to tell him anything. It was such a small thing, really. And after, the enraged townies had set the Sportsman's on fire, had burned up what couldn't be seen.

"Let's go back," the doctor said.

The boy huddled against him. I heard a loon chortle out on the lake, then another. Hodie had told me once that loons were lost souls. I listened to them, then saw the whole thing again, that bright winter day, Netta crossing the lake, snow up to her knees. I imagined what happened at the Sportsman's, Netta tearing Hodie's medicine bag from her coat and dumping it on the pool table, Hodie, hurt beyond what he could bear, swinging his cue around like a bat, and the last of it, the officer turning in the car, Hodie reaching for the officer's gun and putting the barrel into his mouth and pulling the trigger.

That they had died that way was a horrible thing. But I had held on to something in it, had protected myself. Somehow all those years I had convinced myself that Hodie's killing Netta proved he didn't really love her.

The doctor's boy was watching me.

I sat there, stunned.

"What are we waiting for?" the doctor said.

The boy looked like he might cry. He was having a hard time of it, I could see that. I slid down my seat toward him. I had to tell him something.

"Leave him alone," the doctor said.

I shook my head, bent in closer.

"Listen—and don't you forget," I said, my whole chest squeezing down. "What killed those people was love," I said.

THE
LINE

1967 He had expected something different. Maybe a few smiling faces, a little "how's the weather" talk, some joking around over old times. But now, Martin stood at the end of the dock, and the one Indian he recognized didn't even say hello.

"Bear," Tomato said from behind Martin.

Bear lifted his head from the rod he was repairing. It had been raining and Bear was standing in water. The water went halfway up his legs, darkening his khaki pants. In the front of the boat another Indian, about ten or so from what Martin could see of him, bailed with a coffee can.

"Eli," Bear said. "Could you stop that for a minute?"

The splashing of the water stopped and Bear got a hold on the dock and in one motion drew himself up to where Martin and Tomato stood.

"Well?" he said.

Tomato nudged Martin forward. Martin stretched out his hand and Bear looked over Martin's shoulder at Tomato.

"I've been busy with the tackle—that dumb SOB, what's his name, fucked the open-faced reels up—so we haven't gotten the boats dry."

"That's okay," Tomato said. "This is Doc Sorenson's son, Martin. You remember him, don't you? They used to come up quite a bit. He's going to work with you."

Martin felt his hand in front of him and wondered what would be best to do with it.

"Eli!" Bear hollered. "Get up on the dock here and bring that can with you."

Eli scrambled onto the dock and Martin and the boy looked at each other. Bear turned to Martin and Martin looked into his hard brown eyes, his pockmarked face. He knew Bear couldn't be more than a year or two older than himself, but there was something in him—aside from the fact that he was just plain big, wide in the shoulders, his neck as muscular as a thigh—that made him seem much older.

Bear took the can from Eli and thrust it into Martin's outstretched hand. "Start with this boat here," he said, pointing. "There's fourteen others like it, and I want them all done. Bailed and cleaned." He turned to Tomato and nodded his head in the direction of the lodge. "Got a minute?" he said.

Tomato squeezed Martin's shoulder brushing by him, and then they headed up the dock, Tomato leading, Bear behind him and Eli last. Martin looked down into the coffee can, saw his face there, long and dumb-looking, distorted. He lowered himself from the dock into the boat and felt the water trickle into his shoes, then soak them, then the water wet his legs and he dipped the can in, lifted it and tossed the water over the side.

In front of the lodge Tomato stood holding the railing and Bear was going on.

"It's enough that I gotta take a load of crap from those bullshitters out on the lake," he said, "but now you want me to work with one of 'em too. What's the idea, is he gonna spy on us or something?"

"His name's Martin," Tomato said. "And if you don't—"

"He's Doc Junior to me."

Martin, in listening, had quit bailing.

"Hey!" Bear yelled. "You done already?"

Martin dug into the water with the can and pitched it over

the side. His feelings ran from disappointment, to self-pity, to anger. Now he was angry. That son-of-a-bitching fat Indian. He'd show him. He looked up and Tomato was giving it to Bear. It embarrassed Martin in a way—if Tomato had been sticking up for him because he liked him, that would be different. But this was because there was bad money between Tomato and Martin's father. When Martin's father wanted him out of the house, he'd asked Martin if he'd like to work at the resort.

"I thought Dick could only hire Canadians or Indians," Martin had said.

"I think we can get around that," Martin's father said.

So now, out in the boat, with Tomato giving Bear the business, Martin wondered if he should have taken this on at all. It had a very bad taste in his mouth, and it was only when he looked out across the lake and shut his mind on it and let his arms pump away at the water that he felt he had done the right thing. The lake stretched away flat and calm, a gray-blue, the islands cutting up out of it like gems, the granite black and laced with white veins. On the point birches grew up, their leaves shimmering, and behind them dark firs rose in a jagged line.

"You're going to have to move a lot faster," Bear said. He stood with his hands in his pockets, looking down. "You got a hell of a lot of boats to empty."

"You got a bucket instead of this can?"

"Nope."

"Mind if I go up to the boathouse and look?"

"Yup."

The thought crossed Martin's mind, how he could get up on the dock and slam Bear one in the face before he got those huge arms pumping. It was a dumb idea, and Martin felt his lips tighten.

"What do you want me to do when I get the boats done?"

Bear grinned. "You let me know when you get there," he said.

In the sun, and sheltered by the big, pierlike dock, Martin felt his hair heating on the top of his head. At the boathouse Bear untangled masses of fishing line and organized tackle boxes. Martin bailed. He was on the fifth boat now and when he thought about it, a half hour a boat, and then there was the launch, too, the whole day stretched away into the infinite tedium of bailing. He'd started with the joy that comes in adventure—he was on the Canadian side of the lake, what seemed like real wilderness, he was going to learn to be a guide, even when he wasn't supposed to be able to, and he was working with the Indians he had feared and been so curious about when he was just a boy. But now, with the can cutting into his hands, his feet numb with cold, the adventure had become something else.

"Hey!" Martin yelled up to the boathouse. "My feet are really cold. You mind if I take a minute out to warm them up?"

Bear opened a tackle box.

"You mind if I get out of the boat to warm my feet up!"

"What?"

"My goddamned feet are frozen!"

"All right," Bear said. "Get out of the boat for a while."

Martin braced himself against the boathouse. Beside him Bear yawned. His head slowly sank to his knees, his hands relaxing on the daredevil he held.

"Bear," Martin said.

Bear didn't move.

"Hey, Bear," Martin said, tapping Bear on the shoulder.

Bear bolted awake, his eyes wild.

He jerked his hands up to his face, the daredevil tearing into his thumb.

"Jesus Christ! Don't creep up on me like that!" he said.

He shook the daredevil. The hook was deep in his thumb. He jerked at it and blood ran down the back of his hand.

"Goddammit!"

Martin watched the blood run. He got a strange satisfaction watching, and he felt a little sick and somehow on the edge of laughter.

"You think it's funny, don't you, D. J.?" Bear said.

Bear squeezed his thumb and another stream of blood traced down the back of his hand. "Don't creep up behind me like that again," he said. He stood and cradled his hand to his stomach.

"Really, Bear—"

Bear stooped, then lowered his mouth to Martin's ear. "I'd be howling if this thing were stuck in *your* thumb," he said.

Martin checked his watch. Ten o'clock. The hours were beginning to stretch out, each minute longer now than the one before it, and waiting for Bear to come back out it seemed the morning would never end. Martin looked through the rainbow-colored skiff of gasoline at his feet. His feet were bone white, his toes shriveled and toenails blue.

The lodge door slammed like an explosion.

Bear held up his hand. It was orange down to the wrist.

"Thanks," he yelled.

Martin dipped into the water. His shoulders burned. He wanted to tell Bear to shove it. He knew Tomato was going back to Wheeler's Point around dinnertime, and he thought he could quit now. Quit before anything worse happened. He would sit in the front of the boat, under his jacket, and when they got to Wheeler's Point he could get a bus to International Falls and from there he could take the train back into St. Paul. But that's as far as he could go with it. He could see his father's face, swelling, and the word he wouldn't say but that Martin would know he was thinking. Martin didn't even like the thought of it. It felt a lot worse than his feet and his back and the heat of the sun on his head.

"What are you waitin' for?" Bear yelled.

Martin dipped into the water. Son-of-a-bitch. He raised his head over the dock, emptying the can. Bear was putting new line on the reels, his back against the boathouse, the tin roof protecting him from the sun. Eli was with him now.

"You hungry?" Bear said.

Eli shook his head.

Bear nudged Eli and smiled. "Come on," he said.

There was a candy machine against one side of the boathouse and Bear looked around it and up to the lodge, then slammed the machine with his fist and a candy bar dropped out. He ran his knuckles over Eli's head and Eli tried to push him away.

"I'll get one for myself," Bear said.

Bear turned in the direction of the dock and Martin let loose with a canful of water. It splashed over the side. There was a metallic thump.

"Watch out for Doc Junior," Bear said.

And then it was quiet but for the noise of the water splashing out of the can into the lake.

Around noon Tomato came down from the lodge. He stopped at the boathouse and talked to Bear, then sauntered up the dock.

"How's it going?" he said.

Martin drew his forearm over his face. He was sweating pretty bad now, and the wind off the lake was chilly. It was one of those hot-cold days.

"Fine," Martin said.

"How's it going with Bear?"

"Fine."

"Aren't you a little cold without waders?"

Martin straightened. His back was on fire and his feet were frozen.

"What do you mean?"

"We got a whole wallful of waders in there, in the boathouse."

Martin felt his face flushing.

"I guess I didn't see 'em," he said.

"Well, here"—Tomato reached down and took Martin's outstretched hand, pulling him up onto the dock—"we'll get you a pair."

Martin followed Tomato to the boathouse. Bear busied himself with the tackle, absorbed in lead shot and frog eggs. The boathouse was dark inside and Tomato opened a window. It was long, long enough to fit three or four boats. Old Evinrudes and Mercurys lined the walls, red tanks beneath them, some stacked on one another.

"You remember coming in here?"

"Sure I do," Martin said.

The boathouse smelled of wood rot, gasoline, rubber, and

mothballs. It brought back a time when Martin and his father had spent weeks each summer out on Muskeg Bay, just fishing, their guide in the back resting against the motor and smoking. Martin remembered his father hated smoking, but Martin had always liked it, had liked the smell and that the Indians rolled their own cigarettes out of papers and tobacco they kept in a pouch.

"You want a puff?" Osada, one of the older guides, had said to him once.

He hadn't thought his father was watching and when he took the cigarette his father gripped his arm and said:

"Take a deep—no, don't spit it out—I want you to really smoke it."

Martin had coughed, rasped, and Osada, the muscles tight in his face, had looked back over the motor and Martin's father had said to Osada:

"I don't want you giving him any more tobacco, understand?"

Tomato stooped down the long line of waders, looking for holes in them.

"Is Osada still around?" Martin asked.

"What?" Tomato said.

"Is Osada still—"

"Oh, he's around all right." Tomato slid a pair of waders from the rack. "Here, these'll do you," he said.

Martin jammed a foot into one leg of the waders and Tomato put his hands on his hips and laughed.

"What?" Martin said. "What's wrong?"

"Jesus," Tomato laughed, "you don't put those things on without socks. Where are your socks?"

Martin shrugged.

"Did Bear have you out there with bare feet?"

"No," Martin said, trying to keep the anger out of his voice. He tugged at the boot, trying to get it off, a bitterness filling his hands. This place did not belong to him after all. He'd been a fool to come back, much less to work. He felt stupid and out of place and he hated Tomato now, too, for making him feel this way. He'd been at it barefoot all morning and his goddamned feet were killing him and that son-of-a-bitching Indian had tricked him.

Tomato watched Martin tug at the boot, his hands over his chest. "You young guys . . ."

"It's no big deal," Martin said.

"I wouldn't last a half hour in that water barefoot," Tomato said.

Martin jerked his leg out of the wader. "I just thought it would be *easier*," he said, looking out the door of the boathouse where Bear sat smiling to himself.

The wool socks and waders felt wonderful. Martin's feet warmed and his back didn't ache so badly now.

"Anything else you need?" Tomato said.

Martin looked down at his feet.

Tomato reached for a gas line that hung from the wall and turned it in his hand. "Bear," he said.

"Yeah?" Bear drew his legs up under himself and stood.

"This line's bad. Could you get to it this afternoon?"

Bear nodded.

"I don't suppose you've got a bucket around here, do you?" Martin said.

Bear reached into the boathouse behind the outboard motors and pulled out a bucket.

"How about this?" he said.

Tomato nodded. He rubbed his hand over his chin. "You weren't using that can, were you?"

Bear slammed a tackle box lid with his foot. "What time will the first bunch be coming in?" he asked.

Tomato set his hands on his hips. "They said around seven, but you know what that means. . . . You want those ducks for lunch?"

Martin shrugged.

"Sure," Bear said.

Past noon Martin was still bailing. The cold that had started in his feet had worked its way up his legs and into his chest and now he was shivering. He clutched the pail, dipping into the cold water. He would make it to lunch. He wouldn't think about anything after, just lunch, the duck on the table, waves of steam rising off it, stuffing, more steam, the fork in his hand, the sound of silverware on china, the coffee mug hot against his lips.

Martin dipped the pail into the cold water. The water had a dead smell to it now.

What was he doing up here, anyway?

It was dumb, Martin thought, coming up here. He had had no idea it would be like this. All those years he had thought there was something different about the way the guides had treated him.

"My quiet little one," Osada had said once, ruffling up his hair.

Martin turned his head back and around, trying to ease the burning above his shoulders. He looked out across the lake. The sun cut off the water like sharp glass.

He didn't want to think about it.

The bell would ring soon.

It just had to.

Martin stood in the door, his eyes adjusting to the dark. The lodge dining room wasn't as big as he remembered it, but still it was impressive. The ceiling was a good twenty feet high where the logs came together, and ten heavy-legged tables stretched away to the far wall. The room had the look of candle flame, the walls paneled in pine yellowed with age, the windows overlooking the bay letting in shafts of sunlight.

Marceline, Tomato's wife, came in with a tray. She set it in the center of the table nearest the window.

"Hello, Martin," she said. "How are you?"

"Pretty good, I guess," he said.

"And your folks?"

Martin smiled. "They're okay."

Bear and Eli pulled chairs out from the table.

"Hi, Marcy," Bear said. He forked a duck onto Eli's plate and one onto his own.

"If you're short just let me know," Marceline said.

Martin nodded, poking at what was left on the tray.

"We'll be okay," Bear said.

The meat was dry, and Martin had a hard time swallowing it. Bear sat across from him chugging down glasses of milk between mouthfuls. Eli sat beside him. He carefully cut with his knife, forking small pieces of duck into his mouth. Bear jabbed him in the side.

"What are you, some kind of fairy?"

Martin swallowed without chewing.

"We'd better get out there," Bear said, looking up at the big red clock over the door. "They'll be coming in soon."

"Is it going to make any difference?" Martin said. He reached for his glass and took a long drink. His stomach was knotted and he felt sick. He had hardly eaten anything.

"See that?" Bear said, pointing to one of the windows.

"What?"

"What else? The lake."

Martin set his fork down. He felt his arms swell and heart jerk.

"What about it?"

"It's opening season tomorrow. Don't you know that? There's gonna be a shitload of guys up here."

Martin nodded; be reasonable, he thought, then felt his mouth working. "I mean, what the fuck, Bear? Am I supposed to know every fuckin' thing around here?"

He stood and Bear stood with him.

"I mean, you're giving me a bunch of bullshit down there on the docks and there you sit—"

Tomato stepped into the room.

"That's enough," he said. "We've got a hell of a lot to do around here before they get in. So you get your asses out there on the docks if you want a job."

Eli dropped his fork on his plate. It clattered like a bell.

Bear mumbled something.

"What was that?"

"We were just goofin' around," Bear said.

"Like hell—"

"Weren't we, Martin?"

Martin crossed his arms over his chest. "Sure," he said, nodding. "Sure, that's all it was," he said.

On the dock he was still fuming. He pitched the water out of the boats with a ferocious speed. He didn't pace himself and he went like that up to the last boat. It had been a long, horrible day, but now he could almost laugh at it. He had done it, it couldn't get worse. He was thinking about the roast beef Marceline said she was making. She was making it for the men who were flying up from St. Louis, the Clark brothers and their sons, who Martin remembered as being very fat but funny, and for those drunks, the Ludemans, who always got into fights playing cards.

Martin climbed out of the last boat and set the bucket down. He thought his shoulders would never heal. He never wanted to see another candy wrapper as long as he lived. Bear adjusted the needle jets on the big Evinrude and yanked the starter. Now it seemed like an adventure again. The sun was setting—the men were late, just as Tomato had thought they would be—and gulls flew high and graceful over the lake. A bass jumped, cutting a circle in the water.

"Gimme a hand, will you?" Bear said. He struggled with the motor, the propeller end dragging along the dock. Eli had gone across the bay to Osada's and now Bear and Martin were alone.

"Pick up the back," Bear said.

Martin lifted the motor off the dock and Bear shifted the weight, so to Martin it felt as though he were lifting the whole thing.

"Could you lift up a little more?" Martin said.

Bear grunted. It was the big one, the eighty, and they should have used the dolly to get it over to the launch.

"Just a little bit farther," Bear said.

"Let's just roll it over there with the—"

"No," Bear said.

"It'd be much easier if we'd—"

"Can't you take it? Or what's the problem?"

Martin hoisted his end higher. The crankcase levered into Bear's chest and he grunted with the weight. He pushed down and Martin lifted with his legs. They felt like rubber but he lifted anyway. He'd show the bastard. And like that, Bear pushing the motor down on Martin, and Martin shifting the weight of it into Bear's chest, they made it to the launch. Chests heaving. Legs wobbling. Now Martin could see the blood pounding in Bear's neck.

"Gimme the goddamned thing," he said.

Martin let go, resisting the impulse to heave up on it one last time and send Bear into the lake.

They got the motor on the back of the launch and Bear waved for Martin to untie the ropes that held it to the dock.

"Get in!" he said, the motor burbling and spitting. "We'll go for a test ride."

Bear eased the launch away from the dock and Martin watched the lodge shrink, the tall pines high and dark now. Around the backside Tomato waved to Bear and Bear brought the throttle up, the launch almost planing now, as fast as it would go, the island growing smaller behind them. All Martin could think about was the beef dinner. He was really spent now and wanted to go back in. He could see the big smoky lodge, and maybe Osada would have come in from the marshland where he had his cabin. He could just smell the beef and potatoes and onions, could taste the gravy in his mouth.

"Seems to be working good enough," Martin yelled from the front of the launch. "Let's go back in."

Bear smiled. He had one silver tooth and it shone in the near dark.

"Didn't Tomato tell you?" he said.

Martin didn't need to hear the rest. The lake stretched out in front of the launch, endless, deep, black. It was forty miles in to Wheeler's Point, and the men would be fooling around with their duffel bags and all the booze and bullshit they brought with them. They'd be talking and jabbing at each other, bragging, and then they'd get on the launch, not more than one or two of them saying anything to the guides doing all the work. They'd pass around a pint and one of them would want to stop to piss off the side and then they'd all be stopping the launch to piss off the side. Someone, someone very drunk, would toss someone else's bag into the lake and they'd have to go fishing around for it in the dark. Even when he had been little Martin had been embarrassed by all of this.

And it occurred to him now that the men in the boat, the Indians who had done this for so many years, might have been hungry, too, or might have felt lost as he did now, all he knew stripped away and people angry with him and treating him like a dog for no reason. It was terrible, and crazy, and he hated it and he thought, for sure, when the launch stopped at Wheeler's Point, he would go home, he would go home with his tail between his legs. And as he was thinking this, and thinking how tired and hungry and alone he was, Bear reached under the tarpaulin in back. He pulled out a bag, set a sandwich, carrots, and two candy bars on his knees. He wouldn't ask. He would not ask, he thought, not if a gun had been put to his head. Not like this. It was too awful, that was it, the end, the line reached and crossed, and when Bear brought out another bag, set it on the hull between them and said, "Here, you'll need it to get through this load of rummies," Martin didn't know whether he felt like laughing or crying.

SAFE

1968 The day Martin Sorenson and I set the Muskeg Marshland on fire started out bad. Tomato Burke had dumped more garbage on the south end of the island, not far from our cabin, and my uncle, Osada, was furious. Red Deer was taking most of it—he could speak Ojibway—and while Osada was cursing and yelling, Martin stopped by to ask for Bear. From where I was sitting on my cot it looked like he was yanked off his feet.

"You tell Tomato to come here," Osada said, shaking him by the shoulders. "Understand?"

Martin nodded. His eyebrows were pulled down and his mouth was set in a frown.

"I didn't do it," he said.

Osada opened the door and pushed him out. Red Deer went out with him. Through the window I could see them standing under a fir. Martin was holding his fists at his sides and Red Deer put his hand on Martin's shoulder.

In Ojibway Osada said to me, "He won't even leave me this wasteland."

I felt terrible. Osada glared at me. He walked circles around the room, rubbed the bear pelt on the wall, picked up and examined his rifle, an old Browning he'd bought from Tomato. I was glad he wasn't mad at me. He was a huge man, with big hands and a big nose. There was a scar down the right side of his face, puckering his cheek so his eye was nearly pinched shut. He looked fierce, and now, with his forehead ridged, and his good eye staring, I had to stand up.

In Ojibway he said, "Good, you go now too, Eli."

I was stuck between Osada and the door.

"I'm going," I said.

Outside I felt terrible, too. It was a low overcast day, the light dull and oppressive. The firs drooped as if their limbs were too heavy and the lake had an oily, lifeless sheen to it.

"You gonna talk to Burke?" I said to Martin.

"Why doesn't Osada talk to him?" Martin said.

Red Deer had taken out his knife and was whittling on a stick. He sliced the bark off smooth and clean and cut the ends down so he had a good solid piece of pine. He shifted the wood in his hands, looking to see what was in it.

Martin kicked at a tuft of moss.

"You don't have to do anything about it anyway," I said, but as soon as it came out I knew I'd said the wrong thing.

Martin looked at me out of the corner of his eye.

I shuffled my feet in the dirt, embarrassed. I knew it hadn't been easy for him. He'd worked like crazy before any of us took him for serious, and some of the guides still didn't like how Bear was hanging around with him.

"Think it'll rain?" he said.

Red Deer shrugged. "Could go either way," he said. He had something coming out of his piece of wood. The shavings were getting smaller as the figure came out and the ground was white around his feet.

"You think Bear'll be back tonight?" Martin asked.

"What did he say to you, Eli?"

I felt queasy thinking about it, and told them what Bear had told me *not* to tell them.

"The bone was growing kinda funny."

Martin tossed a rock into the lake. It went in with a loud plunk. "So what did the doctor tell him?"

"He said they might have to reset it. The doctor wants to take him down to Duluth."

Martin found another rock. "Too bad he's missing all this fun," he said. He hurled the rock out onto the lake as though he were smacking someone with it. He'd been in a weird mood since Bear's leg had been broken in the accident with Bill Miller, and now he was showing it.

Portaging with Bill, Bear had taken the downside of the canoe on a steep, rocky slope. When the canoe had come down heavy on Bear, he'd gone rolling ass-over-teakettle with it, all the way to the lake. It'd taken a day and then some to get him out, and by then Martin was saying how he thought maybe Bear'd been pushed, only no one, not even Bear, listened.

"I suppose Osada was giving Bear a load of shit about the garbage too?" Martin said.

Red Deer laughed. "What do *you* think?"

Martin shook his head. "That's what you get for workin' for Tomato around here."

Red Deer ran his knife up the wood. A long slender strand peeled out over it. "What are *you* gettin'?" he said.

"I didn't put that—"

"You eat over there, don't you?"

I climbed the fir behind them. Now I could listen to them and watch for bears. The pine pitch smelled good and the bark was rough under my hands. On the marshland the garbage heap rose out of the sand like the carcass of some dead animal. It was almost high enough now to be above the reeds. It was as big around as a pond and it was getting wider all the time.

"You want to go fishing?" Martin said to Red Deer.

Red Deer peeled away another smooth shaving. As it came off he turned and looked at Martin.

"No," he said.

I didn't dare move. A jay settled in the tree, calling to another down on the marsh.

"I think you'd be a fool to go over there now," Red Deer said.

"Why?"

"You know why."

Martin shifted nervously from one leg to the other. "If Bear were here he'd—"

"I don't want to hear it," Red Deer said.

"But it wouldn't take more than . . ."

Red Deer stood, brushed off his pants. "Just don't come cryin' to me later," he said. He pushed his knife into his pocket and turned up the path to the lodge and Martin watched him go. When Red Deer was over the ridge Martin tugged at a branch, pulled it away so I could see him.

"Eli!" he said. "You want to go fishing?"

I felt like a traitor, down at the dock with Martin. We'd gotten everything stowed in the boat, the rods and reels, tackle boxes and nets, and were just about ready to take off when Tomato Burke rushed out of the lodge.

"Hey!" he yelled.

Martin was tugging on the rope starter like he didn't hear him, and he was even doing it when Tomato's feet hammered up the dock.

"That one's got a bad diaphragm in the carb," Tomato said. "You'll be way out there someplace and it'll die on you."

I didn't know whether to say hello to Tomato or not. He was a big man, as big as Osada, but he had a happy face and it was very hard to dislike him.

"Hi, Mr. Burke," I said.

Martin was fidgeting around like he was afraid I'd see how he talked to Tomato now.

"Hi, Eli," Tomato said. He had one of those faces that turn real red, and after the way he'd come running up the dock I could see why they called him Tomato.

Martin looked up from the motor.

"You want me to take another boat?"

"You can do that or you can go into the boathouse and get one of those Evinrudes."

They stood looking at each other, Martin leaning against the motor in the back of the boat and Tomato up on the dock, his hands on his hips.

"You want this off anyway, don't you?" Martin said.

Tomato nodded. "Yeah, it'll have to come off."

There was something weird about the way Martin was acting, and I could see Tomato saw it too. He was jerky, and as he turned the motor mounts out on the transom, his hands went at it as though he were screwing the things out of Tomato's chest.

"Something wrong?" Tomato said.

Martin rubbed his nose. "I thought you said you weren't going to dump any more garbage out on the marshland?"

"I really don't want to talk about it, Martin," Tomato said. "Okay?"

Martin had his hand on the rope starter and was twisting it. "It really doesn't seem okay to be dumping that crap out there by Osada's place. I mean—"

"I said I didn't want to discuss it."

"But how you could think—"

"Look," Tomato said, "you don't know what I was thinking. Understand?"

Tomato gave Martin his businessman's smile.

Martin shook his head. He heaved the motor up onto the dock and Tomato carried it to the boathouse. The motor swung from Tomato's right arm, his shoulders at least half again the width of his waist.

"God, he's big," I said.

His back to me, Martin shook his head. "There's no arguing with that man."

I picked up my rod and acted like I was trying to put a leader on my line. "How do you do that knot?" I asked.

"Here," Martin said, taking the line.

A breeze had picked up and it tossed his hair over his forehead and he kept brushing it away.

"You get screwed either way," he said, pulling the line tight, looking up. "All he's got to do is smile and what can you do? *I'm right you're wrong.*"

"Martin," I said.

Tomato was coming up the dock with the new motor.

Martin spun around. "Hey, thanks, Tomato," he said, his voice all syrupy like they were best buddies or something.

On the bay we trolled for northerns, cut across the center where it was deep, headed toward the point. It had gotten dark and looked like it might rain.

"Any strikes?" Martin said.

I said no, wondering what was wrong with him. Even I knew the bay was no good for northerns.

"Why don't we drop line for walleyes?" I said.

The motor was puttering and he didn't seem to hear me.

It had gotten colder, too, and already my sweatshirt and windbreaker weren't enough. "I want to go in if it starts raining," I said.

Martin cut down on the throttle. "What?"

"I want to go in if it starts raining."

He pointed to the canvas bag he'd brought along. I was wondering what was in it since he'd gone all the way back to the lodge to get it.

"I brought enough gear for both of us," he said. "You'll be okay."

The boat bounced down on the lake, spraying us.

"It's too cold," I said.

Martin reached out and grabbed my arm. His eyes were pinched, angry. "We're not going in until we catch something," he said. "Got it?"

Where my suit had rotted the rain came through. I hunched over, my back to the bow, trying to stay warm, watching my lure cut through the water.

"Slow down!" I said. I was getting pretty mad. "Look," I yelled back to him, "there's nothing out here."

"Just keep that lure in the water," he said.

He was smiling. I could see him inside that army-green poncho, rain running down his face, his eyes staring. He nudged the gas can in back with his foot.

"We got enough gas?" I said.

Martin nodded.

I turned around to look where he was steering us. He'd turned south, veered around the point and now the marshland came up. There were no fish here, and I was going to tell him so.

"Martin!" I said.

"What is it now, Eli?"

I leaned toward him, the rod tight in my hand. I was trying to figure out what to say.

"Look," I said.

And then I got the strike.

It hit so hard it bent the rod double. I snapped on the release and the line sung out of the reel like a siren. Martin had given me a crappy old open-faced reel with this heavy braided nylon line, the kind nobody in their right mind uses, and now I was happy. So happy. It was high-pound line, and the fish, cutting through the reeds, would have broken any monofilament. The rod jerked, and I got in a few feet of line, and then the fish headed back into the reeds and the line was whining out like a siren again. The fish made a big circle around the boat, twice, and I reeled in some more and let out a little less. The fish was beginning to feel like a big log on the line, it was tiring.

I got the whatever-it-was right up alongside the boat, could see its shiny, green-gray pebbled back, the big dorsal fin like a blue plume. God it was big.

"Get the net!" I yelled.

The fish gave a tremendous thump on the side of the boat and I tried to hold him there.

Martin shoved a hand into his pocket, as if he were deciding something.

"Hey!" I said.

The fish slammed the boat again.

"What are you doing?"

Martin leaned over the gunnel, grasped the line, and with his knife cut right through it. The rod shot up in my hands and I fell on my butt. The boat rocked, nearly taking in water, then calmed. We just looked at each other.

"Notice where we are?" he said.

I looked around. While I had been fighting the fish Martin had pushed us up into the marshlands with an oar. It was so quiet you could hear the raindrops on the lake.

"Got any idea what we're here for?" he said, grinning. "You probably know we're not fishing, right?"

He looked a little crazy, the hood of his poncho over his head like the hood on a monk. He put out a hand, watched the rain fall.

"Perfect," he said.

We beached the boat right up at the garbage dump. Martin looked at his watch.

"We'd better get going or the bears'll be around."

He snapped the gas line off the motor and lifted the tank out of the boat.

I stood with my hands in my pockets. I couldn't believe it. There was more junk there than I'd ever seen in my life. Old furniture, plates, all broken, ruined axe handles, rotten lumber, what was left of the old boathouse—what they hadn't simply dragged out into the lake and sunk—and garbage. So much garbage. Pink plastic bags and green plastic bags and bags all bleached out. Chicken bones and coolers full of rotten old stuff, torn apart by the bears. All that garbage must have done something to the sand because the reeds grew at least eight feet high around it.

"You've never been over here, have you?" Martin said.

I said I hadn't.

Martin set the tank on the sand. The rain made a light pinging noise on it.

"It's a lot worse than it looks from the ridge, isn't it?" he said.

I didn't know what to say.

Martin marched right up the side where they'd dumped the furniture and waved his arms. "I can even see the lodge from here," he yelled down.

I still didn't get it.

He almost looked funny, standing up there, king of the heap.

He turned a circle, then ran in huge, floating leaps down the garbage and skidded to a stop in the sand.

"You know what we're going to do?" he said.

I got a sick feeling in my stomach from the way he said it.

He reached for the gas tank, held it shoulder high. Eight gallons and he was swinging the thing around like it was nothing.

"We're gonna burn the whole goddamn dump down," he said.

I looked at the mound of garbage. "That's funny, Martin," I said, the knot in my stomach tightening. "Really funny."

I followed Martin around the island side of the dump, the crotch of my suit chafing my legs and my whole back cold and wet. All I could see from under my hood was his swaying green shoulders and his legs kicking through the reeds. Then we were around to the lake again and Martin charged through the last of the reeds.

"No big deal," he said, striding to the boat.

I stumbled out onto the sand after him.

He spun around and held his index finger up. "One more thing."

He tore a cattail off its stalk, tossed the fluff up over his head. The seeds floated in toward the marshland.

"Good," he said, "the wind's blowing in off the lake. We'll only have to cut down the stuff on the island side."

He dug a sickle out of the canvas pack and handed it to me. It was one of those jobs you use for cutting weeds down, small, rusty, and dull. He pointed to the water's edge on the left side, said, "Just cut from there"—then swept around the dump to the water's edge on the right—"to there."

I raised the sickle, turned it in my hand. "With this?" I said.

"What the hell else would you use?"

I was thinking of a big power mower, the kind with shears in the front. Then I was thinking of going home, sneaking off through the reeds, climbing the ridge, and walking down to Osada's cabin. I wiped the rain off my face.

"It's not that bad, Eli," he said.

I ran my thumb up the blade of the sickle and looked at the streak of rust it left on my skin. "You're crazy," I said.

It was an impossible job. The sickle was worthless and a lot of the burnable junk was buried in the sand. I hacked and stomped the reeds back and Martin struggled with the beams from the old boathouse. Six men couldn't have made a neat fire in two days, but in a couple of hours I had the reeds cleared back a good fifteen feet and Martin had gotten what he could up off the sand. He was slowing, and some of that crazy look on his face was gone. He hauled a charred four-by-six up the heap, and, dropping it, wiped his hands on his pants. He'd tore them, and a wet flap of corduroy hung from his knee.

He crossed the sand to the boat and we stood admiring what we'd done. For a minute there I felt pretty good.

"Ready?" Martin said.

"We don't have to," I said. "I mean, it looks better, doesn't it?"

But then Martin got up on the heap with the gas tank.

In the green light the can glowed reddish-orange, looked explosive. He sloshed the gas over the furniture, then the old lumber, and down on the stuff that stunk so bad, and he had just enough to get us back to Tomato's when he stepped off at the bottom.

"You sure there's enough?" I said.

The gas was stinking something unbelievable. Even in the rain. Martin raised the can and I could hear the gas sloshing.

"I'll just put it on the boat and start the motor," he said. "We'll be one-hundred-percent-safe."

He hooked the gas line up and pulled the rope starter; on the second pull the motor coughed into life—the way old outboards *never* start.

"It's a sign," Martin said.

The sky had turned black. There was the distant rumble of thunder. A big fork of lightning ripped into the lake. I counted: one-thousand one, one-thousand two, one-thousand—

The thunder boomed like a gunshot, rippling away into nothing.

"You sure we can get across the bay before it hits here?" I said.

Martin tugged at the hood of his poncho. "Just a couple minutes more," he said.

A bear ambled over from the high side of the island and I pointed him out to Martin. The bear was sniffing the air, turning his head in our direction. He came down the embankment and Martin banged on a broken pot. It sounded like a drum. The bear sat back on its haunches and trained one eye on us. Martin banged on the pot again. Hair stood up on the bear's back.

Martin dropped the pot and dug through the pockets of his rainsuit. "I think this is it," he said, pulling out a big pack of waterproof matches, his hands shaking. "Stand back."

He struck a match, leaned out like a dancer, balancing on one leg, the flame cupped in his hands, then tossed the match onto the pile.

The match flickered, went out.

"Don't worry," he said. He fumbled with the pack, his hands jerking, and lit another match and threw it on the pile.

That one went out too.

"Shit," he said.

We stood there in the rain at the base of the garbage heap, all of it stinking like rotten oranges, rust, and gasoline, the bear, snarling, his lips curled back over his teeth.

"We could just leave," I said.

Martin stared at me from under his hood. "If he comes any closer, get in the boat, okay?"

I knew it wouldn't do any good but I smiled at the bear. I was thinking "Nice bear, good bear," smiling like some retard while Martin got the tank from the boat. He sloshed gas on the bottom of the pile and ran back and set the motor up again, but didn't start it.

"Well," he said, watching the bear, "here we go again. Stand back."

He pulled the box of farmer's matches out of the pocket of his poncho, his hands all palsy, struck one match and touched it to the others. The whole box sputtered, and he held it out, delicately, like some kid giving flowers to his girlfriend. He lifted his arm, and in the warm light from the burning matches I could see a wavering of fumes. A cool, blue-green streamer shot from Martin's hand into the pile and blossomed at his feet. His eyes widened, and before he could move a sound came like a jet taking off. An orange ball of fire swept around his head. He stood in it, and the flame shot upwards, and he ran toward me, his hands over his face.

"Get in the boat," he yelled.

The wind blew the flames down into the water and the reeds started up, crackling and snapping. Martin pulled like crazy on the rope starter. The motor puttered, then died. Puttered again—it sounded so good, I couldn't believe it—then died.

"Get the goddamned oars, Eli," Martin yelled.

I rammed the oars into the oarlocks and pulled hard at them. We slid away from shore, cutting through the reeds.

Martin was pulling at the starter with both arms now.

The fire curled up behind us, washed over the boat. I got down in the bottom and Martin jerked me back up to the oars. He kicked the motor mounts free, and I stopped rowing.

"Hey!" I said. "What are you doing?"

Martin turned the big Evinrude on its side and it dropped off the back.

A wall of flame hit the boat and we scrambled into the bottom.

"Get out of the boat," Martin said.

I was not going to get out of the boat.

"Get out of the boat!" he shouted again.

He reached down and grabbed me by the shoulders. His fingers poked into my armpits, hit a nerve, and I lost my grip on the seat stays. He lifted me up and over the gunnel and the boat shrunk below.

I flew.

The water struck my forehead like ice. I got my boots off, then my jacket, and kicked up through the water, a cough trying to burst out my mouth. I pushed through the surface, heaved out the bad air and got a lungful of hot, raw smoke.

In the fire Martin rocked the boat up on its side. As if sighing, it held there a second, then went over. I tried to push through to the boat but the reeds burned my hands.

"Martin!" I yelled.

Martin reached through the reeds, his hair all burned and ratted back. I went under, coughing, scrabbled to the surface, got a mouthful of water, and just when I thought I would drown Martin grabbed me around my neck. He pulled me under the boat, and it was dark and I was choking and I couldn't see anything.

"Here," Martin said. He put my hands on the seat stays. "Don't let go."

He was gone then, and in a second I heard a splash inside and felt a blast of air and water on my face.

"Can you kick?"

I said I could.

The air was sharp, like needles, and I couldn't stop coughing. Now Martin was coughing too. I started to drift off, and something hit me in the face.

"Don't stop breathing."

Martin would disappear, then surface inside again, blasting out the bad air. It got terrible hot, and I reached up and touched the bottom of the boat. It burned my hand and I let out a yell.

"Don't touch it," Martin said.

"It's all your fault," I choked out.

It was orange around the sides and I could see the back of his head.

"I mean, what's the use—"

"You shut up," he said, jerking around to face me, his eyes black holes in his face. He grabbed me by the jaw, poked his fingers into my cheeks. "You shut up," he said, "or I'll put you out in the fire, understand?"

I gripped the seat stays for all I was worth, too stiff to even nod.

. .

The air in the boat cooled and the water dropped off, bottomless and black. Martin went out, and seconds later splashed up in the bow, exhaling.

"Come on," he said, jerking me along with him.

Outside the air was cool and fresh. The south end of the island was in flames, and there were lightning strikes now, huge white forks cutting into the lake and the islands. I was shaking. My lungs ached so bad it felt like they were stuck full of pins. We'd lost the oars, and to paddle the boat across the bay in that cold water was impossible.

I lay out on my back, holding on to the keel. The clouds were orange.

"Come on, Eli," Martin said.

"Leave me alone," I said.

"Come on. We're gonna swim around the point to Osada's," Martin said. "Let go of the boat."

He sounded drunk.

"Let go," he said.

I felt him prying on my fingers.

"Let go of the boat."

A big orange cloud reared up. It looked like a horse, all fire and swirling. "Okay," I said.

Tomato had pulled up a chair and a dim light shone below Osada's faded calendars.

"I have no idea where the boat is," Martin said.

I was still in bed, half-asleep. The chill hadn't left my legs and I woke with a start, for a second thinking they had cut my legs off.

Red Deer was carving, his back angled against the bed where Martin sat. Osada was looking at Martin. There were blisters on his forehead and nose, and his hair had been cut off in clumps.

"You still haven't told me what you were doing in there," Tomato said.

"We were fishing," Martin said.

"Nobody fishes over there."

"Christ, I said we were fishing."

Martin was looking pretty tough. Osada wouldn't stop looking at him. Not mean, just wondering like.

Tomato looked at his watch. "They sure are taking their sweet time," he said. "Now tell me again what you were doing over there."

"I told you," Martin said. "We were trolling for northerns and Eli got a great strike and we went into the reeds for it."

"I still can't understand why you didn't get off the lake."

Red Deer lit a cigarette. "I've fished over there," he said. He said it as though with great difficulty, the words coming slowly and unnaturally.

There was a knock on the door and Osada motioned for Red Deer to open it. A jowl-faced man wearing a black poncho and peaked ranger's cap pushed into the room.

"I'm looking for a Richard Burke," he said.

Tomato nodded and stood. "That's me," he said.

I looked at Martin. It was as if his eyes had sunk farther back into his head.

Tomato shook my shoulder. "Get up," he said.

Red Deer gave me a robe and a cup of hot, bitter coffee.

"You know why I'm here," the fire marshal said to Martin. He pulled a chair out from Osada's table and sat, one leg crossed over the other.

Martin looked across the room at me.

"Let's make this as easy as possible," the marshal said. He drew a small notebook and a pen from his breast pocket, then smiled a stiff smile. "All right?"

He was slow, methodical, and he scribbled in his little book even when no one was saying anything. Especially when no one was saying anything. Martin went through how the motor wouldn't start and how when the fire swept into the reeds he had turned the boat over and we had paddled out. But the marshal kept going back to one thing, how the fire started, and he didn't let up.

"And you say you were fishing?" the marshal said to me.

I nodded.

He had a habit of pulling on his earlobe, then turning to you and smiling. Now he did it again, pulled on his earlobe and smiled.

"I can't hear you," the marshal said.

"Yes," I said. "We were fishing."

"And *you* saw the fire start . . ."

Here I lowered my head, so I could catch Osada's eyes.

He was immobile, and stared back.

"I want it from both of you," Tomato said. He was smoking into his second pack and the room was lousy with smoke. A pile of basswood slivers had grown up like fungus where Red Deer sat carving.

"I told you," Martin said, "we didn't see the fire start."

"You say you were *in* the fire?" the marshal said.

"Yes," Martin said.

"But you didn't see the fire start?"

"How many times do I have to tell you?"

"Just as many times as it takes to get it straight. Now, you say the lightning started the fire. Is that right?"

"Yes."

"But you didn't *see* it start the fire, right?"

"Right."

"So how do you know it was the lightning?"

Martin slumped in his chair.

"I don't know it was the lightning."

"But didn't you just say it was the lightning?"

I thought Martin was going to break down. He had that *all right, that's enough* look in his face. I think the marshal saw it too, because right then he put a hand on Martin's shoulder.

"I think you're lying, boy," he said.

Martin shook his head.

"He's lying, isn't he," the marshal said to me.

He tightened his grip on Martin's shoulder and lowered his head to Martin's. "I don't think that was any lightning," he said, "I think you and this pip-squeak here, Tonto, or whatever his name is, set that dump on fire. Isn't that it?"

Martin's lips were working.

Osada's eyes narrowed; he stood, and kept on standing. He was even bigger than Red Deer.

"Get out of my cabin," he said.

"This is park property," the marshal said, standing. You could see he'd done it before, the same way he pulled on his earlobe and smiled at you.

Osada's scar twitched. He leaned toward the marshal, his big hands popping, and in a low, throttled voice, he said, "Get out."

"I'll do what I want here," the marshal said.

Red Deer was gouging away huge chunks of basswood. He turned to look up at the marshal. The marshal unsnapped his holster. He slipped his hand around the butt of his pistol and clicked off the safety. Red Deer reached under the bed. Before the marshal had the pistol out Red Deer had Osada's rifle trained on the middle of his chest.

Tomato sat in his chair, a trail of smoke rising from his cigarette.

The marshal turned to him, his face angry now. "You with them?" he said.

Tomato looked at us and then back at the marshal.

"You'd better be sure about what you're doing," the marshal said. He crossed the room, opened the door and stood in it. "You've got a lot to lose here."

Tomato crushed out his cigarette. "I don't believe this," he said.

The marshal shook his head.

Tomato stood, patted his pockets for his cigarettes and couldn't find them. "Okay," Tomato said, turning to the door.

The marshal lifted his chin, as if he had won something, and stepped outside.

Tomato turned the doorknob, testing it. You could see the veins on the back of his hand. He scratched his head, balanced there, then leaned out the door.

"Hey."

"You coming?" the marshal said.

"I'd rather go to hell than anywhere with you, you son-of-a-bitch," Tomato said, and then he pushed the door home and the latch caught.

Bear was back the following day. The whole island still reeked of burned pine and reeds. Across the bay I could make out Martin on the docks; he loaded boats, helped the old guys in, the ones who needed it, and filleted fish like a machine in the fish house. Tomato came down from the lodge, loaded up a boat, and a few hours later he was at the dock with what was left of the Alumacraft. The gunwales were melted down and the motor was in back.

"What the hell happened to the boat?" Bear said.

We were sitting outside Osada's cabin, playing gin rummy. Bear was no good at it, or he just didn't care, and he was looking all over the place or scratching under his cast and I could cheat— just for fun, the game was so bad—look at Bear's cards when he had his head turned.

"I'll take the aces," I said.

"Now wait a minute . . ."

Osada stepped out of the cabin and stretched. He sniffed the air and smiled a little bit. Martin was out on the end of the dock with a couple old duffers. He helped the last one into the boat, and then straightening up, he looked out across the bay. Tomato was behind him, watching. Martin waved to us, and then something I'd never seen happened. Osada, standing on a rock outcropping, raised his arm, his hand held palm out. He didn't move his arm or anything, but we could see what he was doing.

CROWNING
GLORY

1969 *Tonight I will have him,* Vonny thinks, straining at the lodge kitchen window on her toes, her strong brown hands gripping the rim of the sink. The transistor radio on the window-sill jabbers baseball, but she isn't listening. Can't listen now.

Out on the bay, Red Deer stands to cast; Bear balances the boat in back. *Little pig!* Vonny thinks, watching Bear pump his legs to steady the boat.

For the past month Vonny has secreted charms away in Red Deer's meals: a circle of her hair, a tiny figure of tobacco no bigger than a thumbtack, a spray of chokecherry. She has carefully, lovingly, hidden each charm, in the batter of a pancake, in the center of a deer steak, at the heart of a salad, but in the lodge dining room, at the moment of her triumph, Bear has eaten each one, has shoveled onto his own plate what Red Deer has left on his, digging like a beast with his fork. But tonight, *tonight* will be different.

The small boat dips in the wake of a larger, flashier boat, and Red Deer and Bear wave. They are an odd pair, Red Deer, in his early thirties, tall, sure on his feet, but sullen and quiet, Bear like a fireplug, short, squat, with laughing eyes, just out of his teens, a boy, really.

But she has their number now. She knows their secrets, their habits in the boat. And this, her latest plan, is foolproof, is powerful. *Powerful.*

Bear's laughter carries up through the window, high, full of animal pleasure. *Little pig!* Vonny thinks, thrusting another dish into the water. This time, Vonny thinks.

Getting this charm right has taken Vonny nearly a year, and it is *foolproof.* Vonny's mother, Okitchita, had been a sorceress, and had taught her well. Even Vonny's name is a charm— *Yvonne*—something her mother had seen in a movie in town. As the credits had rolled up off the screen, Vonny had kicked in her mother's belly and the name had flashed like a vision across the theater.

"Why-vonne," her mother had said, some curious charge settling deep in her.

And Vonny's charms are powerful.

She has calmed stormy seas between lovers with the shaking of a bell, has given others things they wanted: marriage, babies, jobs. She has driven away nightmares and has cured more than a few cases of the croup. An early learner, her charms have been sought for years, and she has administered them where they have been needed, all for the asking. But now she is the one doing the asking, and it has set her off balance. That her charms have been ineffective—totally ineffective—on Red Deer makes her furious, and that it is a *man* makes her even more so. She has taken men down with just a wink, has pleasured more than a few—for her twenty-five years she doesn't like to think how many—who liked her silky brown thighs and sumptuous breasts. She even monied for it once, she was so sought after, but Red Deer doesn't seem to notice her at all. She isn't like the skinny white girls she sees him with in town—high-fashion Kenora girls in their jewels and dyed hair. No, she is round like these lakes, raven haired, and hard as ice when she has to be.

No, you may not have noticed me, Vonny thinks, looking out the window, but just you wait, buster, just *you* wait.

She turns to stack the plates in a rack, her movements full of bravado. "Take That!" she says to no one there. But she aches from holding herself up at the window, and she fears that at some moment—some mundane washing, or scrubbing, or polishing—she will turn away and the snare she has set will go KEE-WUNK! and she will have missed her moment of glory. So she cranes her head over her shoulder, her eyes fixed on the boat, gun sights on game.

There isn't much to see. Just Red Deer and the boy, hunkered down in the boat, their lines in the water.

For months they've spent their evenings out in the boat like this. It's baseball season, and they make pretenses of fishing— Red Deer with his muskellunge lure, the size of a rolling pin, Bear with his too-shiny spinners. They sit out in the boat till after dark, a radio wired to the bow with a coat hanger. A few nights a week, game nights, they take the boat out, just distant enough from shore so Tomato doesn't call them in, but close enough so they are never more than minutes from the lodge and the pies Vonny bakes—gooseberry, blackberry, blueberry. If it is a still night they will circle the island, trolling, and almost miraculously, they will step through the lodge door the moment the pies are out.

One night Red Deer stood up in back and shouted. Vonny could hear him all the way up to the lodge.

"Strike the son-of-a-bitch out!" he yelled.

She had been slipping birchbark charms into his pockets that week, ones she had stayed up nights making: beautiful, painted pairs bound with horsehair.

"You listening to baseball out there?" she had asked when they came in.

Red Deer had stared off across the kitchen. Bear had blinked at her.

"You want a piece of gooseberry pie?" she said.

Bear took a step in her direction. He was all appetite.

"No," Red Deer had said, pulling Bear outside with him.

It was a confusing thing to her, a hard nut to crack, but after that night she'd had a lead to go on—there was something important in this baseball business. So she got herself a radio, and listened to the games. Now she knows Rod Carew's batting average. How Blyleven pitches. She knows all the scuttlebutt about Oliva, and wonders if it's true. She buys baseball magazines, and wakes in the middle of the night, saying strange things like *Force play*, or *Down-the-pipe*. And waking, she always gets to thinking about bases, runs-batted-in, and then she gets to thinking baseballs and biceps and bats. And then she tangles herself in her bedsheets, and wants him worse, as she wants him now. Sitting big and pretty in the back of the boat, she wants him, wants him, oh! how she wants him.

From this window over the sink, she will see it all—unless—her heart skips a beat, a cold knot of fear in her stomach—unless Marceline wants her to do the laundry, in that windowless loft, but—

Tonight is the big game with the Cardinals, and *tonight* is Red Deer's birthday. She can see it all coming together now, the Twins victorious, Red Deer ecstatic, the charm so powerful fighting it would be like trying to hold the sun down at dawn. She so thrills with the knowledge of her power she nearly breaks the dish she is scouring. No, this time she has it right. If Marceline comes for her, she will bake pies, fifty of them if she has to, but she will stay at this window to see her charm do its magic.

Somehow all along she had known it was in this baseball thing, and it amuses her now to watch Red Deer stand and cast again. Such ardent fishermen, such poor luck!

For weeks she had watched them out in the boat, new up at the lodge and stricken with Red Deer, until one evening, at the sink and up to her elbows in soapy water, it occurred to her that she had never seen them catch anything. It so intrigued her that when it got dark she stole down to the point and in the red willows slipped out of her dress. The water was cold, and she kicked away from shore, her legs carrying her powerfully through the water. A radio was playing and she swam toward it and the boat. The game was in a fury.

"Give it to 'em, Harmon," Red Deer said.

He brought his arm back with his rod and reel, cast out onto the lake. The lure went in with a loud splash.

"I'll bet they lose again," Bear said.

Red Deer reeled in and lay his gear over the gunwale. Vonny could hear Bear shifting around in the boat and she got hold of the anchor rope. The rope was covered with bristles that stuck like needles in her palms, and she struggled to hold her head above water.

A roar came from the radio.

"Goddamn," Red Deer said. "Those goddamn Twins. Leave it to Blyleven to throw him one like that. Shoulda walked him and went for the play on third."

The boat splashed, Red Deer digging through his tackle box in back.

"Gimme that," he said.

There was the whine of a reel. Something heavy hit Vonny in the forehead. It was that goddamned lure. The reel whined a second time, and when the lure came down again she caught it—to hell with the hooks—gave it a powerful jerk. There were no hooks.

Vonny clung to the anchor rope, holding the lure, dumbfounded.

"What's goin' on?" Bear said.

Red Deer gave a sharp tug on the line. Vonny tugged back.

"Ho!" Red Deer said, and Vonny dove, kicked under the boat and headed for shore.

Bear was shouting. Red Deer heaved in on the line, but the drag wouldn't take Vonny's weight. Offshore she let go of the lure and climbed up into the willows.

"But I saw it!" Bear was saying. "I really saw it."

"Don't you say nothing," Red Deer said.

"But I—"

"You going to shut up or not?"

"I saw—"

There was a hollow thumping, an immense splash, then Bear was hollering.

"See? Nothin's out there," Red Deer said.

In the morning Bear and Red Deer had come in for breakfast. Red Deer had eyed Vonny suspiciously, and Bear had asked, "Where'd you get that shiner?"

But now it all seems worth the trouble!

In a little time the matter will be settled and she can nearly feel Red Deer in her bed, his sinewy arms around her. She thrills to think of it, swoons over the sink, her hand darting through the hot water to pluck the plug from the drain. She watches the last of the soapy water swirl down and away, and catching something out of the corner of her eye, she raises her head, her heart turning over like dough being kneaded.

Out in the boat, Bear has lifted the box, is turning it, then shaking it. She had given Red Deer the box after dinner.

"Just something for your birthday," she'd said. "Open it after the game."

It is a hat box, wrapped in aluminum foil, with a huge blue ribbon; the foil flashes in the evening sun. Red Deer reaches for the box, gets a hold of the ribbon, and Bear tugs back, laughing.

"Let go you little son-of-a-bitch!" Red Deer yells.

But Bear's laugh is infectious, and Vonny is caught up in it, laughing almost hysterically herself, rescued for the moment from her fear that Bear might ruin the charm. She closes her eyes and counts—beef, onion, celery, carrots, peas, potatoes, marjoram, basil—stew! she thinks, opening her eyes.

Red Deer stands to cast and Bear's voice carries in off the water.

"Hope you drown," Bear says.

But she can see the bright box in the boat now, the anchor like a huge hook set on top. Though the box is secure, it bothers Vonny that Red Deer would set the mucky anchor on it, the carefully folded foil, the frilly ribbon.

Vonny slides the plastic tray of glasses across the counter to the sink, runs the tap, then dips the first into the sudsy water, pokes a washcloth in and scrubs.

Red Deer, he's a strange one, all right. After that night out on the lake she had asked around about him, but nobody would tell her anything. Not Dick, the manager, or his wife, not the other guides, and as a last resort she had baked a pie and brought it over to his father, Osada, across the bay.

"Ahhh," he had said, opening the cabin door.

She slipped under his arm and into the cabin, setting the pie on the table.

"Well," she said, beaming.

There had been a scrabble years back, between the Finedays and the Jacksons, and now she could see Osada was out to tease her about it.

"And your mother?" he said, squinting across the room at her.

Vonny got a knife and plate and fork, swung herself over to the table, the way men had liked at the restaurant when she'd waited tables. She cut a piece of pie and slipped it onto Osada's plate. Osada had a forkful halfway to his mouth when he stopped, smiled, then pushed his chair back from the table.

"What kind of mischief are you up to now?" he said.

"Eat," Vonny said, but he didn't. "Eat," she said.

Osada stood and led her to the door.

"Thank you," he said.

Rowing to the lodge she had watched the back of Osada's cabin; halfway across, the pie tin, fork, and plate tumbled out the loft window.

Vonny holds a glass up to the ceiling light, a skin of milk stuck to the bottom. She balls the washcloth into a tight, knotted mass, then thrusts it past the lip of the glass, in and out, trying to rub up inside. She stops, suddenly struck by the glass, the washcloth.

It is in her like a hook. Thinking about Red Deer she gets all soft inside, feels her legs trembling. She thinks about his fine head, his braids, his . . . She thinks about his dark eyes, his hands, long-fingered, his . . . Oh! she thinks, slamming the dishware into the cupboard, her eyes on the boat. She *won't* think about it, but she does. She thinks about his powerful thighs, his little rear, his—

The boy laughs.

Vonny laughs. Even though she is wound up now beyond laughing, she still can't help laughing with him. He always makes her laugh. He's funny, the little pig! She likes his funny little gut and the way he stands, his feet out to the sides. He's like an otter, and she—Shouldn't think about him that way, Vonny thinks, scrubbing at another glass—fifty to go. God she hates church groups! She scrubs in small circles, screws up the volume on the radio, her body moving in time to the beer commercial, her eyes held on the boat. It's meant to be, she thinks. It has to be. The charm is perfect.

She had poked around all over, had given herself to the finding of the charm—couldn't find it. And then, just like that, it had revealed itself to her. Joe Big Otter had come into the lodge with his son, Eli, and Vonny had winked him into the kitchen.

"Like a piece of pie?" she had said.

There was something strange going on—she recognized something in the man's squat figure, his laughing eyes—and then it struck her. This was Bear's father, and it all connected up and the current was going strong.

She set the pie on the table.

"Picked the blueberries myself," she said. "Ice cream?"

"Don't mind if I do," he said.

She swung around the table to the freezer, brushing by him. She was enjoying this now, how his eyes perked up. In his own way he was handsome, but too old. Scooping out the ice cream she thought how Bear's face would slim out like his father's, all craggy and handsome, but with that joking, quizzical look.

"Enough?"

Joe poked at the mound on his plate. "I'd say," he said.

Vonny sat across the table, her hands in her lap. Joe dug into the pie. He ate with the same gusto Bear did. He took great pleasure in his eating. She liked to watch him eat.

"Good?" Vonny said.

Joe smiled, then laughed to himself. "You make the best damn pie on the lake, Vonny, and I'd say so any day," he said. He had that same infectious laugh, that smile.

"You been following the Twins?" Vonny asked.

She went through the whole litany, the players, batting averages, the games the team had won and lost. She tried to turn things around to Bear, so she could get to Red Deer. Joe finished and was eyeing the pie.

"I see Bear and Red Deer are nuts about it," Vonny said. "They get that from you?"

"No," Joe said.

"They're just nuts about it."

Joe was eyeing the pie. "Goes way back with them."

"Is that so?" Vonny said.

Joe ran his fork across his plate. "Guess so," he said.

Vonny slid the pie across the table and stood. She turned toward the refrigerator.

"Did either of them ever play?" she said, opening the refrigerator door.

"Well," Joe droned. "Like I said," Joe said, "it goes way back—"

Vonny held the door open.

"—Ah, I guess I may as well tell you," Joe said.

Vonny slipped back to the table; she cut a huge slab of pie from the tin and slapped a mound of ice cream on it.

"So you were saying," Vonny said.

Joe poked at the pie with his fork. "You won't say nothin' now . . ."

The radio on the windowsill roars.

Vonny clutches at the washcloth in her hand. Ninth inning, but the Twins only have a one-point lead. Please, please, pretty please, Harmon, Vonny thinks, straining at the sink, her eyes fixed on the boat. Bat a homer for me.

It is almost too much now—it is all taking far too long and any minute now Marceline will be in with something for her to do, worst of all laundry. Vonny hefts the tray of glasses, her hands shaking, carries it across the kitchen to a rack in the wall. In a second she is back at the window. Red Deer casts, deftly sending the huge lure out across the lake.

Since that night Vonny had talked to Joe, had learned that Red Deer had played double-A baseball, had even made it to the minor leagues, but had lost out to a car accident on the way to his last game—Joe had even been there, or so he said—she had seen Red Deer out on the field, a star. "He could pitch like nothin' you've ever seen," Joe had said. Nights the Twins played Vonny imagined the lights on the field, the crowd cheering, the photographers, the triumphant players, and she had settled on this last charm.

A hat for Red Deer—a *magic* hat.

She took the bus down to St. Paul, the RedHawk Special, for the seniors who wanted to see a game. She had never been in the Cities, and when she got off the bus with her ticket, and went up and into the stadium with the others from Kenora, she had seen what seemed like all the people who had ever lived, under blinding blue lights, and not so much as one Chippewa among them. It scared her, the immensity of the stadium, and she wondered how she would do what she had come to do. It seemed impossible now. The roaring in the stands was incredible, and then the booing started. It was a terrible game, and Blyleven's pitching was terrible. Everyone was drinking beer around her and she got terribly thirsty and had a few and then she started in with the others, shouting and cursing. In the last inning she went down to stand behind the dugout. There was to be an autograph signing, and she intended to get Blyleven's hat. She hadn't thought about how she would get the hat, but she was determined to get it whatever it took.

The game ended, and what looked like a waterfall—all boys and girls, and their parents—went through a narrow steel gate onto the field. Vonny went too. In the mob she pushed, then shoved. There was an overwhelming animal smell, sweat and anger and fear. The ball players were signing like mad—Oliva, Carew, Kaat, and Perry.

"Gotta run!" Blyleven shouted, then strode across the field with the others.

Vonny watched him go, an enormous defeat sucking the life out of her legs; she felt as though she might fall. Blyleven turned to wave, and then—something spoke to Vonny, said, how much do you want this?—like a shot, Blyleven hurled his cap up over the field.

Vonny charged.

Only problem was, when she got back up to Morson, she found that Blyleven had a small head. Red Deer took a seven and five-eighths. She'd measured his hats. She got a sheet of blue felt, and widened the hat in back, took the stitching out from around the bill. Under the sweatband she sewed in duck feathers and witch-grass and the thighbone of a hawk. She took some hair from between her legs and put it under the Twins logo in the front, where it would go straight to his brain. It was a powerful charm, and she was even a little afraid of it herself when she was done.

It had taken her the better part of a month, and she'd worked like mad up till the last, because she couldn't miss this day. It has to be *this day*, Vonny thinks: Red Deer's birthday, the Twins playing the Cardinals.

And now the game is almost over.

Vonny bends over the wide sink to turn up the radio. She can hardly stand listening to it. The dishes are done now, and she fears even more now Marceline catching her standing dumb at the sink. A sun of desire and fear bursts and fades away in her heart, bursts and fades away.

Out in the boat Bear turns the box over and over in his hands. He laughs, poking Red Deer with the box, and Red Deer takes it from him. Vonny is on the verge of screaming, but the radio stops her. Twins lead. Cardinals' last batter up. Please, please, please. Just one game. The Twins have been on a losing streak and winning this game now would be no small miracle. Two and one. Blyleven rears, stretches.

"There's the pitch!" the radio spurts.

And with the last heavy thud of Vonny's heart the ball crosses the plate, a strike, and the crowd roars. Vonny pushes her face up to the screen in the window, so anxious she wants to climb out. She can't see well and she squints. Bear dances in the front of the boat and Red Deer sits in back smoking.

"Cut it out, will you?" he shouts.

Then Bear has the box out again, is pushing it at Red Deer. Red Deer tears at the ribbon and the foil, then has the top of the box off. He lifts the hat out of the box, turning it over and over in his hands, and in that moment Vonny cannot breathe for holding herself still. She can see the hard line of Red Deer's shoulders, the disbelieving, angry tilt of his head, and in one heart-wrenching jab he punches a finger through the felt in back and spins the hat on his finger like a propellor.

"Christ!" he says in a loud, angry voice, laughing, then reaches out with the hat and jams it on Bear's head.

"Here," he says, "this one's for you."

It is a strange moment. Bear stares up into the kitchen window, the hat cockeyed over his ears, Vonny peering, horrified, down into the boat on the lake. A horrendous, tearing moment. Bear turns his head away and down, his shoulders slumping— she can tell he is crying—and something shoots across the water with the power of all her magic, something she's been blind to all along.

COOTS

1970 The light from the island outside crept across the ceiling, an enormous, gray cat. Wait, he thought. The cat dipped, stretched, eased over the big knot in the middle, slid, lengthening, across the remainder, and bunched up around the tin stovepipe in the corner, where it waited, and waited, and waited until it leapt—burst against the loft wall.

It was time.

Eli reached out from his cot and shook his brother's shoulder.

"Bear?" Eli whispered. He could hardly contain his excitement. Bear blinked his eyes open and raised himself off his bed.

"What, Eli?" he said. His hair hung down his forehead into his eyes, and he brushed it away, squinting.

"You goin' out this morning?" Eli said.

Bear drew away the curtain over the window beside the bed. A gray light filled the room. It was drizzling—there were beads of water on the window. A wind tossed the pines.

"It's miserable out," Bear said, dropping the curtain over the window. "Go back to sleep." He flattened his pillow with his head and stretched out his legs.

Eli watched Bear sink into the bed. He could hardly stand more waiting. It was the morning of his twelfth birthday, duck hunting was in high season, and Bill had slipped, and now he waited for the time when he would be out on the lake with the men, not bailing anymore, not leaning over the bow sighting for deadheads, but *hunting* with them.

"Bear," Eli said.

"What now, Eli?"

"You going out hunting with Martin today?"

Bear drew in a deep breath. "Eli," he said, "if you ask me that one more time—"

"I was just thinkin'," Eli said. "If you were going out maybe I could sit in the front."

Bear yawned. He pulled the curtains away from the window again, then shook his head. "I wouldn't count on it," he said. "It looks like it's pretty mean out there." Bear dropped the curtain back over the window. The light went away and it was dark in the loft.

"Bear?"

Eli listened to the ticking of the big red clock at the end of Bear's bed until he couldn't stand it anymore.

"Is it Sunday?" Eli asked.

"Christ!" Bear said. He rolled over and slapped the bed with his palm. "And what other day would it be?"

"I don't know."

"For Christ's sake! Go back to sleep."

Eli slid under his covers and stared into the ceiling. He would have to wait, and he imagined foxes now, in the knots in the rough pine, then saw them digging under the fence behind the house on the reservation. The first got under and Eli raised his gun and *Kerpow!* knocked him back. Others came through after the first. Three shots. Each dead on. It was over in a matter of minutes. Eli imagined carrying them up to the house, their bodies bumping against his legs. On the porch his father, Joe, waited, smoking a cigarette.

"I'll take those," he said.

Joe went inside the house—Eli could hear his mother and father arguing—there was the sound of a slap, and the second-story window was thrown open, and Eli's mother flew out like a crow, her dress billowing black behind her. In the house someone cried. Eli waited on the steps for his father to come out with his gun. He waited a long time.

"Eli!" Red Deer said, raising the end of the cot and dropping it. "Get up!"

Eli gripped the cot, and when Red Deer raised it again, he spun his feet onto the floor and rubbed his eyes. The cabin shifted, and he tried to find his balance. It was light out, and Bear had gone.

"Where is everybody?" he said.

"In the kitchen," Red Deer said. "Come on, sleepy."

Eli pulled on his pants and followed Red Deer down the ladder. At the table Bear was shoveling pancakes into his mouth as if he hadn't eaten in weeks. He dug slabs of margarine out of a tub and spread them on his pancakes. He slapped the chair beside him and Eli bumped down into it. Osada sat on the other side, smoking and writing on a pad of paper. He was a big man, with a scar running down his right cheek, and he had a calculating look on his face now; he struggled to get what it was on the page to come out right. Red Deer shook a big iron skillet on the stove. He tossed a pancake in the air and caught it in the skillet.

"How many do you want?" he said.

Eli shrugged, looking for the package in the room. He couldn't see it anywhere, not under the car seat that served as a sofa, not by the lopsided refrigerator, not in the loft. It didn't make sense that it would be in sight, but still, he was beginning to think that Bill Miller had been pulling his leg. Eli had run into Bill down on the dock the week before, when he had been filling the minnow buckets. Bill was casting a daredevil into the bay from the launch. Standing so he could lean against the boat lift, he worked the rod in his usual, agitated way, and Eli had stopped to watch him, amused.

"Catchin' anything?" Eli'd said, teasing Bill. Walleye season had been over for a month.

Bill tugged at the brim of his hat.

"So, how do you like that gun?" he said. His voice was high and nasal, and he snorted when he talked, his pipe clamped tight in his teeth.

A burst of excitement ran down Eli's legs and he looked into Bill's long, sunburned face.

"What do you mean?" Eli asked.

Bill took his hat off and scratched his head. He was nearly bald and he had burned his scalp. The skin was peeling on the crown and he scratched it.

"Wasn't your birthday a couple days ago?"

"It's *next* week," Eli said, "on Sunday."

Bill tossed the lure out onto the lake. The daredevil cut the water with a musical plunk, and Bill set the drag on the reel. Eli could see the hairs in his nose.

"Guess I was mistaken," he said.

Red Deer stepped around the backside of the table and slapped a big pancake on Eli's plate. It was shaped like a rabbit, had long ears and legs.

"Not bad, huh?" Red Deer said. He elbowed Eli in the back.

"Eat," Osada said, looking up from his pencil and paper. "There's all you can eat."

Eli cut the head off the rabbit, then the legs. He poured syrup on the pancake and pushed a forkful into his mouth. He was wondering why no one was saying anything, and he was wondering if anything had come in the mail.

"Did Tomato go in to Wheeler's Point yesterday?"

Red Deer jerked the skillet up, flipping a pancake. The pancake sizzled in the bacon grease.

"I went," Red Deer said. "Remember?"

He reached with a long arm into the loft, slid his hand along, scrabbling with his fingers, then tossed Eli's comic book on the table. Superman soared across the cover, a bright red and blue.

"Now do you remember?"

Eli paged through the comic book. The bright colors that had been so exciting yesterday were somehow irritating now, too bright. Eli threw the comic book on the car seat and stuffed another forkful of pancake into his mouth.

"Make my next one so it's not so mushy inside, okay?" he said.

Red Deer's eyes narrowed. "Your next one, huh?" He twisted a knob on the front of the stove and the grease in the skillet sputtered. "I'll make you one."

Smoke rose to the ceiling, then down over the lamp. Bear waved his hand in front of his face, the smoke swirling in front of him like tissue.

"Hey!" Osada said.

He reached over to the stove and turned off the burner. Red Deer slapped the burned pancake on Eli's plate and Eli sat in front of it, his eyes watering.

"What's wrong with you?" Osada said.

Red Deer shrugged.

Osada pointed to the pancake. "You think he's going to eat that?" he said.

Noon came and no one made lunch. The cabin was deadly quiet. Drizzle collected on the roof and dripped from the eaves in front. Red Deer was carving a raccoon, one with a pinecone in its hands. He had got the angle of the head just right, as if the animal had raised itself in curiosity, and now he struggled to get the hands on the cone and the back just so. He held the carving up to the bulb in the ceiling, then returned it to the tabletop. Bear cleaned his shotgun. He very carefully disassembled the gun, scraping the rust from the workings with a penknife. He sloshed turpentine on a rag, and holding each part up to the light, buffed and polished. Osada played solitaire at the kitchen table. He slapped the cards down, looking up every so often, frowning with displeasure. He cheated—Eli could see the cards were bent—but still the game wasn't going well, and Osada, with each draw, slapped the cards with more energy onto the table. Eli sat on the car seat, trying to force himself through the Superman comic book again. He had been in the loft with it earlier, but he had read it too many times already and now he shifted on the seat, trying to think of something to do.

"Can I go out?" he said.

"No," Osada said, slapping down a card. "It's raining."

Eli looked out the window facing the lake. The lake was the color of steel, and now rain came down across it in irregular, wavering sheets.

Eli kicked the car seat with the heels of his boots. "I want to go out," he said.

Red Deer raised his head from his carving.

"You heard what he said."

Osada snapped down another card. He shook his head, his mouth rounded in an angry O. "Help Bear with his gun," Osada said.

Eli sat with Bear on the floor. Bear had arranged the parts of the gun in a neat pattern on a sheet of linoleum: stock; hammer, springs, and firing pin; breach and barrel. Eli didn't want to touch any of it—it was all so dark and shiny now, perfectly polished—but he picked the barrel off the floor and raised it to his eye.

"What are these whirls in here?" he said, staring up the barrel at Bear. Bear's eye swam in the dark, a brown-centered moon.

"It's a twist chamber," Bear said, pushing the barrel out of his face. "Spins the shot around so it doesn't wear grooves. And don't do that anymore. Not even in fun. You understand?"

Eli set the barrel down. Seeing Bear with his gun now was terrible. A rabbit pancake! Red Deer hadn't made him a god-damned rabbit pancake for years. He looked out the dark windows streaked with rain—the firs in front of the cabin all seemed to be drooping in the rain—then around the room. Old calendars hung from the walls, their pictures faded, like watercolors. The floor was warped and sagged down toward the kitchen. The cabin smelled of burned pancake now, and tobacco, rain, and damp rot. It was quiet. Osada, Red Deer, and Bear were all busy with themselves, and Eli wished he could be with his father—even if he was on another bender, even if he had sent his mother running off to who knows where. It made him sad, and a little angry, to think about it. His father tearing the house apart back on the reservation and his mother staying with family in the Dakotas. If only things had worked out somehow.

"He's pretty late," Red Deer said to Osada, jabbing at the raccoon with his knife.

Osada pursed his lips. His bad eye twitched. He lay another card on the table, and shaking his head, pushed himself up from his chair. "Bad cards," he said. He snatched his jacket off the hook on the kitchen wall. "May as well go and see Tomato," he said.

Eli sat beside Bear, pulling at the gauze on his finger. Osada had been gone nearly an hour, and in that time Eli had tried to carve something with a meat knife, had cut himself, and had knocked one of Bear's hammer springs through a crack in the floor, so they had had to pry up a board to get it back. Now he sat beside Bear. He was trying not to say it. That they had all forgotten him. That even his mother hadn't sent him a card. He wanted to know if they even wanted him here, and if they did, why were they being so mean?

"Bear," he said.

"What?" Bear asked. He was refitting the springs and firing pin in the gun. He held the hammer back with his thumb, the springs in his mouth.

"What day is it? I mean, what's the date?"

Bear looked up from the gun, his eyes narrowed in concentration.

"Just a minute, huh?" he said sourly.

Eli turned to the window. It was getting darker, the drizzle heavier on the windows. They *had* forgotten, and they *didn't* care, Eli thought. He watched Red Deer at the table with his raccoon and Bear with his gun on the floor. He added up everything that had happened in the past day or two—the strange silences and Red Deer making that stupid pancake to shame him—and now it all meant they did not want him. It had all been because his mother had called them and they had had to take him in. And realizing this, he wanted nothing more than to get out of Osada's cabin. He wanted to go home, wanted to be back on the reservation, even if it had been crazy. He wanted his books and his father, and worst of all he worried about his mother, and he wondered where she had gone. He thought of her voice, how soft it was, and he remembered how she had combed and braided his hair; and when he felt his eyes watering, he thought about running away. He wouldn't say anything to them. Red Deer or Osada. Not even Bear. He would wait until the middle of the night and then he would sneak out the backdoor and take one of the boats. They would miss him in the morning and he would be gone. He saw the dark water, felt the rumble of the motor in his hand, imagined how it would be out on the lake, the boat rocking, the smell of water and gasoline. If he got lost he could fish, there was plenty of tackle and he could even eat the minnows if he didn't catch anything. Maybe he'd die out there. And now that didn't seem so bad either.

A dripping started in the kitchen.

Red Dear, without raising his head, reached for the skillet on the stove.

Eli listened to the patter of the water.

"It's behind you," Bear said, pointing.

Red Deer set the skillet on the floor so the water dropped into it. The water sounded to Eli like a clock—*plip, plip, plip, plip,* and he turned to watch Bear buff his gun. Bear turned the gun around in an old T-shirt.

"You gonna be done soon?" Eli said. He had to say something. He couldn't listen to the water in the pan.

Bear shrugged his shoulders. "I don't know."

Red Deer ran his knife edgewise along the raccoon's tail. He raised his head from his carving and looked out past Eli through the window on the north wall. He blinked, then whistled the Hamm's Beer song. Bear stopped his polishing.

The door swung back, banged against the wall.

Bear and Red Deer got to their feet. Osada dodged across the room, one arm held behind his back.

"Run!" Osada yelled.

Eli bolted for the loft but Bear blocked him. Osada caught him with his free arm and spun him around and around. It all went into a blur, and Eli clung to Osada's jacket, his fingernails scraping on the thick canvas.

"Now I've got you!" Osada bellowed.

Eli banged his fists on Osada's back and Osada thumped him down on the bench seat. The room was still spinning. His breath came short.

"Give it to him," Bear said.

Osada stooped to brace one arm on the back of the seat. Eli could smell the whiskey on his breath. His bad eye stared off to one side.

"For you," he said, pressing the long package into Eli's arms.

•

Eli carried the new gun over his shoulder. In front of him, Bear and Martin cleared the rise down to the lodge. The rain had slowed to an even drizzle, and the bay looked deserted now, the boats straining against the ropes that held them to the dock.

"Vonny's been crazy," Bear said.

Martin grasped a branch along the path, breaking it off and slapping his leg with it as he walked.

"What's wrong?" Bear said.

"I don't know. It's just—"

"Hell, he can hear it," Bear said. He spun around, caught Eli's head in the crook of his arm, rubbed his knuckles over Eli's scalp.

"Cut it out!" Eli said, pushing Bear away.

Bear wriggled his eyebrows. "She's crazy," he said, pretending to reach for Eli's head again. "Usually they're runnin' like rats from me, but Vonny"—he cupped his hand over his groin—"It's *sore.*"

Martin laughed. "Goddamn," he said. He put his hand to Bear's ear and Eli followed close. He stepped into Bear's heels, and with a gut-wrenching lurch forward, felt his feet slip out from under him and he stumbled, the gun pitching forward so it nearly poked Bear in the back.

"Hey! Watch out back there," Bear said.

Eli scrambled to regain his balance, his heart pounding. Men died falling with guns. But then Bear was laughing at Martin's joke, and they were talking again and everything was all right.

Bear eased the boat around a sandbar, into a small, reedy cove. The reeds grew high and in clusters, and up near shore, white, diseased trees sagged in the drizzle.

"How does this look?" Bear said.

Martin stood. "Looks good to me," he said. He pointed off to the right. "Why don't we put down anchor over in those reeds?"

In the reeds, Eli couldn't see anything. Overhead, clouds drifted by low and dark like smoke. The drizzle was coming down lighter now, but everything smelled of wet canvas and water. Martin pulled his gun out of its case and loaded the pump with shells.

"Here," Bear said, in back, opening a case of twenty-gauge.

He handed Eli a shell and Eli slipped it into the breach of his gun and drew up the barrel. It made a sharp oily click.

This was the moment he had been waiting for. Or was it? He was excited and afraid now. He had fired Osada's gun at the range out by the point, had blasted holes in paper targets, and another time Osada had taken him out to the range and they had shot clay pigeons. He'd been good with the clay pigeons, but that evening had ended badly.

A lone coot had flown over the sand pit and Eli had followed it with his gun. He knew no one ate coots—they were small, dirty birds—but he had seen white men shoot at them for practice.

"Coot," Osada had said.

Eli got the end of his gun lined up on the bird.

"Like this," Osada said, swinging his arms around.

Eli fired. The coot veered slightly, then dipped over the ridge and was gone.

"I told you not to fire," Osada said. His mouth was puckered, as if he had eaten something sour. "Give me the gun," he said.

Eli opened his mouth but nothing came out.

"I said, 'Give me the gun,'" Osada said.

Eli handed him the gun. Osada cracked the barrel open and shoved the spent shell into his pants pocket.

"You don't know, do you?" he said, and Eli had cried.

THE SNAKE GAME

The ducks came in fast and low. Martin missed the first, pumped up a shell and got the second. Eli braced himself against the hull of the boat, pulled for all he was worth on the trigger of his gun.

"Safety's on!" Bear yelled.

Eli scrambled to find the safety and pushed it off. He followed the ducks around, fired, missed, then frantically cracked the breech open, digging in the bottom of the boat for another shell, the barrel pointing in all directions. The gun up and loaded, Eli followed the last duck, the duck rising high and far away, and when he squeezed the trigger, nothing happened. Bear grasped the barrel.

"Listen," Bear said. He reached for the small, red button behind the trigger guard. "I put this on while you were swingin' the damn gun around like nobody's business. Don't ever be goofin' around with the safety off or somebody'll end up with a mouth in their belly. You understand? You feel for it—"

Martin smiled. "You'll get your chance," he said.

"You gotta lead 'em, see?" Bear said. He shouldered his gun, and pointing to where the bird would be with his finger, swung the gun around. "Like that," he said.

"*I know it,*" Eli said.

Bear winked at Martin. "Okay," he said.

It was getting late, and Eli glowered over his gun now. He hadn't managed to shoot anything. Martin had shot four ducks, Bear five and now he was thinking how he hated everything, the boat, the lake, Bear and Martin and their stupid jokes.

"Is it time to go back in?" he said.

Bear nudged the ducks in the bottom of the boat with his foot. "You hungry, Martin?" he said.

"I could stay out," Martin said. "What about you?"

Bear poked Eli. "We need one more duck to make it even," he said.

Eli tightened his grip on his gun. He didn't like being teased.

Martin lit another cigarette. "You ever shoot a pump, Eli?" he said.

"No," Eli answered.

Martin handed Eli the gun. It was heavy, much heavier than his own. It had a reddish-brown stock, varnished so it shone, and a blue-black barrel. Eli felt the rubber pad on the stock against his shoulder. All the men he had been out with—they had had guns like this too. Wealthy men's guns.

"Where'd you get it?" Eli asked.

"It was my dad's," Martin said.

Eli raised the gun to his shoulder. His arms shook with the weight of it.

"Can I shoot it?" he said.

Now, more than anything he wanted to bring down just one bird. Just one slow, sick bird. He had to shoot one, had to throw it in the bottom with the others. He just had to, and he could just feel it in the gun in his hands, that this gun would do it.

Martin looked over at Bear and Bear shrugged.

"Sure," he said.

Eli held the gun up as long as he could. His anger and fear drained away, and then he was tired. He stared into the weeds, feeling lonely and sick, and it all came back to him. He tried not to let it get ahold of him; it was his birthday, after all, and birthdays were supposed to be happy. But now, with the quiet, he saw his mother in the dream, flying out the window. It made him curdle up inside, and he held himself against it. He hadn't let himself think about what his father was doing or where his mother had gone to since he had come up to live on the bay, because for the longest time he had thought they would come to take him home. Every day he had waited.

"Eli," he had imagined Red Deer saying, "I talked to your Old Man. He wants you back on the reserve."

Bear was humming to himself, a tune Eli knew from when they had lived at the house together.

"Bear," Eli said.

"What?"

Eli couldn't look at him so he looked out across the lake, past the reeds and the dead trees.

"You ever think about back home?" Eli said.

Bear picked at a spot on his pants, scratched the back of his head. He turned his head one way, then the other, cleared his throat. He reached for the box of twenties by his foot, opened it, took one of the red shells in his palm, rubbed it with his thumb.

"I don't want to talk about it," he said, and holding out the box of twenties asked, "Do you need some more shells?"

The sun had gone down over the island, and Eli lay with his back against the cold aluminum hull. The boat turned in slow, irregular circles. In back Martin and Bear smoked and talked.

"He's pretty tired," Bear said in a low voice.

"You think we should—"

A shot boomed in Eli's ears. Then another.

"Son-of-a-bitch!" Bear was shouting.

Eli gripped the seat with his thighs, and kneeling, brought the gun to his shoulder. Late and behind the mallards, he fired, then fired again, his heart in his throat, missing again.

Two wads of smoke drifted high and away from the boat. Eli's ears were ringing.

"Closer," Bear said. He pointed out toward the island where three small birds dropped down toward the water.

"Coots," he said.

The coots pinwheeled across the weeds. Eli could hear their wings cutting the air, a frightened warble in their throats.

Coots.

They loomed up like spots in his eyes, greasy black, bellies exposed, more helpless than anything had a right to be—yellow feet, dirty, pitiful birds. He raised the gun, pumped a shell into the chamber, and in a shallow sweep, led the first, the rage in him pointed down the barrel of the gun.

"Just like—" Bear said.

Eli fired. The bird in front burst, tumbling into the water. Eli snapped up another shell.

"Hey!" Bear yelled.

Eli swung the gun around.

"GODDAMMIT!"

Eli fired and winged the second, then brought the gun around to follow the third and felt Martin's hand on his neck, squeezing so hard he thought his neck would break.

"Stop," Martin said from behind him.

Eli lowered the gun. He was trembling.

"Don't you ever," Martin said, "shoot something you're not going to eat, understand?"

"You hear what he said?" Bear said.

Eli nodded.

The wounded coot cried out on the lake in a high, desperate warble.

"Goddamn. He's in the reeds already," Bear said.

He started the motor and brought the boat around in a wide circle. The coot swam in zigzags, and Bear reached into the water and pulled it up by the neck, its legs frantically paddling the air. Spinning the bird around, Bear broke its neck and set it on the shell packs. Eli watched the small black bird quiver, then finally settle against the bottom of the boat.

Martin took the gun from Eli.

"I see those other guys shooting coots all the time," Eli said, his voice shaking, his eyes on the coot. "They shoot whatever they want to."

Bear craned his head around. With both of them looking at him, Eli had a momentary impulse to laugh, and it welled up in him, twisted his mouth and he was choking.

"I just wanted—"

"Don't ever do that again," Bear said. "Not with me around."

Eli nodded.

"You understand?"

"It was just that—"

"Don't say you're sorry to me," Bear said. "Hell, the other one isn't even worth going after."

Bear straightened the coot's head. The coot looked small and frail now. Bird lice ran across its wings and into its eyes.

"What do you say, Martin?" Bear said. "Should we call it a day?"

Martin cocked open the pump on his gun. "Why don't we stay out a little longer."

Bear tossed Martin a pack of shells. "All right," he said.

Eli sat with his hands in his jacket pockets, staring into the bottom of the boat.

"You want the gun?" Martin asked.

Eli shook his head.

Martin pushed three shells into the chamber. He snapped up the first. It had the sound of something breaking. Martin held the gun out to Eli. Bear stubbed out his cigarette.

"If you're not ready, Eli," Bear said, "don't take it."

Eli grasped the stock of the gun.

"You're sure now?" Martin said.

Eli tugged at the gun and the awful weight of it passed from Martin's hands to his own.

"Yes," he said.

HIPPIES,
INDIANS,
BUFFALO

1970–71 The letter arrived on a cold, rainy Wednesday, a month to the day after the news that Toby had been killed somewhere south of Khe Sanh. The thin blue envelope was traced with postage markings as if with veins, some of them obscured by handling and water damage, some of them razor sharp, strange lions and elephants and multi-headed people with angular limbs. Martin had come home early from the university, and digging through the mail in the box outside the house, he came upon the letter as if upon a ghost.

In Toby's usual facetious way, the letter was addressed, *Center for Deviate Recruitment, Sir Martin D. Sorenson Esq.*

A shiver ran up Martin's legs, and he took the remainder of the mail, a sheaf of bills and advertisements, into the house with the letter. He set the bills and advertisements on the kitchen table—he was tempted to throw Toby's letter in with the rest—then went into the living room and lowered himself onto the couch and switched on the lamp. He turned the letter in his hands, watching the clock on the wall across from him—his mother would be home soon—and finally, his heart pounding, he edged his thumbnail up the back and slipped out the thin paper inside.

"*So, you little son-of-a-bitch,*" his cousin had written, "*you did open this without telling M & D. Am I right?*"

The doorbell rang, and Martin, his hands clumsy, tried to neatly fold the letter. The doorbell rang again, and Martin squashed the whole mess flat on the coffee table, then shoved it into his pants pocket. At the door Martin's mother butted up against the bell, two overstuffed bags of groceries in her arms. Martin opened the door and his mother nearly toppled over onto him.

"I'll get the rest," he said.

Coming up the drive with his first armload, he watched his mother through the kitchen windows. She took a deep breath, then assailed the refrigerator, tossing the frozen things into the left compartment, the others into the right. When he had carried in the last two bags, he stood for a minute watching her. She spun around and smiled.

"So, how was your day today?" she said.

Over dinner, Martin's father got into it again. The spaghetti sauce had too much sage in it, and the garlic was—too much. Martin shoved another mouthful in, aiding and abetting his mother.

"I like garlic," he said.

But there *was* too much garlic—and it was garlic salt Martin's mother had used, so the spaghetti was too salty as well—and Martin was determined to just get it down and get away from the table. He could feel something brewing, something bad.

"Did you hear about the communists?" Martin's father said.

Martin shrugged. He didn't want to talk about it. Martin's father was in private practice, and all this Kennedy talk about socialized medicine set him off.

"Don't you read the paper?"

"Some," Martin said.

"You've got to keep up with what's going on."

Martin looked up from his plate. His father's forehead glistened dully. He reached out and gripped Martin's forearm, manfully. Martin didn't like it. Martin's father had never had a father, and he was forever trying to be one, something he wasn't very good at.

"It's Cambodia now," he said.

Martin tried to pull his arm out from under his father's hand. His mother, at the other end of the table, ate slowly, and his sister, across from him, carefully picked at her bread.

"Did you hear?" the doctor said. "They've moved into Cambodia now. This whole thing might escalate into something big."

Martin bent his head over his plate.

He felt his father's eyes boring into him. He felt the weight of it, the man's money, his anger, his certainty.

"Stop staring at him," Kristen said.

At the sink, the radio on, Martin and Kristen washed dishes. The light from the bedroom upstairs was on and Martin felt relieved. His father would be reading the paper and his mother some inspirational thing. *Make Love Your Aim* had been the last one.

"He's just tired," Kristen said.

Martin pulled a fork from the water and cleaned between the tines. He didn't know what to say, and what he'd read in the letter bounced around in his head.

"So, you little son-of-a-bitch, you did open this without telling M & D. Am I right?"

"You okay, Marty?"

Martin slipped another plate into the water, scrubbing, then rinsing it. He handed the plate to Kristen. He wanted to say something to her, but that wasn't the way. Everyone was holding everything in and had always held it in. There was Martin's grandfather, the alcoholic, who no one talked about, and his uncle, who was Martin didn't know what, though he sensed the uncle was the source of some family embarrassment. There was the disappointment of what some people had told him would be the best years of his life—how could they get worse?—and now there was this thing. At the dinner table Martin had lied. He *had* heard about the communists in Cambodia. He had read all he could about it. There was talk of a big offensive, possibly a full-force offensive to the east, and lots of troops. He had watched Huntley and Brinkley, and Cronkite, and had seen Toby's snapshots and had read his letters, over and over. For two years Toby had been sending Martin letters, most of them rambling, sardonic, and Martin couldn't make much sense of them. They were composed of cryptic lyrics from songs he barely knew ("Johnny's in the basement, mixing up the medicine/Twenty years of schooling and they put you on the day shift/Watch out Kid!") and weird exhortations—"Beware of the Stobor!" Martin had saved all the letters in a shoe box under his bed, though none of what was in them had seemed real, the heat and the mud and the death, not until they had gotten word about Toby and how he had died.

Martin handed a dish to Kristen.

"You want to wash and I'll dry for a while?" he said.

They traded places. Kristen churned away in the water.

"Hey," she said, bumping Martin with her elbow.

In his room he sat on his bed, a calculus text open beside him. He leafed through a copy of *Goldfinger*. He'd nearly finished the book—it was pure escape, right up there with pot, a real slug in the arm—only now, he couldn't so much as get through the last few pages for thinking about Toby's letter. He wondered what was in it, and why it hadn't come earlier, and when Martin heard his father's heavy tread down the stairs he tossed *Goldfinger* under the bed and opened his calculus text.

Martin's father smiled bitterly in the doorway. He was holding a glass.

"You're not fooling anyone," he said.

Martin felt his face heat.

"The only person you're fooling is yourself," Martin's father said.

Martin scratched at the open book with his pencil, trying to think of some way out, but nothing came to him. It seemed there was no way to fight this man, and the small victories he had won over him in the last year he saw now as nothing more than self-inflicted injuries. He had failed three classes, had gotten in some small trouble with the police, and had refused to have his hair cut. A counselor had straightened him out on the classes ("You won't get into the better schools if you keep this up"), and the mess with the police—a drunken driving charge and a night in jail—had convinced him of the consequences of screwing up for real. But the hair stayed. Somehow it was the hair that got to his father. It was a simple, tangible thing—he had grown it long, and had made a braid of it, like the Indians up at the lodge, where he worked summers—and as silly as it seemed, it had come to represent something, something even Martin didn't quite understand.

Martin turned to face the window. His father stood in the doorway turning the glass of soda in his hands.

"Marty," he finally said, "why don't you tell me what's wrong?"

Martin drew his breath in. He picked at a hole in his jeans. A car rumbled by outside. They hadn't talked for so long there was no place to start.

Upstairs Kristen's door shut, and then the house was silent. Martin waited ten long minutes, then carefully tugged the letter from his pants pocket. He lay the letter on his calculus book and smoothed the creases out with his palm.

"So, you little son-of-a-bitch, you did open this without telling M & D. Am I right?"

Martin shook his head. He was afraid to read the letter. He held it under the lamp, and the blue letters seemed to rise up off the page.

December 3, 1969

Dear Marty,

I'm gonna make this short, and I hope to God you get this, only I don't know. We've been held down under mortar fire the last day and a half and I'm damn near deaf. Yesterday that kid Boehmer (remember him from grade school? The guy with the buck teeth?) got gut-shot and was screaming like you wouldn't believe. We were pretty close. He said he'd take this stateside (guess how

*and where? I'll give you a clue—it's a place where the sun
don't shine), only he didn't pull through, after all. But this
is it, Marty, you smart-and-screwed-up little bastard.*

Here the longhand ended. The remainder was printed, in large
block letters.

*Whatever you do, don't let them talk you into coming
over here. All we're doing is dying like pigs out in this
fucking muck. Don't listen to grandpa, and don't listen to
your old man. Just keep telling yourself, it's not something
worth dying over.*

*Don't show this to anyone. You were always an okay
guy, Marty. I'd say "pray for me" if I believed in that, but
I don't, so I'm saying "wish me luck" instead.*

Yours,
Tobe

Martin read the letter again. Then again. He read the letter
ten times before he shut his light off, and after what seemed like
an endless time lying in the dark, he turned on the light and read
it five times more. When he finally fell asleep he didn't know,
but in the morning he woke with the light on, the letter still in
his hand.

"Marty," his father called down the stairs.

Martin rammed the letter behind the bed. He felt as though
he had been caught doing something shameful, and he tried to
make his body look sleepy.

There was that heavy tread on the stairs.

"Marty," Martin's father said. Then, shaking Martin by the
shoulder, he said, "Come on up, I made breakfast for you."

Thanksgiving Day 1970 The gravy tureen made
its way around the table again. Martin's grandfather, Spencer,
was corralling his peas against a mound of mashed potatoes.

"I'll have some of that," he said, taking the tureen.

Martin watched him pour the gravy. He ate with his usual gusto, though Martin's cousins, Jane and Lucy and Todd, at the smaller table with Kristen, held back.

Nearly a year had passed since Toby's death, and this Thanksgiving was the last of the firsts—the first Christmas without Toby, the first Easter and so on. Without Toby around, these times together had been different, an adjustment, and this was the last. Martin looked from face to face around the table. They were all carefully talking around anything having to do with what had happened to Toby—his aunt red eyed, his uncle poking at his plate, his mother smiling nervously, his father and grandfather chewing forcefully.

Martin wiped his mouth with a napkin and excused himself.

In the bathroom he sat on the toilet. He held his hand over his mouth. A bitter laughter bubbled up in him.

"And Lord, let us remember Toby today," Spencer had prayed, "that he did not die in vain but that it is through such sacrifice that our lives are possible."

There was a knock on the door.

"Marty, you coming out?" Kristen said.

"Just a minute." Martin flushed the toilet for effect and ran the tap. He opened the door, and Kristen smiled at him.

"Come sit at the other table with me," she said.

Martin's father and uncle were talking politics again.

"At least he wasn't one of those goddamned draft dodgers," Spencer said.

Lucy and Jane and Kristen were talking about orchestra. They talked loudly, filling in the gaps. Todd was listening to the other table, and made no pretenses about it. Martin liked that about Todd, and angled his chair to see better.

"I'm proud of Toby," Spencer said.

Martin's father shook his head. "I'm not saying it's a happy thing, but we can't just let them go wherever they want. It's world expansion they want, after all. You know that"—Martin's father gestured with his fork—"you were in right after I was. Remember how it was in Korea?"

Martin's uncle slowly pushed his chair back from the table. He had an especially long face, and it went through a transformation now as he turned to face Martin's father.

"We'll see what you have to say when Marty gets sent over there," he said, grimacing.

Martin's mother set a pie on the table.

"Dessert's here," she said.

The letter from *Uncle Sugar*, as Toby had called the armed services, came in December. It was a Monday, and it was snowing, one of the first really big snows of the season. Martin opened the letter with a knife in the kitchen. He was to report for training at Ft. Hood, Texas, on May 16.

Martin sat at the table waiting for it to sink in.

He tried to imagine himself with thousands of other bald-headed kids, running around in green uniforms, practicing killing people, and then, if worse came to worst, actually going off somewhere and doing it. He'd killed plenty of things, when he thought about it—a deer every fall for the last six seasons, ducks, pheasants, and he was a crack shot, a natural, with a gun. But up at the lodge, with Bear and Osada and Buck, there was a certain reverence in the killing, thanks given, and a reason. This was senseless and evil, and as Toby had put it, *political*. Martin didn't want to be involved in these political things, and he didn't really see why he had to. It wasn't a matter of national threat. Any idiot could see that. In some ways it had been over since that mess with Lieutenant Calley. So what was going on?

Martin stood and opened the shutters.

It was so bright out, so *white*. The elm in the front yard was covered with snow. Above the trees snow tumbled down, a boiling curtain of white. A plane cut across the horizon and disappeared into the clouds. Something in the letter caught Martin's attention and he held it up in the light.

May 16, that was it.

And then it struck him, like a fist in the stomach, that May 16 was also Opening Day on walleyes, and if it hadn't been for this mess, he would have taken the train up to Wheeler's Point, where he would have caught the launch over to Big Island.

In February, Martin bought the car from a dealer on Lake Street. He didn't know *why* he had to have the car, but he knew, somehow, that it would be important. The car was an old Nash, one that looked a bit like a bathtub turned upside down. For months Martin had joked with two of his friends about it.

"The World's Ugliest Car," he had said, pointing it out to them.

It had a grille like that on the bottom of a refrigerator, and bumper guards that looked like chrome tadpoles.

"We ought to paint LOVE BANDIT on the side for you," his friend Tony had said the afternoon Martin bought it.

And for months after, Martin had gone out to look at the car mornings and new slogans had been spray-painted on the fenders and hood. This also had a sense of rightness about it. In some slow way Martin felt himself turning, but in which direction he wasn't sure. In a way he felt as if he were destroying himself, but then it felt good, too. He had decided he would give as little of himself as possible to the things he didn't believe in, and the war was one of these things. It wasn't his war. It wasn't even his country he would be fighting for—it was some *thing*, and Martin was damn sure it wasn't freedom. So he drove around St. Paul in the Nash, feeling out this new direction, and feeling it was not possible for things to be other than they were.

How things were came to him in bits and pieces and angered and saddened him. Everywhere he saw people divided against one another, and at home it was no different. Mowing his grandfather's lawn one hot afternoon, Martin stopped to cool off. He lifted the braid off the back of his neck, draping it over the bench. Spencer shook the newspaper he was reading and set it on his knees.

"You look like a *goddamned hippie*," he said, his voice filled with disgust. "Or worse yet a *goddamn Indian*."

Martin scratched his forehead. He fought an impulse to say

what he was feeling; he was afraid he might say things he could never take back.

"What's happened to you?" Spencer said.

Martin stood. The words caught in his throat.

"Nothing," he said.

He dragged the mower around to the front yard, then attacked the hill bordering the street. The mower shuddered through the high grass, snapping over spring deadfall. Martin felt hurt, and angry. What had Spence meant? That he was like the Ojibway in the housing projects, people who lived as if in a war zone? Is that what he had meant? That he was defeated and pitiful? If that was it, then Spence was *wrong*. For if Martin had learned anything from working with the Ojibway up north, it was that they had not been defeated, *couldn't* be defeated, and for that reason they had been destroyed. It made him think of something Osada had said.

They had been out in the boat, duck hunting, and a plane had flown low over the lake.

"Boy, what I'd give to have one of those," Martin said.

Osada looked at him, cocked his head to one side, then the other, as if he were measuring him up.

"What would you give?" he said.

Martin felt himself caught in it, and tried to come up with an answer, one that was not a lie.

"I guess I don't know," he said finally.

Osada laughed to himself, then quieted.

"Listen to me," he had said. "The way against the spirit is the evil way, is the way of destruction."

Lifting the mower into the trunk of the Nash, Martin glanced over the hill into the yard. The bench, newly painted, glistened a bright maroon, the grass flat as a crew cut around it. Martin opened the driver's door and got in. He sat for a few minutes in the heat, fanning his shirt over his chest. Out of the corner of his eye he could see Spence in the front window. When a big bead of sweat ran down Martin's forehead and dropped onto his hand, he turned the key in the ignition and started the car. This time he wouldn't back down.

. .

The car was not popular.

Martin's sister, Kristen, when he asked her what she thought about the car, hesitated, a studious look on her face, and said, "I like the steering wheel. . . . It looks like pearls." Martin's mother offered to sew him some seat covers for it. Martin's father's friends ignored the car, parking in the street so as not to put their Lincolns or Cadillacs beside it. Martin's father hated the car.

"I want you to get that hulk out of the driveway," he had said the morning after the first spray-painting had been done.

Now Martin stood beside his father, surveying the damage of this last night's raid. The white paint dripped, then ran in curtains from the letters on the doors.

"The Lone Ranger" the letters read, and on the trunk they had sprayed, "Zooks!"

"I want it out of the driveway," Martin's father said. "I mean it."

Martin shoved his hands into his pockets.

"I don't think it's so—"

"Oh, come off it. It looks like hell."

Martin could see this was becoming something much bigger than a ruined two-hundred-dollar car, and he tried to ease away. His father caught him by the arm and spun him around.

"Just what do you think you're trying to do?" Martin's father said.

Martin shrugged.

"I want you to tell me—just say it straight—what the hell do you think you're doing with this car?"

Martin got a boiling sensation in his chest, and then he imagined himself banging his father's head against the car until his head split open.

"Don't worry," Martin said.

"What?"

"I said, 'don't worry,' " Martin said.

"What do you mean, 'Don't—' "

"Goddammit!" Martin said. "It doesn't make a goddamn bit of difference because three goddamn weeks from now I'll be in goddamn Texas! You hear that?" he said, his hand jabbing the space between them. "Tex-ass!"

Sunday night the week before Martin was to take the train down to Ft. Hood, the house was quiet. Martin's father rummaged around in the basement for his old duffel bag.

"You'll need this," he said, setting the bag at the end of Martin's bed.

Martin had packed everything away, had cleaned out his closet, and had piled the clothes he would take on the bed. It amused him, in a grim way, the concern over these small things now. He knew none of it mattered. In his mind, the army would strip him of everything, and he imagined, with bitter humor, showing up in a Bozo the Clown outfit, complete with the red nose, ruffled neck ring, and oversize shoes.

"Hi! I'm Bozo," he would say. "And you must be Commander Bozo . . ."

Martin's mother brought towels up from the dryer.

She laid the towels on the bed and wrung her hands. She was a birdlike woman, funny at times, sad at others.

"Here's some towels for you," Martin's father said.

Martin smiled at his mother.

"Thanks," he said.

Kristen leaned against the doorjamb.

Martin looked from Kristen, to his mother, to his father.

"I got to get some air," he said.

Hours later, his feet sore and legs tired from circling the chain of lakes in town, Martin turned the corner of the service road home and went up the drive. The house was dark, and he was tired, and he didn't see his father standing with his back braced against the car.

"Hey," his father said.

It startled Martin, and he could think of nothing to say. They stood like that, staring up into the low-hanging clouds. The night sounds grew in volume and faded away, fireflies blinking across the lawn. It was the fireflies that got to Martin. He thought of catching them in a jar with his father. They had run across the yard, nabbing them off grass stems, two jars, a contest with no winner, a *fun* game, really.

But there was always more to remember.

"A chemical process makes them light up," Martin's father had explained.

Martin had looked into the jars, curious.

"You aren't listening," his father said.

"Yes I am," he said.

Martin's father stood. "No, you're not," he said.

He took the jar from Martin, and in one heart-rending swoop of his arms, he tossed both jars up into the air, where they turned end over end until they shattered on the driveway.

"I'm sick and tired of this," his father said, and Martin had tried not to cry.

And now, here they were again.

Martin could sense his father was trying to say something. But he just stood there, a big, mute presence in the dark, but dangerous, like a buffalo. It was as if his standing like this, against the car in the middle of the night, was his way of saying he was sorry. Martin slapped a mosquito. Now that he had stopped moving the bugs were biting.

"Can't stand out here all night," Martin said.

Martin's father rubbed his forearms.

If he were to say he was sorry now, Martin thought, *I would let it all go, this night, right now.*

Martin's father shuffled, ran his hand over his thinning hair. He picked at a scab of paint on the Nash, and pulling up on it, a whole strip of paint came away from the rusty metal underneath. Martin looked up into the dark sky. A jet lumbered in from the west, its lights cutting bright holes in the dark.

"What are you going to do with the car?" Martin's father said.

"What?" Martin asked.

"The car—what are you going to do with the car?"

Martin turned to face his father; he had been hoping for something else, but this is what it had come to.

"The car?"

"Yes, the car," his father said.

Martin slipped out of bed. In the dark he dressed in his jeans and moccasins and denim jacket, shouldered the duffel bag, and without turning to look at the nearly bare room, climbed the stairs to the front door. He was turning the knob when it occurred to him that he had forgotten something. He set the duffel bag down, then was in the bathroom and in the cabinet under the sink. He pulled Toby's letter and a small blue envelope from the hollow behind the sink, and stuffed them in his breast pocket. He hadn't realized before why he had kept his savings out of the bank, but it all came clear to him now. The daydreams he had had for months, had dismissed as fantasy, now took on real proportions.

Out on Highway 35, Martin geared the Nash up, and the old six crooned. Martin hung his arm out the window, singing to himself. He tried not to think about what he was doing and he switched on the radio. He had gotten the radio a few weeks before, and now he turned it up, pretending to enjoy the music. What the hell, there were a lot of things he could do, he thought. A highway patrol car drove by, then spun around, lights flashing.

On the side of the road, the officer held a flashlight beam in Martin's eyes.

"What are you doing out at this time of night," the officer said, looking down at Martin's license.

"Going fishing," Martin said.

"Let's see your gear."

Martin got out of the car. He reached for the trunk key in his pocket.

"Hold it," the officer said, the gun out of the holster and ready now.

Around four, Martin cleared the last of the plains. To the north the lights of Duluth held off the dark waters of Lake Superior.

There was a huge trucking complex off the highway, a diesel stop, and Martin drove the Nash through the labyrinth of roads to the squat brown restaurant in the middle. He took a booth at the far end, away from the door and the counter where two heavyset truckers sniggered.

"What do you want?" the waitress said.

"I want a cup of coffee."

The waitress gave Martin a sour face. Behind her the two truckers laughed.

"You've got to get something to eat with it," the waitress said, holding a menu out. "We can't have people just drinking the hell out of our coffee for nothing."

Martin took the menu.

"What do you have?"

"You can read, can't you?" the waitress said, bracing her hand on her hip.

Martin could see now the truckers had put her up to it, but she was enjoying it as much as they were. The two truckers nudged each other and laughed. The bigger stood and strode to the back, pushing through a red door. Martin patted his breast pocket.

"Two eggs," he said, "hash browns, biscuits, and lots of coffee."

The waitress went around to the kitchen and the trucker nearest the door caught her arm as she went by.

"Is it a boy or a girl?" he said.

Martin tried to ignore them. He traced the markings in the tabletop, thinking about driving north now, and the gravity of what he was doing struck him as something having these kinds of effects. He hadn't thought about it, he had just gone on what he thought was right. He had believed Toby, but he hadn't thought about what it would be like *not* to go. All he had thought about was what *going* would mean.

The food came and the waitress slapped down the ticket.

"Anything else?"

"No," he said, poking at the food with his fork.

The energy that had driven him this far, a wiry, unthinking

energy, had gone away, and now he felt sick. He wasn't so sure about anything now, and he felt as though he were poised between two starting points all over again, the Nash outside, waiting, this food on the table in front of him, and the big man out of the toilet and laughing with his friend.

He thought of going out to the Nash and getting his .30–06.

"Like deer hunting, Fat Boy?" he would say.

But beneath the anger was something else, and it got all tangled up trying to come out. Martin belted down the hot coffee, trying not to think about it. What was he doing anyway? Who was he fooling? The big trucker gave out a belly laugh, and Martin stood and went into the Men's. On the wall was a large vending machine, naked women spreadlegged across it, their mouths big O's of pleasure. Martin stepped up to a urinal. He could hear them laughing out in the restaurant. He stared into the wall, and something in it came clear. Someone had cut through the wallpaper, in big, jagged strokes,

HIPPIES ARE LIVING PROOF THAT INDIANS FUCKED BUFFALO

It stuck in his head like some hot poker, and then he was striding up past his booth to the car, all of it bursting out of him now. He didn't trust himself to drive this way, and he leaned against the fender, watching the waitress. She went over to the table, and when she saw Martin hadn't paid his tab, she marched to the front door and out, the truckers behind her.

Martin got into the Nash and started it.

"You son-of-a-bitch!" the waitress yelled, pointing.

The big man took off across the gravel drive and Martin swung the Nash around, headed for the waitress. She blinked twice, then saw he meant murder, her face a brilliant moon of fear, and in that moment Martin saw himself, what he had been running from, and he veered off to the right and burst up the road onto the highway, and with the blood pounding in his head, and the highway howling under him, he went a long time, the Nash swaying from side to side, barreling along as close to death as it would take him, and not until he passed a road sign and slowed down did he admit to himself that it wasn't an accident, he hadn't taken the wrong entrance onto the highway, and the lights of Duluth were now far away and to the south.

IT'S NOT
WHAT
YOU THINK
IT IS

1978 They were looking for an island, one with a dry, open stretch of stone where they could build a fire and make dinner. They had passed five or ten islands, all heavily forested, and Martin was beginning to worry that in this latest of diversions they had gotten lost. Bear, in back, poked Martin in the shoulder and brought the boat around, zigzagging.

"That's the one I was looking for," Bear said.

Miles off to the north an island rose out of the water, a low stretch of sand on one side and a high, bald dome on the other. Martin was thinking it looked like a hat, when Pete, the younger of the two brothers up in the bow, said,

"Looks like a hat!"

Andy, Pete's brother, shook his head. "That's the dumbest thing I ever—"

"It is not!" Pete said.

"It is not!" Andy said in a high voice, imitating Pete.

Martin nudged the stringer of walleyes in the bottom of the boat with the toe of his boot. He was hungry, and wanted to go in. He'd listened to the boys bicker all afternoon, and now he had just about had it.

"I'll tell you how dumb it is," Andy said, raising his fist.

"Cut it out," Martin said. "You hear me?"

Andy jabbed Pete with his elbow.

"You got that?" Martin said.

Andy glared over his shoulder, then hunched down beside his brother. The boat bucked over a rough section of water and planed out again.

"Andy," Martin said, "when we pull up on shore I want you to scout around for some firewood. Okay?"

Andy tossed his shoulders.

"This is all so stupid," he said.

Martin fought an impulse to spin Andy around. He thought about the boy's grandfather. He had talked with the old man at the lodge, and the old man had given him a word or two on handling Andy.

"Don't let him get away with nothing," the old man had said. "That Andy, he thinks he's always right. Since his dad ran away he thinks he can get whatever he wants—it's his mother, see. Just don't give in. . . . Petey, he won't give you no trouble."

"Hey," Martin said.

Pete leaned over to his side of the boat and Andy squared his shoulders. It irked Martin to be caught up in the kid's meanness, and now he felt more than a little angry with the boys' grandfather. Martin hated keeping other people's secrets, and from the way Andy had behaved all afternoon, Martin suspected Andy knew already. He would have to be careful now.

"Pete," Martin said. "You think you could round up a little firewood?"

Pete spun around, smiling. "Sure!" he said.

Andy grunted. "He already asked me, *Petey*."

"Well—" Pete said, rocking back on his seat "—you said you wouldn't."

"I never said anything."

"That's what you *always* say."

"And I'm not saying anything now, either."

"Yeah, big woopie," Pete said.

"What do you mean by that, pip-squeak?"

His hands ready, Martin watched the boys out of the corner of his eye. Andy sat up, much taller than Pete. Pete held on to it as long as he could, then let fly.

"You're always *mouthing off*," he said.

Andy tossed his head and sneered. "Well, if it isn't *Grandpa's* little parrot!"

"I'll tell," Pete said. "Really I—"

"Just shut up, okay, Petey?"

Pete turned to face the island. He smiled a small, clever smile, and Martin leaned back against the gunwale.

The island swelled off to the right, the dome high and bald. Bear eased the throttle back. Pines bordered the shore, dense, heavy limbed elderberry brush dark beneath them. The island had a hollow to one side, where the rock sloped into the lake from the big dome.

"I don't see any place to make a fire, Bear," Martin said.

Bear brought the boat in closer to the island and the trees shot higher, then higher yet. Martin craned his head back to see the tops. The trees were so heavy and dark and high the island had the bulk of an ocean liner.

"Those are the biggest trees I've ever seen," Pete said.

Andy spit into the water. "No they're not."

Pete held the gunwale. "I should know what's—"

"They're not as big as the redwoods we saw out in California," Andy said.

In the shade the air was cool and damp and Pete pulled his jacket on. The air had a musty, damp smell.

"Makes me feel like we're in one of those dinosaur movies," Pete said.

Bear stood in the back. "Hey, Andy," he said.

Andy was kneeling on his seat, his head bent back.

"You see any yetis in there?" Bear said. He drew his shoulders up, like hackles on a dog, and growled.

"Real funny," Andy said.

. .

There was a good thirty feet of bare stone and a large blackened circle where others had built fires.

"What do you say, Marty?" Bear said, cutting in close. "I told you it was here."

Martin jumped from the boat onto the ledge, taking the anchor rope with him. He fastened the rope to the trunk of a small, sad-looking pine, one with rope burns around its base, and gave the boys a hand up. Bear tossed over the rucksack with the flour and oil and coffee, and mounted the ledge, the stringer of walleyes over his shoulder.

"Son-of-a-bitch, I'm hungry," he said.

Martin set the rucksack outside the blackened circle. "First things first," he said, turning to look at Andy. "Let's get a fire going."

Andy stood with his arms crossed over his chest and Pete kicked at something on the ground beside him. *Well, isn't this sweet,* Martin thought.

"You going to get that wood, Andy?"

"How about if I clean the fish?"

They all turned to watch Bear. Across the rock shelf, on a board, he cut through the belly of a fish with his fillet knife and tossed the guts into the lake.

"Andy," Martin said, "I asked you to—"

"You asked Pete."

Martin dug into the rucksack and pulled out a hatchet. "You can use this," he said.

The two boys stood, shoulders nearly touching, their hands in their pockets.

Bear had turned to watch now. "Aw, come on!" he said.

"Go ahead, Petey," Andy said.

Pete looked up from his shoes. His eyes darted nervously from Martin, to Bear, and back again.

"Christ," Bear said. He tossed a handful of offal out onto the lake, the guts spinning around the spine, then strode across the rock shelf. He took the hatchet from Martin.

"All right," he said. "Which one of you two pansies is big enough to go back in there?"

Martin dug deeper into the rucksack. Had *he* been one of the two boys, he thought, it would have been hard to resist that jibe.

"Who's it gonna be?"

Andy shrugged.

"We'll both go," Pete blurted out.

"Yeah, we'll both go," Andy said.

Bear reached out with the hatchet. Pete lunged for it but Andy beat him.

"You always—"

Martin smacked a can of beans down. "That's enough," he said.

The boys' voices carried through the woods, the hatchet hacking away in spurts.

"Bear," Martin said.

Bear tossed another handful of offal out onto the lake. The gulls circled now, calling to one another, fighting for the offal.

"What?"

"You ever seen the likes of those two?"

Bear held up a fish on the stringer. "Look at the size of this one," he said. "I think this one was yours, the one you caught with that daredevil."

Martin nodded.

"Hey, really," he said, kneeling beside the pack, setting out the big, cast-iron fry pan. "What do you think of those two?"

"Oh, I don't know," Bear said.

"What don't you know?"

"Hell, they're just kids," Bear said. He looked up from the fish, pointing with his knife. "I remember somebody not a whole lot unlike either one of 'em."

"You think so, huh?"

Bear stretched his back, his hands on his hips, the knife jutting out sharp and shiny. "Holy mother, am I hungry!" he said.

"You want me to take over?" Martin asked.

"Sure, if you want to."

Martin crossed the shelf to Bear and took the knife. There were five more walleyes on the stringer. Martin held the first up and behind the gills, then cut behind the head, running the knife down the spine and folding the fillet back. The meat was white as popcorn, the entrails still-healthy greens and reds.

Bear lit a cigarette. "Pretty nice, huh?"

There was the sound of chopping, and Martin stopped to listen. The chopping had a heavy, solid sound.

"Knowing Andy he'll probably bring back a tree," Martin said.

Bear laughed.

"What's so funny?"

"You," Bear said.

Martin slipped another fish off the stringer, cutting up the backside, his hand jerking the knife along.

"Now don't go gettin' pissed off," Bear said. He took a drag on his cigarette. "Only, seems to me we had somebody up here about ten years ago who Andy wouldn't be any match for."

The chopping stopped, then started up again, lighter and faster, and Martin worked with the knife. He could just see it, Pete, hacking away for his life, and Andy teasing him, but scared, too.

Martin glanced over at Bear.

"You forget all that up there at that fancy school in Toronto?" Bear said.

"No," Martin said. He didn't want to talk about it.

"Remember that time I showed you how to fillet fish?"

Martin nodded. He did remember. He had been so eager to show Bear he knew what he was doing he'd nearly cut his thumb off, and they had had to take him into Wheeler's Point for stitches. The scar was still there, a long white line starting at the base of his thumb and running all the way up past the first digit of his index finger.

"I didn't know if Tomato was going to let me stay," Martin said. "You know how that work stuff is."

Bear smiled. "And then there was that time you damn near set the whole island on fire and got you and Eli—"

"That's not fair," Martin said. "I didn't do that just to be nasty."

"Why did you do that?"

Martin craned his head around. The thought of how badly Bear and the other Indians had treated him his first few weeks up at the lodge still made him angry.

"You tell me," he said.

Bear knocked a cigarette out of his pack. "I guess you were trying to prove something," he said.

Martin lifted the offal from the shelf, and with a wide circle of his arm, hurled it into the lake. The gulls dipped in after it, screeching and pecking at one another. Martin set the knife on the board and wiped his hands on his pants. The gulls were really going at it now.

"That's right," he said, eyeing Bear. "You're absolutely right," he said.

Martin stretched his cramped legs. Andy and Pete were sprawled out farther up the rock shelf, dozing, and Bear was fishing down by the lake. Bear brought his rod back; the lure made a high arc, then cut into the lake with a watery plunk!

Martin checked his watch, shifting uneasily beside the fire. Past nine, it would be dark soon and he would have to think of something to say to the boys. The old man had given Martin instructions not to bring them in before one—"Tell 'em we're having a *Firemen's Ball* if they really want to know," he'd said—and now, dinner over, Martin wondered what to do. He watched Bear cast the lure out again, unwilling to start it all. He hated being caught up in the old man's lie, and he wished the old man had just told the two boys what was going on. After dinner at the lodge, the men would play poker and drink until late in the morning, and if things went as they usually did, a boatload of women would come around the backside of the island, and To-mato, who owned and managed the resort, would play along with it all, pretending he didn't hear the sound of the outboards and the titter of laughter behind the lodge. It had been going on as long as Martin could remember—back to when he had been even younger than Pete—and he felt foolish, being drawn into something so secret, but so obvious.

THE SNAKE GAME

Andy stirred in his sleep, and mumbling, eased down again. Martin poked at what was left of the fire with a stick. Things had gone well enough so far, but he would have to think of something better now, something that would keep them going. *Muskies really strike well in the moonlight.* But that wouldn't be any good, because a low bank of clouds was rolling in from the west. *They're having a secret meeting, like the ones the Masons have.* And then he'd have to explain the Masons, which he didn't know a *damn* about—they wear funny signet rings and maybe they knock some people off. Were the Masons right-wingers or left-wingers? Or just plain reactionaries. And that would do it, too. It was all bullshit, and Martin could tell Andy was on to him already, and Pete was right behind.

Martin looked up and back of the shelf. Andy had made a pillow with his forearm. Pete, his hands curled under his chin, looked half baby and half boy. It hurt Martin to think about Pete. All day Pete had defended his grandfather against his brother's criticisms.

"Grandpa doesn't know shit," Andy had said, and Pete had shot back, "You're wrong—Grandpa knows *everything.*"

It would all come to a bad end, Martin thought. It had to. There was no getting around it. Sooner or later it hit you, that a whole lot of what people said and did was a lie, and you just went on living with it. The lies weren't even about big things, when you thought about it—people were just trying to make themselves feel better—but the lying made you feel as though you had to be ashamed of yourself.

Sometimes now, it seemed to Martin his whole life was a lie. *School in Toronto!* Who had told Bear that one?

Martin pushed what was left of the stick into the coals. The stick bent, then caught fire. No, he thought, it wasn't a very nice thing to find out, but sooner or later you had to know it, and here Pete was, right on the edge. It made Martin think about what had happened with his father.

He could still remember with absolute clarity the night Bear had brought him back early so they could peep into the cook's cabin. They had come around the backside of the island—the men were still gambling and drinking in the lodge—and there, right in the cook's cabin with some woman he had never seen, was his father, naked.

There was a secret to match his own!

Martin held his hand out over the coals. He lowered his hand until his eyes watered.

Martin stood and brushed the dirt from his pants. He carefully crossed the shelf and lowered himself to the sand where Bear stood.

"Bear," he said, "what do you want to do with the boys?"

Bear braced himself on the big rock outcropping, smoking and casting with the daredevil. He flicked his cigarette into the lake and shook his head.

"Are they still sleeping up there?"

"Not for long."

Bear snorted. "We'll just give 'em the old walleyes-in-the-moonlight business. 'Big as a goddamn canoe!' Hell, I had two kids who wouldn't come in until they saw the abominable snowman. And it wasn't anywhere near winter."

Martin found himself a place to sit up and behind Bear on the rock. Bear brought the rod back, the hooks swinging from the lure.

"Watch out," he said.

Martin ducked and Bear heaved the lure far out onto the lake. In the lake the sky was reflected as clear as a picture, high, billowy clouds and stars coming through. The lure made circles in the clouds.

"I wouldn't worry too much about it," Bear said.

"Why's that?"

"Hell, it's not as if they don't know," Bear said. "Andy's wise to it all and, Pete, he's real smart—he smells the fire, only he doesn't want to." Bear cast out again. "I got something for you to take a look at," he said, reeling the lure in. "Come on over here."

Bear stooped behind the boat. He reached for the live net, and pulling it up a little, something thrashed madly. Martin jumped into the boat. The sound echoed across the lake, a clunking, hollow sound.

Andy called down from the fire. "What's up?"

"Nothing!" Martin shouted.

Bear lifted the live net out of the water. A huge black-eyed northern bit at the mesh.

"Don't let on this is under the boat," he said. "If they get cranky we'll just hook this leader here onto your line and let him run."

"Why don't those loons shut the fuck up?" Andy said.

"Why don't you shut up," Pete said. His rod drooped over the side of the boat, sorry-looking. "Are we going in pretty soon?"

Bear stretched in back, yawning. "Pretty soon."

Martin fixed a huge, articulated lure to his line and stood. He swept the lure out and away from the boat. The lure went into the water, heavy, graceless, and he reeled in, tired of waiting. Everyone was restless now. The sun had dropped below the trees and a chill was coming over the lake. Andy, in his boredom, wrapped the anchor rope around his neck. He made choking sounds, and when no one paid him any attention he tossed the rope in the bottom of the boat. "You guys are a load of thrills," he said.

"You ever see 'Batman'?" Pete asked.

Martin reeled the lure up to the side of the boat, and lifting it, tore the weeds off the hooks. "Sure," he said.

The boat dipped to one side, and Andy and Pete hung their arms over the gunwales, poking their fishing rods into the water.

"Marty," Bear said.

Martin turned to face him. He was grinning and pointing to the back of the boat.

"You want to try another lure?" he said.

Bear had been pestering Martin the last half hour, and now Martin had had it.

"Fine," Martin said.

Bear mouthed the words asshole, and Martin mouthed them back.

"Here," Bear said.

He had tied the leader with the northern on it to the back of the boat, and now he fixed it to Martin's line. He nodded to Martin, and Martin set the drag low on his reel, so that when the fish got going it would take nearly all the line. Bear scrounged in the bottom of the boat, then hefted a fist-sized stone. He wriggled his eyebrows, and as if shot-putting, heaved the stone out in front of the boat. The stone plunged into the lake, off to the side opposite the boys, and Pete came off the gunwale like a shot.

"What was that?" Pete said.

Andy tossed his head back, adjusting his arms. "Just a goddamned rock, is what, Petey," he said. He shook his head and turned to face Martin and Bear. "Boy, was that clever," he said. "I'm really fooled."

Martin fought an impulse to slap the boy, but then the fish hit hard, drawing the line out in a whirr.

"I told you," Pete said.

Martin cranked at the reel, but the line still played out.

"Set your drag," Bear said.

Martin set the drag back and tugged hard at the fish. The fish was going to bottom, digging into the weeds. At least a fifteen pounder, he could cut the line there, or at least tangle it, and Martin heaved back, the rod slapping into his shoulder.

Andy balanced on the edge of the boat. "Don't let him go down there!"

"I know what I'm doing," Martin said. The fish tugged hard again, and then it occurred to Martin what to do. "Here," he said, holding the rod out to Andy.

He could see it was a mistake as soon as it came out—Pete turned away, kicking the tackle box. The rod bent double in Andy's hands.

"What should I do!"

Martin reached out to set the drag back farther, and Pete, his face bloated with rage, reached up for the rod.

"GODDAMMIT!" Andy yelled. "IT'S MINE!"

Pete pulled the rod down, and the line, unsupported by the rod, stretched, singing higher and higher.

"Let go!" Andy shouted.

With a high Prinnnnng! the line snapped, shooting out from the boat, and the two boys tumbled back. Andy got onto his knees and gripped Pete's coat. "You little fucker!" he shouted, shaking him. "You've been givin' me shit all day!"

Pete swung at Andy, hitting him in the throat, and Martin pinned Pete's arms to his sides.

"I ought to smack you one!" Andy threatened.

"Shut up!" Pete yelled. "Shut up!"

"Andy," Martin said, "say you're sorry."

"I'm not sorry," Andy said. He took a swing at Pete and Martin caught his arm.

"Bear," Martin said.

Bear cleared his throat in the back of the boat. "Cut it out," he said.

"I'm not about to," Andy said.

Bear stepped over the two seats and knocked the rod out of Andy's hands. The rod hit the side of the boat and went into the lake with a loud splash. Andy bent over the gunwale, watching the rod and reel sink away, and Bear jerked him back on the seat.

"You can get away with talkin' to your grandpops like that," he said, "but don't you think for one second *I'll* take that kind of shit. You got it?"

Andy nodded.

"I want to hear it."

"*Yes.*"

Bear shook him.

"I said 'yes,' " Andy said.

Bear stepped back and sat by the transom. Martin slowly released Pete. He was angry that his rod had been lost, was angry with the boys, but most of all he was furious with the boys' grandfather now, for having shucked this job off on him.

"Sit down, Pete," Martin said.

Pete looked up at Martin, his eyes puffy and hurt-looking, then sat beside his brother. "I want to go in," he said.

Martin lowered himself into the boat. He rubbed his forehead.

The boat drifted up a narrow spillway and the anger left him; in its place was a feeling of futility and sadness.

Pete turned on his seat. "I wanna go—"

"We can't go in, Petey," Martin said, shaking his head.

"Why not?"

Bear tossed something over the side of the boat.

"What are you doing?" Martin asked.

"I'm dragging for the rod," Bear said.

They all looked down into the water. Beneath the reflection of their faces, Bear's line stretched far and away into the green water and out of sight. Martin ran his eyes around the shoreline to the island.

"Tell me what you're hiding," Pete said.

Andy looked away. "*I'm* not hiding anything."

Pete looked into the back of the boat, then at his brother. "Yes you are," he said. "You've been weird all day. It's about Dad, isn't it?"

"No," Andy said. "No, it isn't about Dad."

Pete blinked, shifting gears. "What about Grandpa then?"

"I'm not sayin' anything, Petey."

Martin watched Pete now. He felt suffocated, his mouth dry.

"Is he leaving Grandma?" Pete finally said. "Like Dad left Mom?"

Andy shook his head.

"I'm gonna tell on you for all those things you—"

"Shut up," Andy said. "There's a lot goin' on here you don't know about, Petey."

Pete looked at all of them; he kicked at a rib in the hull of the boat. Martin poked at the burn in his palm. He wondered what he should tell Pete, and he remembered running from the cabin that night, the noise the falling stones had made, his father behind him. Looking for someplace to hide, he had climbed through the boathouse window and his father had stood outside, breathing deeply. When they had both quieted down, his father had said,

"Marty."

Martin, in the dark, had huddled against the wall. He felt

enraged, betrayed, and worst of all he felt terribly a part of something he wanted no part of.

"Marty," his father had said. "Listen to me, Son."

Martin's father had never used that word with him; it made him feel as though he were being turned inside out.

"It's not what you think it is," his father said, his voice imploring. The voice hesitated, then went on, so deep and aching that Martin crept across the boathouse floor to escape it. He was climbing out the back window when he heard the last of it.

"Son," the voice had said. "Son, are you there?"

Martin glanced over at Bear. He scratched at the back of his head.

"Just tell me," Pete said.

Bear hunched over his rod and reel. "Go ahead and tell him, Marty, for Christ's sakes!" he said.

Martin could see by the creases around Bear's mouth that Bear thought he, Martin, had failed. What was it to him, anyway? So what that he hadn't been able to pull it off, hadn't been able to tell all those happy lies. So what that he wouldn't be one of them.

"Pete," Martin said, his voice quiet, "what I said before, about there being a dance in town and all that—there isn't any *Firemen's Ball*, and the men aren't going anyplace."

"So why are we supposed to stay out here?"

"They don't want you in the cabins right now," Martin said.

Pete blinked again, his eyes puzzled. Martin could see the vein in his neck pulsing. *Somewhere*, Martin thought, *he already knows.*

"I don't get it," Pete said.

Andy looked out over the bow. Bear searched his pockets for cigarettes.

"Just tell me plain," Pete said.

"It has to do with those girls," Martin said.

"The dancers."

"Right, the *dancers*," Martin said.

Something like light shot across Pete's face. His eyes widened and a high red color came out on his forehead and cheeks. He held the gunwale, breathing hard, trying to swallow. Martin thought to put his hand on Pete's shoulder, but stopped himself. Pete squeezed his eyes shut. His whole body shook. Martin stared out at the island.

"Pete," he said, shocked at what he was about to say.

NOT
ONE
OF
US

1979 Believe me, there were no flags flying when we came home. We came in sullen groups, or alone, some monied and certain of their future, their political exile over, some destitute, looking for something they'd lost. I came back twenty pounds heavier, three inches taller, and six years older. COs, deserters, draft dodgers, evaders, they had a whole string of names for us, which pretty much amounted to the same thing: coward.

I never did take that one to heart.

My reasons for leaving, once I got some distance from it, were quite clear. Among other things, the war, as I saw it, was long over, and people were dying for no reason.

We had two dead.

First, it was my cousin Alex. Out of nowhere, he appeared at our dinner table one spring night, back from the Annamese Cordillera. After dinner, I was sent out into the garage with him. He was handsome, had the sharp, high-boned features some Chippewa do, and I had always admired him. Only now, his left eyelid twitched and his mouth had twisted into a permanent scowl. We hadn't been out there a minute when he pulled a joint from his pocket and lit up.

"This is good shit," he said, handing me the joint.

I'd just turned sixteen, and hadn't had grass more than once or twice; and the first time had done nothing at all.

"Hello," Alex was saying, rapping on my head.

"Hi!" I said, my voice echoing.

"So, you high or what?" he said.

I nodded. My vision had become strangely focused. I could only see things in parts: Alex grinning, lighting a cigarette. His mouth, a wide row of pearly whites. Long, flat-bridged nose. That eyelid flapping like a broken shade in a window.

The garage door opened.

"Coming in?" my mother said.

Later, at the curb out in front of the house, Alex showed me his motorcycle.

"What do you think?" he said.

He'd gotten a Harley and customized it; it looked like no other I'd seen. It was all chrome and spikes, had skulls and the logo AIRBORNE painted on the tank.

"Get on," he said, and I did.

We went out Portland Avenue, just cruising along. The bike shook, smelled of hot oil and gasoline. The grass was still turning my head inside out. I watched his muscular hands on the controls. He wasn't so crazy after all, I thought. And when we turned up the ramp onto Highway 62, he screwed that thing down so the roar of the exhaust came back off the houses we passed and he didn't let up. The wind tore at my scalp. I couldn't blink the tears out of my eyes. I could hardly hang on. I felt the baffle of air as we tore by car after car. Someone honked and Alex took both hands off the handlebars—you can do that with Harleys—and flipped the guy off. He passed five, ten cars, weaved in and out of lanes, cut a truck off, then nearly rear-ended an import.

"Rice-fucking-burner!" he bellowed hysterically, then gripped my knee so hard my leg shot out and I nearly fell off the back.

"Better'n fuckin' flying, isn't it?" he shouted.

. .

Not long after, Alex ran a stoplight. The policeman who called said he'd been doing nearly a hundred by the looks of the car he hit.

"Was he disturbed in any way that you know of?" he asked.

"No," my father said.

The second death we suffered was of a different order.

My aunt called. Toby was gone, she said, shot down in a helicopter ambush. Just like that.

No theatrics, no noise.

No nothing.

We'd written letters; he'd printed at the bottom of the last:

Just keep telling yourself, it's not something worth dying over.

And up in Toronto I did just that. I got a new name, a new look, new identification. I sold my car and a rifle for rent, and when that was gone, I hit the skids, bought a fifty-pound sack of potatoes, and moved to a flophouse for winos. I needed a job, and soon. I was down to my last few dollars, and the winos weren't helping: one morning I woke to find my shoes had been stolen.

At job interviews I had a whole strategy worked out.

"Home?" they would ask.

"Quebec," I'd say.

The interviewer would invariably nod. "I didn't think you were from around here."

"No," I'd say, then speak a little French.

I got a bitter kick out of it, thinking how all those mornings with Mademoiselle Frobish, four years at 7 A.M., were being put to good use. But without exception the sentiment was the same: the interviewer scribbled on his pad of paper some variation of *Not one of us.*

Then the money was gone; I took anything I could get. I had a string of jobs—janitor, short-order cook, choke-setter on a logging operation, mechanic—and finally settled in carpentry. It was cold up there, which was nothing new to me—even as far south as St. Paul it gets down to forty below—and they needed people who would work outside year-round.

I didn't know why then, but I loved building houses.

This was all before prefab, and we excavated, put in foundations, built from the bottom up. The wood up there was incredible—straight, well cured, manageable, the grain running in the right direction, and all the knotty stuff sent south.

I learned about the whole business. Masonry, carpentry, electrical. Sewage. The whole cycle, and while I had no place in the world to live, I built homes, cabins, offices. Places for people to be and work. The last place I worked was a bowling alley. "We're putting you on the lanes, Rick," my foreman said.

Regulation lanes. Specs you wouldn't believe. Brunswick gear. Miles of wire. And when I was done, I was proud, and so was the foreman. The lanes were perfect. He even said as much.

I remember that moment as if it happened yesterday.

I was testing one of the ball loaders, actually bowling. I had always hated bowling, or had only done it with a bellyfull of beer, thinking bowling was for fat, bored, or old people, but this was incredible. The balls rolled down the lane as if on guiding wires. The lanes were that *flat*. The gate came down, knocked the pins away, sent the ball back.

"Sit down, Rick," the foreman said.

It scared me—I was afraid they'd found me out—but as usual, my fear was mistaken.

"Christ you're touchy sometimes," the foreman said. His name was Glen. He had a wide, squarish face, and sharp brown eyes. He was the kind of guy you'd have wanted for your father but never had. He said he liked my work—how long had I been with them? Almost four years. Exactly, he said. He said he'd been thinking about how I was coming along, and this bowling thing was the last test. He was pleased. He scratched at the back of his neck, then let it out.

"We'd like you to be our fifth wheel," he said.

I could see the others smiling at me from where they stood in a cluster drinking coffee. I looked off down the alley, pulled at my ear. My eyes had clouded up.

"You need some time to think about it?" he asked.

"No," I said.

Two days later, Carter pardoned the whole bunch of us.

I remember it was a Saturday, I was off, and I paced the length of my efficiency. I walked circles within circles, then went outside and did the same downtown.

Somehow it seemed a revelation to me:

I had just turned twenty-five, and was a thousand miles from home.

It horrifies me to think about it, how we all came running. I lost everything, thinking I was taking back my life. And like I said, there were no flags flying when we rolled into town, unvictorious, vanquished, expelled, the last reminder of a war no one wanted to remember. Whereas in Toronto I was a craftsman, a worker of skill and endurance, a finish carpenter, back in the good ol' USA I was looked upon with suspicion, even by those in my own family. Some members of my family wouldn't even speak to me. My uncle, for example, on my father's side, still maintained that the "draft cowards," as he called them, should have been shot like other communists had been, like the Rosenbergs. This he told me at Easter, over dinner. I reminded him, that last time we talked, that the Rosenbergs had been electrocuted, and that he should keep his methods straight if he were going to play the part of the executioner.

At first it was strange hearing my name again.

"Marty," someone would say. "*Marty*, you there?"

I went back to school. Studied like a fiend. Took my MCATs and got in. I didn't think about what had happened, didn't want to, even escaped from it by burying myself in books, ones that were reassuringly concrete in their content.

Classes, eight to five. Labs reeking of noxious chemicals. Rote memorization of every body part, disease, and treatment known to man. Nights of sketching chemical formulas, preparations, and properties on recipe cards. A comprehensive exam every Friday morning. Students and instructors who were deadly serious, anxious, utterly practical in their thinking.

I did not understand these people, that was the worst of it. The party line was: If you can't see, hear, taste, smell, or touch it, it doesn't exist. I felt like I was in jump school: No yakking. No grabass. No yukking it up.

About the last I found out the hard way.

"I vant to tok viss-you, Mister Zorenson," Dr. Zeiss, my lab instructor, said one morning. His parents had come over from Germany in the fifties, and he'd retained some of that Nord Deutsch accent himself.

I followed him back to his office, halfway across campus. Chuffing along behind him, watching his bowed shoulders, I had time to think about what I might have done in class to offend him. For one, I'd nicknamed the cadaver my partner and I had been given "Lucy," short for Lucifer, to make our work less gruesome. I'd done some other things, too, but I finally figured it was my fixing two buttons to my lab partner's coat that had brought on this review from on high, and I was right.

I HATE LUCY, ASK ME ABOUT IT, one button said in big purple letters. The other read LUCY LORD OF DARKNESS LOVES YOU.

I'd fixed the buttons to my lab partner's coat, right out front, over the breast pocket where he kept his pens, where he couldn't miss them. But he had, and while he'd been shooting around the lab in a daze, the others had snickered. In the middle of it, Mike's eyes widened and he tore one of the buttons from his coat.

"This really tops it all," he said, brandishing the button in my face.

"It's a joke," I said.

"It's stupid," he said. "The whole idea is stupid. Where'd you get a stupid idea like Lucy *Lord* of Darkness, anyway, huh? It's like saying *woman* is *man*."

"You've just said something bright," I said.

He looked at me, confused for a second.

"Fuck off, Marty," he said.

.   .

THE SNAKE GAME

I admit it. The whole thing was pretty juvenile. But facing that cadaver mornings was just too much otherwise, and I said as much to Dr. Zeiss in his office.

He tilted back in his chair. "You had better vatch yourzelf," he said, leafing through a stack of exams on his desk.

So I got serious.

Class was that much less tolerable. I was bitter and angry. It was hard for me to take my classmates seriously. One afternoon I almost quit.

"Jesus Christ!" Mike, my lab partner, was saying, over and over after an exam.

During the exam he'd snapped a pencil in two, and after, he had run to a phone. I thought maybe something had happened in his family. He was holding his face in his hands.

"Look, Mike—"

"Leave me alone," he said.

He banged his head against the wall behind the phone booth, spun on his heels, then strode up the hallway and turned the corner.

Later I discovered it was the first exam he had not placed at the top of the class:

He'd missed it by three points—out of three hundred.

What kept me in it, I can only see now. But back then my feelings came to me obtusely, out of the corner of my eye so to speak, surfaced, and were gone.

They came to me like snapshots:

One Sunday, at my parents' church, I survived the sermon (in which "sinners" were compared to "criminals," and Christ to the pardoning officer of the day) by imagining Jimi Hendrix materializing up front of the altar, playing the guitar with his teeth. It was a pretty good scene, full of violence and distortion and rage. He played "The Star-Spangled Banner," set his guitar on fire, as he had at Monterey. My little twist at the end was his setting himself on fire.

I'd gotten to thinking like that:

Cutting a loaf of bread, I would think *I could just shove this knife through my chest.* Or baking something, I'd court the oven: *Why not just stick your head in there?*

It got so I was so wound up I was like one of those games that were popular then—*Mousetrap*, or whatever—a complex mass of cogs and gears and chutes all set up for one final effect: the ball to drop in the cup, the flag to run up the mast, the gun to go off.

But then Bear stuck his fat finger in and jammed the whole works.

Just before Thanksgiving he called me. I hadn't seen him since opening weekend in May.

"Where the fuck've you been, asshole?" he said. It was a way we had of addressing each other, a male thing.

"You wouldn't believe it up here," Bear said. "Most beautiful weather in twenty years. Shot my limit today."

I told him I couldn't make it. Classes, I said.

"That's a bunch of shit, Marty," Bear said. "You got time."

"How would you know?" I said.

Bear coughed. "You know it as well as I do. Get your ass up here. I can hear that self-torment just eatin' you up, Marty. You're full of it, you Swede." He laughed then, a big belly laugh and I laughed too.

"You asshole," I said.

"I got a big surprise for you when you get up."

"All right," I said.

I imagine my getting out of the car at the government dock on Muskeg Bay and meeting Bear was something akin to what my cousin, Alex, must have felt, stepping out of that C-141 from Gia Lam, into sunny South St. Paul.

Home, again. But not home.

Three weeks had gone by since Bear and I had talked; we were into the month of December. The season had changed. I had imagined red oaks, orange maples, yellow poplar. But it was winter now, and the winds came down from the Arctic, the lake white and frozen over, drifts stretching out across Muskeg Bay as far as the eye could see, the trees on shore barren and black.

A truck pulled up, and Joe Big Otter and I waited. I kicked my feet around, nervous. I hadn't seen Joe in ten years maybe, yet there we stood, whole lifetimes between us, familiar, but strangers. I'd heard a lot about Joe from Bear, how Joe had never been much of a father. I wondered how he and Bear were getting along now—*if* they were getting along. I wondered about the other guides, Dusty, Osada, Buck, and Eli.

"There it is," Joe said.

Bear brought the Tucker, a big, slow moving, tractor-type snow machine, and the trailer, up against the dock. The diesel gave one last bellow, then Bear shut it down.

"Get a Mercedes!" Joe shouted.

Bear grinned through the windshield and flipped Joe off.

"Kids," Joe said.

Two days later, up on the spine of Old Woman's Fire, I stopped to shift the rifle on my back. Bear and I'd been out since seven, and we hadn't picked up any new spoor. My neck and shoulder ached where the rifle strap cut through my jacket. The whole weekend we'd circled the islands south of the lodge, up early, back late. We'd gotten a few inches of new snow and with the sun out the light was brilliant. I pushed my sunglasses up my nose.

Bear tossed a handful of turds at me. They pelted off my jacket like hail.

"Goddammit," he said. "I knew it. It's all hunted out."

The air was sharp and clear and filled with the scent of pine; it was enough for me just to be hiking.

"We should go up north," I said. "Take the Tucker."

Bear glanced over at me, then away again.

"The Tucker's too godawful slow," he finally said. He raised his hand—his gloved fingers shot out.

"I've got it," he said.

.   .

Bear proudly pulled back the boathouse doors.

"This is it," he said. "This is the surprise."

I'd forgotten entirely.

"It's a surprise all right," I said.

At first sight the whole mess made me think of a vegetable slicer—the propeller, without a shroud, a sharp, shiny silver; the steering vane like a sluice behind and high off the transom. I'd never seen anything like it. He'd taken the ruined hull of a speedboat, had built a platform in back, and had mounted an engine and propeller on it. He'd finished the hull in brown enamel; the whole surface was pocked with leaves. I ran my hand up the hull.

"Camouflage," Bear said, "all those leaves. I figured—what the hell."

I tried not to say anything. God almighty, was it ugly.

"You don't like it," Bear said.

I could see by the angle of Bear's head that he was angry. Angry and disappointed.

"You think it's—"

"*I didn't say that,*" I said. But I had been thinking it. "*It looks dangerous.*"

Bear shook his head, his hands on his hips.

"What'd you expect?" he said, glaring. "A love seat? Walking across the street's dangerous. What's to say you don't get *wacked* driving home? Shit, Marty, if I was lookin' around like you are now I wouldn't get out of bed."

I took in what he said.

"Do you want to go out there or not?"

I walked a circle around the machine, checked the bolts holding the motor down, turned the steering vane one direction, then the other. Everything was makeshift. I didn't know what to say.

"Ah, come on," Bear said.

"*Ah, come on yourself,*" I shot back.

Bear snorted, then threw his hands up. "All right—Okay!— be a chicken heart."

I looked over the hull at him. "Who's saying anything about being chicken?" I said.

. .

I guess you could say Bear lied to me.

"It takes two people," he said in the boathouse, "otherwise it's too light up front."

He told me Buck and Dusty had gone out with him in the skimmer—that's what he was calling it, "the skimmer." I figured if old Dusty could take it, I could take it, and then some.

Only, Bear did not tell me he had never used the skimmer out of the water, or that ice, like a hammer taken to fine crystal, would shatter the hull.

Maybe.

But I did my part.

"Gimme the goddamn wheel," I said at the dock.

Tomato, my old boss, and Buck, Bear's half-brother, had come down to help us get it out. Bear and I made a few turns around the island—Buck and Tomato standing there by the boathouse, dog faced—then headed north. The skimmer slid and bounced across the ice, shuddered, the engine in back howling. I was just getting the hang of it—there was a kind of raw, angry feeling to driving the thing—when Bear slapped my shoulder.

"You're goin' too slow," Bear shouted. "Let me drive!"

I brought it up a little.

"Jesus," Bear shouted. "You gotta get some *balls*—"

But I didn't hear the rest. I felt something like a hand on my hand, squeezing, and I pushed the throttle all the way up. The machine leapt forward, hammered down on the ice, up and down and up and down.

Bear was punching me in the back.

"Cut it out!" he hollered.

We gained speed and the hull shuddered, snow coming over the front so I couldn't see. The whole thing swelled, roaring, shuddering. We went like that for what seemed like miles.

And then, the bow hit a drift.

The bow rose up, and in that one suspended moment it hung there, over our heads. I watched my hands, frantic on the controls, as if from some great distance. It occurred to me that *this time* I had really done it. I felt my whole body stiffen; I got the most peculiar sense of weightlessness—that's the only way I know how to describe it—and then the bow came back over us and down like a lid.

I heard the *Chut, chut, chut* of the propeller hitting the ice behind us, and everything exploded.

It was quiet lying there. I was on a couch, and it fit my back and spine perfectly, but for a spring that had come through the upholstery. It was a couch I had had at my old apartment, and I thought I should really throw it away this time. The spring kept pushing into my back. I felt something cold on my face and I tried to sit up. My face burned. I tried to brush whatever it was off my face. I tasted blood. I couldn't see, then realized something was on top of me.

I lifted the sheet of fiberglass back and took off my glasses. It was nearly dusk. Bear lay a few feet to my right, facedown in the snow.

I couldn't make any sense of it. I had this piece of one-by-two jutting out my side, and my face had fiberglass stuck in it. I stumbled over to Bear.

He's dead, I thought, turning him over.

And then I heard someone wailing, out there on that sheet of snow.

"Oh Jesus God," the voice blubbered, pleading.

In the end, Bear's loss was primarily blood, and the tourniquet I put on his leg did not result in amputation, as the doctor told him it might have. Barring the hundreds of stitches in his arm and buttocks, he made out all right.

My prognosis and recovery was much the same, only mine took longer. I lost two ribs, a part of my right lung, and the tip of my liver. The leaves Bear had painted onto the hull of the skimmer raised hell with me, infection so bad they had me figured for dead, and had me on pain killers and penicillin until my rear was so sore they had to inject it into my thighs. I sat in an oxygen tent for the better part of two weeks, in a permanent drizzle.

Condensation collected on the plastic and made it hard to see out. My parents came often, even my sister, all the way from New York. I got a card from my classmates, and a few of them stopped by one afternoon to cheer me up and ask when I'd be back.

I said *soon,* but didn't mean it.

I couldn't kick that moment on the ice. It was as if a door had opened, and I had passed through into something else. I had a lot of time to think about it, in that oxygen tent, and even after. I wondered in there, if, somehow, I had brought the whole thing on, the accident. If, somehow, I had had to suffer to pay some debt, or to prove myself, only, unlike Alex or Toby, I had not been killed doing it. Whatever, I was no longer ashamed.

Out on that ice, dragging Bear over the snow on that sheet of fiberglass, I had never in all my life felt so abandoned.

Of course, it had been me, screaming, but nobody came to the rescue. Not Mom or Dad or Uncle Sam. Not the Church, the pope, my girlfriend. Not Tomato or any of the guides, or Buck, who could have lifted us both, Bear and me, under one arm. Not even God.

That much I had done myself.

It was enough.

BEAR,
DANCING

1980 His heart is a drum.

Lub-lub-lub-lub.

The bells on his pants legs jangle; the sleeves of his jacket pinch his arms. No one told him how hot the suit would be, how the beard and moustache would make the skin on his face crawl.

Ho, ho, ho, he's supposed to bellow when Father Lundquist gives him the signal, and he practices, Ho, ho, ho, only now it sounds more like someone choking, a throaty gurgle that echoes up the empty stairwell where he hides behind the door waiting.

Bear has been waiting for this moment, dreading it, since last summer, when he agreed to help Father Lundquist with his Christmas fund-raiser.

You're perfect, Father Lundquist had said at the lodge, up with the church-camp group.

That Father Lundquist remembered him so well amused Bear—it had been thirteen years since he'd left the settlement, dropped out of high school to work as a guide on the lake.

Not once, in all that time, had he seen Father Lundquist.

And suddenly, there he was, in the lodge dining room, smiling, telling Bear how he and his boyhood buddy, Doden, had looked, slipping out the back of the church to throw snowballs at cars.

You two were like a couple of wolves, he said. I'd've liked to come down and toss a few myself.

You should've, Bear said.

Some altar boys you two were!

Vonny, Bear's lover, came in from the kitchen and sat with a cup of coffee.

'Lo, Father! she said.

They talked about the parish. Did Bear remember the week he and Eli stayed in the rectory, the week all hell broke loose on the reserve?

Of course, Bear said. And Father Lundquist launched into the story about the fire, and how they were having a big get-together, a Christmas party, to raise money for the roof, and how they needed somebody who could liven things up, lend a little humor to it all.

Really, Father Lundquist said, turning to Vonny, don't you think he's perfect?

Vonny smiled.

It's just to put on a new roof. What do you say?

Bear rubbed his eyes. I don't know, he said.

And Father Lundquist countered, For your people— Think about it, all right? Just think about it.

And all that week, he had.

Out in the boat, the fishing slow for the August heat, he thought about his half-brother Buck, how he'd gotten caught between, ground up in the gears, and he thought about Hodie, a friend of his father's, who'd gotten worse, a murder-suicide.

Not for him, Bear thought, *never*.

Only, then he got to thinking, too, about his cousins and the family, and how he hadn't seen Old Man Muskeg in ages. He thought about the old place on Turtle Lake, the marsh in back where he and Doden caught crayfish, remembered the flour and soda smell of his mother's pan bread, and ricing in the fall, the rich aroma of grain and smoke. It made him sick for something, and toward the end of the week, after an especially bad day with two fat drunks from St. Louis, he knew he had to go back.

So you'll do it? Father Lundquist had said.

Bear nodded.

December . . .

And Bear nodded again. Sure thing. You bet.

Only later, Father Lundquist's party became something bigger, *grand-er*, as Father Lundquist put it, and they asked Bear to play Santa. Father Lundquist took the launch from Wheeler's Point, crossed forty miles of rough water to Big Island, to ask him about it.

Bear had felt himself blinking with surprise. Santa?

That Father Lundquist had come all the way out to see him made Bear feel important, but he felt pressured, too, this effort of Father Lundquist's working in the way of obligation.

So what do you say? Yes or no?

Bear turned his head from side to side, then up and down. A silence as heavy as snow filled the cabin. Bear shivered, slapped his arms. And months away from it, and feeling the discomfort of the moment, he figured, What the hell! He'd go home and see some folks. It would work out all right. He was just being pushed into what he had to do anyway.

All right, he said, finally, and Vonny brought in a plate of sandwiches and winked at Bear.

Could he still tell a few jokes? Could he laugh?

Could he laugh, Vonny said.

You're a natural, Father Lundquist said.

He's a real clown, Vonny said.

Ho, ho, ho, Bear laughed.

But now, as the last of the party straggle in, a panic squeezes his chest. He feels as if he will burst, and he steps back from the door, his legs shaking. He had had no idea so many would come. Father Lundquist had said fifteen, maybe twenty—mostly kids anyway. You like kids, don't you? But there must be forty—even fifty—people gathered around the tree now. Up front children pull and poke and pinch, their faces bright with expectation. Claire and Dee and Vonny bustle like birds in the half dark, clearing tables; and back of the hubbub, Buck and Osada and Doden, and his cousins and uncles and aunts, stand solemnly, arms crossed over their chests, waiting.

Eli, always the late one, squeezes in on the side, a *this will be something* look on his face.

It irks Bear, his brother's smug assurance; and when Eli turns his head, glances through the crack in the door and winks at Bear, Bear jerks back from the door as if bitten.

It is all so clear now.

If it's awful, laugh, Bear had said to Eli out hunting once. If it's real awful, laugh real hard.

It had always been his way.

You've got a real gallows humor, Bear, one of the guides, Marty, had said. You ever wonder what would happen if you stopped joking around?

Me? Bear said.

Yeah, you.

It was something that had never occurred to him.

It hit him like a blow to the face, dead center, an eye puncher. He got a huge lump in his throat, felt something hurtful blossom in his chest, and when it got too big to fit, he tilted back his head and laughed it out.

Laughed long and hard, ah, ha-ha-ha-ha-ha!

Jesus, you say some dumb things sometimes, Marty, he said, and Marty shook his head, exasperated, but relieved, even pleased somehow.

You're incorrigible, Bear, he said, and Bear laughed again.

Sweet belly laugh, one huge slap in the face of pain.

But now, all he has protected himself from rushes at him, head-long, as if it will devour him. His mother running off to the Dakotas. Joe, his father, drinking himself into oblivion. The whole reserve collapsing in on itself. The thoughts come in a jumble, and at the bottom of it, he remembers the night he left, just took off, the night he and Doden went out drinking with Doden's father, Tossed-About-the-Winds.

Get us a loaf of bread and some bologna, Windy had said, pulling the truck into the lot of a convenience store.

They went in, Doden and Bear, mulled over the racks and racks of candy and pies. They were pretty wasted, and they took a long time, and when they got outside, a fire was going up the road—Windy's truck, the top caved in.

Somehow, Windy had tried to turn around up the block, had raced up Jacobsen's Hill. Two broad, black swatches on the crown veered like arrows into the ditch. Skid marks.

Doden just stood there, that loaf of Wonder Bread hanging from his hand.

Jesus, he coulda waited, he said.

And Bear held his stomach, bent double to squelch the laughter that seized and tossed him till it burst like hot coal out his throat.

Better to die, Bear thinks, than go through that again. But when he looks out from behind the door, the feeling is back, powerful, sharp, like a familiar, awful smell.

Strong Ground, leaning against the wall, pokes Eli in the back with his cane and Eli nods in recognition, grabs Strong Ground's cane and gives it a tug. Eli's hands are scarred, raised skin running up from his wrists in ribs like those on the backs of leaves.

And Doden, who after all these years had had nothing to say, what about Doden?

Doden, behind Eli, nervously pulling at his braids, looks fifty now, his face caving in, caught like an avalanche at his chin. The last thirteen years are there in Doden's face so plain it doesn't take Bear more than a glance to see it, see it in all of them: Osada, his hair gray now; Buck, hollows forming under his eyes; Claire and Dee and Vonny putting on weight like protective padding; and farther back, Old Man Muskeg coughing his lungs out, a stooped woman holding him by his elbow.

Something about the set of the woman's shoulders—defiant—makes him stop there, then, heart leaping, look again.

For a second Bear's scalp crawls.

He is sure it is his mother—but then the woman turns and it is not his mother after all. It is a woman whose eyes turn down in the corners as his mother's had, a woman who has sewn an appliqué skirt and blouse for the occasion, in the old way, as his mother would have.

Something about her speaks to him. A terrible voice. Her eyes say it all.

Laugh, she says, the word sinking like a dagger into the pit of his stomach. Go ahead.

It is all Bear can do to hold himself at the door.

He considers tearing off the costume. He tries to breathe deeply, to calm himself. But then it is time, and Father Lundquist in his vestments swoops from behind the tree to lead them in "O Come All Ye Faithful." The voices rise like smoke, dissonant, strained.

Let's try another, Father Lundquist shouts, and with each new carol the din grows louder, and Father Lundquist sends his arms higher, trying to work an enthusiasm into the singing that isn't there.

Bear can see in Father Lundquist's face that he, too, had expected something different. Father Lundquist's arms aren't working the miracles they do at mass, with the mixed congregation, and it shows in the furrow between his eyes, the line of sweat on his forehead. And when he can withstand his experiment no longer, he glances over his shoulder, gives the nod of his head that is the signal.

Bear, behind the door, cannot move.

He struggles to lift his foot but can't.

He can't breathe right—his chest is bound up like cement—and he grips the doorknob to steady himself, turns to look behind him, then back at the circle of waiting faces, then behind him again. On the landing below him is another door, to the street outside. He imagines bursting through it, into air so cold and clean it hurts his lungs. He imagines kicking through knee-deep snow, free again, to breathe, to not see what he sees here, but then Father Lundquist turns, and with a flourish of his arms, points, the finger of God shooting lightning bolts of responsibility through the narrow space between the door and doorjamb, and Bear is carried out and down to the tree.

Well, if it isn't Santa, Father Lundquist bellows.

Ho, ho, ho, Bear thinks, but his mouth refuses.

Did you come all the way from the North Pole, Santa? Father Lundquist asks, waving his arms again. What's it like at the North Pole?

That's Bear in that suit, a girl in pigtails says.

Hey! Fatty! the boy beside her says.

Why don't you hand out some presents, Santa? Father Lundquist says, pushing a shiny package into Bear's middle.

Bear cannot so much as move to take it.

The woman he had seen earlier has slipped around to the side, her eyes drawing him to her. And then he remembers meeting Vonny's mother long ago. Okitchita, a sorceress—Vonny had told him that much.

I know you, Funny Man, she'd said; and remembering, Bear shivers, a cold finger shooting up his back and into his head, where it sits on his scalp like a cap of ice.

Hand out some presents, Father Lundquist says.

He pushes the package into Bear's middle again. Bear raises his head, holds his hands at his sides and the box hits the floor with a heavy slap. Startled, the little girl in front cries. The whole wretched lot is staring now, and Bear feels it like a hand, pushing him down.

Say something, for God's sake, Father Lundquist whispers. You're ruining everything!

Bear opens his mouth. He can think of nothing to say—a fat man in a Santa suit. A clown.

Say something!

But all he can hear is his heart in his ears. *Lub-lub-lub-lub.* A quiet, insistent pounding.

A drum.

And it comes to him then—

The long-ago–stretching rhythm, the smell of dust and the hot sun on his back, the rising of the earth beneath his feet, the musical warble of Ojibway.

Ho! he says, to himself.

Father Lundquist laughs.

It's all funny now, he thinks, back on track, and he stoops to sweep up the package, and smiling, motions for Bear to take it, but Bear spins away, the bells on his pants legs ringing.

Ho! Bear says, a leg shooting out from under him. Ho! he says spinning, circling the tree, searching out the feel of it, letting his body remember.

What a clown! Father Lundquist laughs out.

Hey, Fatty! the boy says.

But Bear is caught up in it now. His throat swells. His pointing feet carry him around the tree in joyful half-steps, in swirls and spins and dips, the bells on his pants legs ringing like rain. He is grass-dancing, and now Buck's voice carries out, and the others join him.

Hey, Fatty! the boy says again.

Father Lundquist, baffled, stands waiting for things to come back to order. The girl in front, who had been crying, stares, wide-eyed, clutching her brother's arm.

Okitchita, in back, nods.

A joyous uproar fills the room: Something holy is happening, something sacred.

Ho! Bear sings, spinning, his feet half-stepping, taking him around the tree. Ho! he bellows, gaining speed, spinning, turning, singing, *Ya hey ya hey ya hey!*

ARRIVAL

1981 Pushing through the Greyhound depot doors into the crowded lobby, Karen Faber clutches her travel bag, working on a smile. At the water fountain, where Karen is to meet her father, Red Deer, a guide from the resort, stands wide as a horse, his back to the wall. He tips the bill of his red-and-blue cap and steps in Karen's direction, his head bent forward like a turtle's on his thick neck.

"You're late," he says, stopping just short of the seats where Karen stands.

"The bus broke down," Karen says, her eyes on the floor now. The cracked tiles crawl, dizzying, and when Karen raises her head she is shocked—Red Deer reaching to take the bag from her, the row of duck bills wired to the rim of his hat gaping like strange, rounded teeth.

"The car's outside," he says, nodding in the direction of the lobby doors.

"Where's my dad?"

"Your father couldn't come," Red Deer says. "There's been an accident. A guide."

"Oh," Karen says. She tugs at her dress and glances around the room. All the strange people are watching now, the driver at the gate, the ragged man talking to himself, the woman picking at her scalp. "I have to call my dad," she says.

Karen ravels the phone cord around her finger, pulling on it like a spring.

"But *why* can't you—"

"I can't," her father says.

Karen releases the phone cord and draws the back of her hand over her eyes.

"Send mother then."

"I said 'no,' Kit. We'll talk about it later, all right? —So tell me about your first week at the bighouse," her father says. "How's the ninth grade, how are your classes? You there, Kit?"

"Yeah, I'm here," Karen says.

"Let me talk to Red Deer."

Red Deer presses the receiver to his ear. Now Karen's father's voice is loud, the way it is when he is angry, and Karen, standing just outside the booth, is relieved—almost pleased. So what if he doesn't listen? she thinks. Her father will take care of everything.

"Has anyone heard yet?" Red Deer says.

"No," comes the rough, mechanical voice, "but he lost a lot of blood."

Red Deer holds out the receiver and Karen takes it from him.

"Are you all right now, honey?" her father says.

"I suppose so," Karen says.

At the old blue sedan in the parking lot behind the depot Karen takes her bag from Red Deer.

"Door doesn't open on the passenger side," he says.

Karen slides across the bench seat and Red Deer bends into the car.

"Be right back," he says.

Karen runs her finger through the layer of gritty dust on the dashboard, then traces the silver crack imbedded in the windshield like a spider web. A northwesterly buffets the car. Only September and already the weather is changing.

Karen shifts in her seat. Red Deer strides out of the depot, buttoning his canvas jacket with one hand, holding two ice-cream cones in the other. There is something boyish in the way he carries his body, big, but balanced on his toes. His jacket is pinched around his shoulders and the sleeves are too short. When he opens the door he nearly drops the cones.

"Here," Red Deer says, handing Karen a cone across the seat. "No time to stop."

Karen takes a big bite of her ice cream. Her teeth ache with the cold, but it is her favorite flavor, peppermint bonbon, and she thinks of her father, how he has had Red Deer buy the cones.

Red Deer smiles. "Good?"

Karen nods. "Did my dad tell you to get peppermint bonbon?"

Red Deer blinks, then shakes his head and pushes his key into the ignition.

"No," he says.

The peppermint in Karen's mouth turns metallic, and she hands the cone to Red Deer.

"You don't want it?" he says.

Karen shakes her head.

"Okay," Red Deer says, rolling down his window. He reaches out with the cone, and turning it upside down, drops it.

The last of the tar-papered houses on the outside limits of Alexandria slip by and Red Deer presses his foot down on the accelerator. Karen can't get over Red Deer's hands. She had put him together when she first saw him, had him fixed in her mind with huge, gnarled, dirty hands. But Red Deer's hands, lightly gripping the wheel, are *naked* looking, a warm reddish-brown, with short tapered fingers ending in pinkish cuticle and white, cleaned-under nails. They're actually pretty hands, Karen thinks.

"How far is it?" Karen asks.

Red Deer looks out the window. "Three hours," he says.

The car rumbles around a wide sweeping turn. Red Deer reaches for the column shift; his fingers grasp the pearl-colored knob and slip it up a notch.

"Hold the wheel," Red Deer says.

He reaches over the seat and brings up a can of beer. The

wheel shimmies in Karen's hand and she thrills with the way the car veers back and forth across the road when she tugs the wheel one way and pushes it the other. Next year she will get her permit and she will sit *behind* the wheel.

Red Deer pokes through the can with an opener. Foam squirts out onto the seat, fizzling away through the seams. He tilts the can up and his Adam's apple bounces up and down. He takes the wheel again and holds the can out to Karen, his brown fingers pressing little dents in the sides.

"Go ahead," he says.

Karen takes the can, peers in through the holes, then raises it to her nose. It smells like rotten flour, and she tilts the can until some spills out over the top so she can get at it with the tip of her tongue. The last time she'd had beer her father had given it to her. Back then she thought beer would be something special, like pop, but only better, so she had taken a huge gulp and spit it out when the taste hit her.

Karen's mouth is sticky from the cone, and she decides to take a sip just to wash out the peppermint. The beer fizzes up behind her teeth and she swallows it. It doesn't taste so bad now and she takes another sip. She feels silly, but she likes the other feeling she gets, too, for the moment on an adventure and drinking an *Indian's* beer.

Red Deer reaches into the back for another beer and Karen takes the wheel.

"Stay on the black stuff," Red Deer says.

He opens the can and nods to Karen, steering with his knee.

Karen wedges her can between her legs. When she looks through her reflection in the windshield, sees through her impassive, serious face, she sees the pines have thickened along the road. Like some heavy fluid the night comes on, filling up the road and sky. A breeze whips the tops of the pines and the grasses alongside the road.

Alongside the road is a deep ditch. For a second Karen imagines herself lying in the ditch, her panties wound around her neck, her legs bent back at some unnatural angle. Without turning her head, Karen examines Red Deer. Like tiny red suns, the instrument lights reflect in his eye sockets; his nose has a large crook in it just down from his eyes, and his chin is square, covered with stubble. She likes the way his hair rises off his forehead like a black wave. It fascinates her, his being an Indian, and she wants to touch him, to see if he is real.

Karen reaches for the heater knob on the dash and slides it up to high. Now that the sun has gone down the car is chilly. Cold air streams through the heater vents.

"Could you turn on the heat?" Karen says.

Karen wishes she'd worn pants instead of her skirt. It occurs to her now how silly it was to wear the skirt just to please her father at the station. She would have changed into her jeans as soon as she got to the resort anyway.

"No," Red Deer says.

Karen squints. "Why not?"

Red Deer scratches his chin. The headlights make a movie of the road and Karen watches it boom bright with signs:

A high pink sign—FLAMING PINE RESORT, TWENTY-FIVE MILES; then a bent, metal one, nearly cut in half by bullets— CHIPPEWA OUTBOARD REPAIR; and barely visible behind it, a tiny home-made sign—NITE CRAWLERS/25 CENTS A DOZ—goes off like a flashbulb, and the road is dark again.

"Heater's broken," Red Deer says.

His knee on the wheel, he struggles out of his yellow, bloodstained duck hunting jacket and hands it to Karen. It smells musty, like fish and animals and tobacco.

"Are you a Chippewa?" Karen says, arranging the jacket over her knees.

Red Deer smiles. One tooth is silver. It reminds Karen of a pirate, and she imagines Red Deer with a golden earring and a red bandanna wrapped over his forehead and tied at the back.

"Has anyone ever told you you look like a pirate?" Karen says.

A deep, vibrant laugh rises out of Red Deer's chest. When he has finished laughing he speaks into the windshield, shaking his head sadly.

"That was a good one," he says.

Karen smiles to herself. She likes having amused Red Deer.

THE SNAKE GAME

. .

The draft in the car is terrible, like prodding, icy fingers; it works through the seat, around the window moldings, over the places Red Deer's jacket won't cover. For the past hour she has struggled to cover herself with the jacket, but the draft burrows in everywhere.

"Could we stop somewhere?" Karen says.

"No time," Red Deer says.

"It would only take a few minutes."

"Where?"

"A gas station, or a motel?"

Red Deer shakes his head and points to the lights up the road.

"That looks good," Karen says.

The lights loom higher and larger, a sign, a two-story loaf of bread in a wrapper decorated with red and yellow and blue balloons. WONDER, it says, and then the sign flashes by—from the back of a dark rectangle, moths and bugs shooting out from it like sparks.

"Nothing but signs all the way to Lake Carlos," Red Deer says.

Karen tugs Red Deer's jacket tight around her legs, eyeing the side of the road. Her teeth have started to chatter.

"Could you change alongside the road?" Red Deer says.

Karen imagines pulling her pants on out there in the dark with Red Deer watching.

No way, she thinks.

But she is caught up in the thinking of it, anyway. He'll turn, slow, and watch her. But not like the boys at school. He'll do something. He won't tease and laugh, won't yell "Hey! Where's your fuckhole!" He'll lie beside her and pull the tangled jeans from her legs. His hands would touch her *there*.

"I'm stopping," Red Deer says, turning off the highway at a poplar windbreak.

Karen is relieved. Red Deer has decided this. Has brought this about. Red Deer steps out of the car. In the middle of the road he stretches his arms and yawns, steam rising from his mouth in a narrow plume. Behind him the sky is a deep, royal blue, the stars sharp lights in the cold. There is the smell of burning leaves, frost, and decay.

Karen lugs her bag out of the back.

"I'm going to change now," she says.

Red Deer perches himself on the fender, his back to Karen. He reaches into his breast pocket for his cigarettes and snaps the pack on his palm. When he strikes a match to light his cigarette his face glows. He inhales, then blows smoke out his nostrils, tilting his head back to look up into the sky, the corners of his mouth curling with pleasure.

Red Deer shifts his legs on the fender and smokes another cigarette. Karen is shaking with cold but is still too afraid to take her pants out of her night bag. She wonders when Red Deer will turn around.

"I'm almost ready," Karen says.

Red Deer stretches his arms wide and yawns again.

"I'm going to change now," she says.

She digs through her bag—panties, her bra, her new makeup kit, the books she brought, overdue at the library, a sweatshirt from camp last year—and finally gets to the pants at the bottom. Pressed. Folded.

"I'm almost done," Karen says.

Red Deer has cocked his head as if listening intently.

Karen balances on one leg and gives a tremendous, quick tug on her pants. The pants won't go on over her shoes and now she is caught there, heel jammed in so tight she can't get the pants off.

Red Deer clears his throat.

"I'll be done in a second," Karen says.

Then she has the pants off, and she drops her shoes onto the roadside, the gravel cold and sharp under her bare feet. In the moonlight her legs are smooth and white and nearly glow. Her skin puckers with the cold. Bare skin. A breeze. It reminds her of the games she played with the neighbor boy in the park behind her house. So long ago, and here the excitement is the same, dizzy, dream-like, naughty, but now, fear, too, and a vague desire to know, to be touched.

Karen tugs her pants on and straightens down her skirt. It all looks silly, her dress over her pants, the jacket that doesn't match, but it will have to do. She notices the black swatch across the bottom of her dress, and wonders how she will explain it.

"I'm done now," Karen says.

Red Deer peers back at her.

"I'm—"

"*Shhhhh.*"

His index finger raised to his mouth, Red Deer steps around the front of the car. He wraps his arm over Karen's shoulders and turns her to the windbreak. Karen's heart jumps in her chest. There is a puffing overhead, an easy whirring of air. An owl glides over the car and into the poplar windbreak, and Red Deer follows it, one arm held out. He points to a quivering line of waist-high grass yards from the windbreak. When Karen twists slightly under his arm he tightens his grip.

The moon is high and bright and the field is silver.

"Stop it," Karen says.

The owl drops out of the poplar windbreak, a huge gray stone, and near the ground it swoops, darts and veers, its wings tunneling through the air as if on tracks. The owl plunges into the grass, and there is a shrill, almost human scream. Karen holds her arms at her sides squeezing her fists tight.

Red Deer raises his head and turns his ear to the field.

The screaming echoes away, cut short, and Karen shudders.

Its wings spread with tremendous effort, a rabbit hanging from its talons, the owl lofts itself up and over the windbreak. It pumps in great whooshing strokes to the south where tall dark pines rise into the sky.

A gust of wind tosses Karen's hair and she pulls it back over her shoulder. Her hands are shaking and she pushes them into her pockets. Red Deer has taken his arm from her shoulders and now she is cold.

A car sizzles by on the highway.

Red Deer shakes his head. He kicks a boot in the gravel, his eyes level on the trees across the field.

.   .

Past the water tower just south of Lake Carlos and up by the par five, Red Deer blinks his eyes as if to keep himself awake.

"Tired?" Karen says.

Red Deer nods. He pulls off to the side of the road at the golf shack and rolls down his window. It looks warm inside, the men lined up at the bar, their wide backs linked shoulder to shoulder. A stout Indian wearing a white apron pours drinks. Red Deer reaches under his seat, crushes a beer can and tosses it at the storm door window. The can makes a loud clatter, and the moon-faced Indian darts out from behind the line of startled men. The Indian doesn't open the door, he just stares out, shakes his head, and Red Deer nods, sets the car in gear and drops down the big hill to Lake Carlos.

Outside the Fabers' cabin Red Deer cranks on the parking brake. A floodlight on the cabin's porch blazes and Karen's father, a tall man wearing a faded orange jacket, strides around the car. Red Deer opens the door and reaches into the back for Karen's bag.

"Stay in the car, Karen," her father says.

Then the two men stand on the porch, Red Deer only nodding as Karen's father talks and gestures with his hands. Karen rolls the window down a crack.

"There wasn't anything we could do," her father says.

"Was there anyone else in the boat?" Red Deer says.

"No."

Red Deer shakes his head. His broad shoulders droop, then he draws them back again, cocking his head sideways.

Karen's father purses his mouth. "He says it was an accident."

Red Deer shakes his head. "Bear gets his head shot off and all you say is 'He says it was an accident'?"

"What do you want me to say?"

Red Deer holds his small, naked hands out, imploring. "Charley," he says, "you know that man hated my brother—"

"But he said—"

"I don't care what he said. That man, he's lying."

Karen steps out of the car and her father jerks his head around. "Karen, didn't I—"

For a second he doesn't seem to recognize her.

It frightens Karen, his hard, dark eyes, and then she realizes she still has Red Deer's jacket on, the dress, and the pants. It occurs to her how odd she must look, and she shucks the jacket off, tries to smooth her dress over her pants, and walks to the porch.

"Go inside, Kit," Karen's father says.

Karen reaches for her bag and Red Deer steps off the porch and crosses the gravel turnoff to the car. He stands with the door open, leaning into the roof.

"What happened?" Karen says.

"Just another mess with the Indians," Karen's father says.

He holds the screen door open with his foot, and when Karen mounts the steps with her bag, he embraces her.

"There's some dinner left inside," he says.

Karen stares over her father's shoulder through the screen door. Red Deer sits in the bruised-looking blue sedan, his forehead on the wheel. Then he starts the car and crackles out the drive, and Karen watches him, hoping that for just so much as a second he'll turn and their eyes will meet.

A
FIERCE
LIFE

1982 Out front of the lodge, and down by the dock, snow fell in light, uncertain spirals. It was a late spring snow, and the lake, a wide, dark oval, swallowed the snow undisturbed, but for Eli in the rowboat breaking the water with his oars.

Martin tossed the snow from his head, brushed his shoulders dry. It occurred to him that he could slip down to the canoe and around the backside of the island before Eli made it across the bay; but he'd be damned if he'd run from this, he thought, and he eased down the dome to the face, where he sat on a slab of stone, his legs hanging over the edge so there was no mistaking him.

It made him dizzy to look down the face, the flat, dark water beneath his feet, and he thought of summers, how he and Bear had jumped from this ledge. It had been such a drop they had had to wear tennis shoes so as not to bruise the bottoms of their feet. He remembered how when he was seventeen, and Bear nearly nineteen, they'd promised to come back every so often and jump, just to prove they weren't getting old and soft, and it had made sense then.

Widow's Peak, they'd called it.

"No kidding!" Bear had said their first time up on the dome. "I know it for a fact. A guy got all lovesick out here and threw himself off. Only he didn't leap, see?"

Bear had handed Martin the bottle of blackberry brandy, and Martin had taken a slug, sickeningly sweet, and they had peered over the edge.

It was a big jump, seventy feet at least, and it made Martin's stomach rise up in his throat to think about leaping now. At the bottom a long stretch of gray stone waited, barely out of the water, like a blade. Now, a decade and some later, Martin wondered if he would have jumped that first time without Bear's egging him on. It wasn't the brandy, he knew that. And after, when Tomato, the owner of the resort, had told them he never wanted to see them up there again, Martin had discovered what Bear had said was in fact true. Someone *had* died falling off the dome, and Tomato had left it at that.

Martin shuddered. The cold was coming up through the stone and he pulled his jacket around his shoulders. Eli had stopped rowing, and in the middle of the bay the boat held steady, not so much as a breeze, the snow silently tumbling down.

Eli. Oh, Eli, Martin thought. That they all hadn't gone crazy . . . There was so much to think about—he *couldn't stop thinking about*, and it sat in his chest, heavy, over his lungs, or sank down into his stomach where it tangled everything in knots.

Like the business with the war.

Almost six years he'd been away, a very long six years. At first he had thought about returning to the States almost constantly, then less as time went on. He'd had a life up there, in Toronto, though he hadn't thought so at the time. And when he finally did come back, he had been shocked to find how little things had changed.

"You're a goddamned coward," his father had said.

And that had been it.

Only, out in Montana, he'd found that wasn't it, the whole mess over and done with, and mornings at a new job site, he'd roll himself a cigarette, and smoking, the smell of tobacco and fresh lumber and green cement heavy in the air, he'd think about the lakes up north, in Minnesota, and the university—maybe he should have stayed—but the business with the cadaver always came back to him.

"Lucifer," they'd dubbed her.

That part of it still amused him.

It had been a long-standing joke, cutting the "Lord of Darkness" down to size by number, Respiratory, Circulatory, Digestive systems. But when they'd gotten to the Reproductive organs, and Martin had cut through the wall of Lucy's uterus, something had gone wrong. Others gathered around to see.

"Look what Marty's got here," his partner said.

Martin slipped his hand through the incision, then pulled out a tiny lump of flesh no larger than a minnow and held it up under the bright ceiling lights.

"Just put it down," someone said.

"Where?" he'd said, opening his hand, the eyes staring, seeming to follow him however he moved. "Just *where* am I supposed to put this?"

And in the same way, Bear's death had come to him.

"I think you should know Eli called here a few times for you," his sister, Kristen, had written. *"From what he said, your friend Bear has been killed in some kind of accident—he wouldn't say more and I didn't ask. He sounded pretty upset."*

That Martin had read the letter at all was a complete fluke—the letter had gotten lost, and with the mailman waiting in the doorway, apologizing, Martin had felt compelled to open it. He hadn't read a letter from home in over a year, and he'd stood there in the shop, holding the letter up.

Eight months late.

Across the bay the lights of the lodge went out in the snow. Martin pulled himself up on one knee, then rose to a crouch. The ledge was slick—over a slight rise to his right, the stone broke away, a sheer drop—and he carefully balanced himself now, a foot wedged in a crevice for support, peering out over the lake. Eli grasped the oars, raised them out of the water, then dropped them, raised them, and dropped them again.

Martin felt like shouting, but he couldn't settle on the feel of this thing. How would he yell, anyway?

Hello? (mournfully).

Hi! (full of false cheer).

Or, Getchur fuckin ass up here! (confrontative, what he really felt like).

And thinking of the last alternative he nearly laughed; it was Bear's way of doing things, out front, and like it or not he had picked it up. If he thought about it he had picked up a lot of things from Bear. It was unavoidable. Bear had had an exuberant expansiveness about him: a loud, booming voice, arms as thick as thighs, a deep, guttural laugh. He had eaten too much, dug in with his fork and knife, the plate clattering, talked too much, laughed too much.

He was nobody's angel.

He'd had a sometimes brutal sense of humor. He knew people at a glance, and could joke in the most infuriatingly truthful way. He never left himself out of it, and more often than not, people who got to know him felt that here was somebody *alive*, somebody who hadn't gone under.

He nearly glowed with it: *enjoyment*.

"You gettin' fat, Bear?" somebody would tease, and he'd pat his belly and smile, a wide, crooked smile.

He wore a funny-looking Twins cap, a row of duck bills wired to the brim, and smoked green cigars. He looked ridiculous.

"How do you like my lid?" he'd ask, guileless, teasing.

If it was dark, and he was telling a story—and his favorites were always full of carnage and evil spirits—his voice would get softer and softer until he'd howl and slug someone within reach. That Bear had expected the people he teased to swing back, even provoked them until they did, amused Martin, though he was certain now this was exactly how Bear had died.

Out with Bill, drinking, he had pushed too far, and Bill, intentionally or unintentionally, his bitterness and anger pushed too far, had exploded.

Bitter old Bill.

A *hunting accident* they were calling it.

Martin kicked his feet in the slush, prodded himself with it again—*a hunting accident*—thinking if he prodded long and hard enough he wouldn't feel the shock that went through him every time he did, or wouldn't think the same thing every time, what he'd been thinking for two weeks, what everyone was careful not to say up at the lodge now.

Murder.

Everyone but Eli.

Sitting down to dinner Martin's first night up, Eli had said it, over and over again, cutting at him with it, jabbing, always hiding it in some sarcastic remark, some joke.

"Should've been here last fall, Marty," he'd said. "Open season on Bear. You really missed a hell of a shoot." Eli had smiled and pointed with his knife. "It was real bare-assed hunting, right Jal?"

Jalmer, one of the new guides, had glanced over his shoulder.

"Marty is a fine shot," Eli said. "Good as Bill, don't you think, Jal?"

Jalmer had shaken his head.

"What's wrong with you?" Tomato said.

"Is something wrong?—Marty," Eli said, "is something wrong?"

"No," Martin had said.

Out on the lake Eli was rowing again. He bent at the waist, stretching, then pulled powerfully. Whatever it was Eli had been uncertain of, he was determined to do now, Martin thought, and he watched as Eli worked at the oars, legs and arms reaching for the stern, then pulling in unison, up and toward the bow, the boat lunging through the water.

Last week, in Kalispell, when Martin had read his sister's letter, he had been so upset he had tried to call Eli for hours.

Just what would he have said had Eli answered? *I'm sorry?*

And now, what was he hanging around for?

There was so much buried hatred here. It was disturbing,

hurtful; it reminded him of the first summer he had come up to work, when he was fourteen. He had stuck his nose in where it wasn't wanted, had asked the guides all kinds of questions about themselves, how the Chippewa felt about things, and they had put him off entirely. But maybe that was the way it always worked, and looking at it now, he could see a pattern in it: his asking around, then backing off, the guides showing him what they wanted to, finally, in their own time.

And that, if anything, was what he was waiting for now.

He was waiting for Eli.

Eli slipped under the face, and minutes later came up the path, arms swinging, breathing deeply with the effort of the climb. For a second, Martin imagined the two of them scuffling on the ledge and rolling off. That or Eli could give him a kick in the back, sending him over alone. It was crazy, but Martin was ready for it, had his hands set to take Eli with him if it came to that.

"So, you through snoopin'?" Eli said, squatting down an arm's length away. He bent over, looked down the face, and quickly drew himself back. "Whew!" he said. "Pretty damn high up here. Doesn't change much, does it?"

Martin shifted uneasily. There was drink on Eli's breath.

"No," Martin said. "I guess not."

Eli affected a funny cocking of his head. "Looks like a long, long way down." He shuddered and slapped his arms.

"Cold enough?" Martin asked.

"I've seen worse this time of year."

They sat, as if ignoring each other, Eli looking off to the south. It was a game Martin knew he would lose every time, even now he knew Eli's staring off like this for what it was, a cultural thing.

"Look," Martin said.

"Don't *look* me anything," Eli said. He tossed his shoulders. "I got just one thing to say to you, Marty. *Where the fuck were you?*"

"Listen—"

"You got a million excuses for everything, you know that? I mean, I wrote to you I don't know how many times. . . ." Eli smiled, the corners of his eyes turning up. "No, you should've never come back. I mean, what the hell did you think you'd accomplish up here, anyway?"

Martin wrapped his arms around his knees. It was all too big to say anything. All he could do was listen, and he held back the things people said: *I know how you feel, I had something like that happen to me, It's a real tragedy.*

None of it could say what he felt: confused, angry one moment, sad the next, a huge hole in his chest, a hollow where something he'd needed had been.

"You—" Eli smacked his hand down on his thigh. It hurt to even hear it. "I mean—GODDAMMIT!—we took care of you! And now you bring your sorry ass up here, and where the hell were you when we needed you? You know what you are? You're just like all the others comin' up here. Just another rich fat shit. That's what you are." Eli's face narrowed with disgust. "I mean, I just have to say it—You were his *friend*. That fuckin' Bill blows Bear's head off"—Eli made a broad sweep with his arms—"and just walks away. 'It was an accident,' he says."

"Eli," Martin said, but then Eli was off again.

"—all these goddamned cops. They all came to me. I don't know why I stayed. I should've just taken off like Buck. . . . I mean—we are so *screwed* up here.

"You know what I was thinkin' when I came up the path there? I was thinkin', maybe I should just push ol' Marty off the ledge there, that's what I was thinkin'. I could say 'It was an accident!' "

Eli shook his head.

"But it doesn't work that way on my side, does it?—September. Goddamn September Bear gets his head blown off and you show up in May. Well it's all over, Marty. It's all fucking over and what the hell are you doing here? Why don't you tell me what the hell you're doing here, cause I sure—"

"Shut up, Eli," Martin said. "*Just-shut-up.*"

"Okay, *boss*," Eli said. "Anything you say, *boss*. Just say the word—"

"I told you to shut up."

"Who the hell are you to tell *me* to shut up!"

Eli made a sucking sound and spit. The spit dropped away over the ledge, stretched out past the small pines and lichen growing on the face.

"I never got your letters, Eli," Martin said, allowing himself this one alteration of the truth.

Eli spit again, bent his head down to see over the ledge.

"You don't believe me, do you?" Martin said.

Eli shook his head. "I don't know what to believe anymore, Marty. See, there doesn't seem to be that much to believe in. Old Bill, well, there's one. Bear dead, everybody else up and gone. You should've been here for the funeral. Closed casket. Half his face was gone. I don't know why they tried to save him. Wouldn't never have gone for that anyway."

Eli stood, held up his arms. The snow was heavier now, fell in clumps, white on the blue cotton of his jacket.

"Hell, you'd think it was Christmas," he said. "Which reminds me . . ." He dug into a pocket and pulled out a hat.

Martin's stomach kicked.

It was Bear's hat, the duck bills wired to the brim dull and pathetic-looking. The hat looked strange, and Martin was reminded of one afternoon, years ago, driving back to the cities. Traffic had slowed. Martin had rolled down the window. A truck had overturned, a policeman was covering a body with a blanket. The whole scene had had this same stubborn unreality about it, the caved-in roof of the truck, the policeman calmly taking notes, the slow-moving line of cars. But what Martin remembered most was the white socks jutting out from under the blanket. Somehow, in that afternoon light, on the rough shoulder, it had been those shoeless feet, those clean, white socks that said it was all over.

"Buck told me to give you this," Eli said, holding out the hat. "He said Bear would've wanted you to have it."

"No," Martin said. He stepped back from the ledge.

"Go on, take it."

"Eli, don't—"

Eli put the cap on his head. It was too big, hung lopsided over one ear. He skipped along the ledge, the snow turning circles behind him.

"Cut it out, Eli," Martin said. He didn't like the tone of his voice. Pleading. He wouldn't do it.

Eli grinned. "Come on," he said.

"Cut it out, Eli," Martin said. "Stop it."

Eli had worked himself up to the rise in the ledge. He went down on one knee, then caught himself. Martin's stomach leapt in his throat. He got a falling sensation watching.

"Come on," Eli said, smiling bitterly, "walk out here with me. I dare you. Here's your big chance. Take a walk on the wild side, *buddy boy.*"

Martin turned in the direction of the path to the lake. He couldn't watch.

Eli laughed. "Go on, Marty! What are you waiting for?"

"Eli," Martin said, but he would not say it: *please.*

"I got a joke for you, Marty," Eli said. "You just listen. Old Bill was telling it to Rasmussen the day Bear got shot. It goes like this: *What's the difference between a Chippewa and a pigeon?*"

Martin shook his head.

"I'll tell you," Eli said. "*A pigeon can still make deposits on the car at the end of the month,* Marty. Isn't that a good one?" He laughed, high, bitter laughter, lost his balance, teetered, eyes bulging, caught himself.

Martin held himself back. Breathed deep. Already his body bent to it.

It would never be easy, he thought.

And when Eli shouted: "Hey, Marty—Listen! I got another good one," Martin charged up the path, hit Eli at the waist, and lifting him, pushed off the face, a fierce life driving his legs.

OZO'

(tail)

AS
BRIGHT
AND
HOT

1983   That doesn't say I don't love it, but I'm an *Urban Indian*, and what I see is backwards isn't the way at all. No, what we got to have is a big curve, off this damned track everybody's so nuts about, or it's gonna be like that snake the Greeks had, swallowed his own tail.

It's gonna surprise some people, I think. How the whole world's gonna turn in on itself like that.

Progress.

Years ago, they got somebody up on the moon, sent down pictures, and there was a whole lot of braggin' about what got done, but up at Turtle Lake, it took our breath away, seein' those pictures the first time, out of the slip of the moon a drop of water in a sea of darkness, a spirit bubble.

"Spaceship Earth," they were sayin'. Like it was a machine. Take it apart. Make it work better.

A guide from the cities calls us the day after the picture's in the papers.

"Eli," Marty says on the other end. "Did you see it?"

"Yeah, I saw it," I says.

There was a lag on the line, a real disappointed silence.

"You don't sound too excited," he says.

"Tell me what everybody's seein'," I says.

"I got it right here," he says. I could hear him snapping the paper straight. "It says 'Spaceship Earth' right at the bottom. Just look at it. 'Spaceship Earth.'"

I got a big lump in my throat and couldn't say anything.

"Say something," Marty says, and I look around the room. Bear doesn't want the phone.

"I'll call you back," I says, and hung up.

They really think we're idiots.

Like the other night. Some guy invites me to a barbeque. It's a nice thing and we're all havin' a good time—chicken and beans and pie and ice cream. I like this guy—he really gives me a lot of space, doesn't crowd me—but he says some dumb things sometimes. We're up in his place after most everybody else is gone, and I'm standin' up close to a print of Monet's *Water Lilies* he's got on the wall and he comes and stands beside me.

"I got a thing about water," he says. "Archetypal."

I nod. "I like the Impressionists," I say.

We stand there a minute, and then he says, "You ever heard of Carl Jung?"

I catch myself staring into his face, then turn back to the painting and there is a lot of water between us. He'd like a boat to get over to this side, or maybe what he needs is just a paddle, and the boat is already there? Anyway, he coughs, embarrassed.

I want to say, "Kimosabe, fresh tracks! Man with forked tongue come here not long ago."

But instead I say, "It goes way way back with my folks."

"That's funny," he says, and I went outside.

I guess my life is just a load of laughs. I'm a facetious son-of-a-bitch. A real comic. One night a month I go down to the Comedy Club on Seventh and Hennipen—just a stone's throw from *Tonto Town*, what they call Franklin Avenue around here—and there I do standup.

Urban Indians and Other OxyMorons, I call it.

I like the play on the words, Indians and Oxy and Morons, it really gets them. (And it's true: what the hell is an *urban Indian*, anyway?)

I wear the full regalia: Headdress, chaps, and a necklace of plastic quills (I made them from Bic Banana pens).

"A Cigar Store Indian," I say, under the hot, bright lights. I hold myself as erect as I can, pull my arms over my chest, hold up my head. You know, the proud, silent, suffering Indian thing. I do this until I catch some bored looks, then sniffle, run my hand under my nose, stand straight again, look from side to side, as if to see if anyone is watching me, press up with my lungs, so my face is holding a lot of air, straighten again, make like somebody is walking past, and by this time everybody is snorting and when I mimic holding myself up again I let loose with a huge sneeze.

A classic story-line. Attention getter. Small drama. Complication of the drama. Explosion. Denouement. Laughs all around, and I just cut back in.

"You all remember Columbus, right? Sailed the ocean blue." I balance myself as if in a rocking boat, swaying one way and then the other. "They're at sea forever, going this way and that"—I cross my arms over my chest, point in opposite directions—"and somebody sights land. They pull upshore, think they're in the Indies. Some natives greet them with food and drink, and they call them—"

One thousand one, one—

"Indians!" someone in back shouts.

"Right," I say. I got it down to how many seconds it takes for someone to yell. One thousand one is all the further I get, and I pick it up, keep it rolling. "How right you are! And just think what would have happened if old Columbus had taken a left turn there"—I cross my arms one way and then the other, knots, all directions—"when he took a right. He would have sailed right around the coast and into Istanbul, and I guess we all would have been—"

One thousand one, One thousand—

"Turkeys!" someone shouts.

"Which is what Uncle Sam's been callin' us for years anyway, right?"

"Boo," a few people shout.

"You're telling me it's a load of crap! No, I gotta tell you about these guys," I say. "You know how sometimes we get our names from something about us, right? Indians, I mean. Well, there were these two bloods down by the railroad tracks, Muscatel and Night Train, see. Night Train is hunkering down, he's got a bottle.

" 'Big song singing along steel road,' he says.

" 'Gimme that,' Muscatel says, taking the bottle.

"You see, Muscatel is an—"

One thousand one, One thousand—

"Urban Indian!" somebody in back shouts.

"Right! So he doesn't get it. Night Train's wavering back and forth.

" 'Night Train, Night Train, Night Train,' he's sayin'.

"All the while, selfish old Muscatel is taking one long pull after another off that bottle.

" 'You'll get yours,' he says.

"Pow!" I slap my hands together. "The train shoots by."

And always my audience looks stricken. Where's the punchline? What's funny here? I wait until they really are sitting on pins and needles.

"That isn't funny!" my plant yells.

"Try telling that to the bums along that track," I say. "It's the first *red meat* they've had in months. Maybe they'll call the cops down for a look see. 'Hey!' the big cop's yellin', and the bums are up and off the tracks. 'Leave some for me!'

"But seriously, folks, not to worry, it's all a big cycle, right? What comes around goes around. Right? That's an Indian thing. We're all interested in recycling things now, aren't we? They get that stuff off the tracks, dilute it a little bit, and Presto! It goes right back on the shelves. You ever notice that sediment in the bottom of a bottle of Thunderbird?"

· ·

But I was telling you about my *job*.

Days I'm a welder.

I don't have much to do with the men I work for. Joe and Harry. Harry is from the Southside of Chicago, a huge, barrel-chested Irishman, and Joe is from around Ann Arbor, a quiet guy who does the books. But we get along okay. Our shop is off Hennipen and Lake and we do pretty much anything, got a yard in back that'll hold even farm implements and that sort of thing.

I do it all, but they put me on specials now. Hot rods, motorcycles, old cars.

I got the touch. Oxyacetylene, Tig, Arc. You name it, I can lay a bead down so fine it'd take your breath away. It's a thing with me. That's the way it is with welding. You've got to get it all in your head, the thickness of the metal, the temper, how much expansion or shrinkage there'll be, and you've got to know if you're gonna need a heat sink, something to take the heat off if you're going weld hot. Every job is different. Take the implements. Most of it's cast or forged iron. Heavy stuff. You run the amperage up, use a heavier rod to carry that current, and then lay into it like buttering bread. Just a nice even sweep, and you got to, *absolutely* got to, watch for carbon deposits. If you're goin' too hot, your rod will start to burn, will leave big carbon scars and they'll crack. And that's absolutely N. G. Now sheet metal's something else, takes a sharp eye or it'll warp all to hell. Like I said, a heat sink'll work, but there's more to it than that. With sheet metal you got to be able to run that old steel in with the new. There's always some catch to it and some guys end up with work that looks like popcorn's trying to burst through it, all mucked up and lumpy, and then there's people who got a feel for it. Thin rod. Easy on the heat, the right pressure and pull to suck the metal up so when it cools it runs right up with the old. If I told you it was an art you wouldn't believe me, but sometime you should see one of them old-time lead workers or brazers. They may be dumb as dirt, but they got a feel for things.

It's like X-ray vision, and you can see it right away if they got it.

Most anybody can weld implements, and that's why Harry

and Joe hired me. Just another hard-lookin' son-of-a-bitch who could work in the heat and lay a line of weld no better than a load of bird shit. That's the Indian they hired, and I didn't even know any better. I'd been doing implements for nearly a year: diskers, harrowing equipment, tractor axles. Just took it for work.

Then, right around closing time one night, this guy Kosmoski come in. I didn't know him from Adam, but he says,

"Kosmoski," like he's some king or something.

I don't say nothing, and he's looking all around the shop.

"Is Harry in?" he says.

I shook my head. I'd been stuck with closing late, had a combine in back that still needed work.

"What can I do you for?" I says.

So Kosmoski tells me that Harry owes him one, and that there's some kind of big car show in town and he's going to lose his ass if this car isn't done for it. I said I'd try calling Harry at home, and I did, with old Kos there kicking around like a stone in a tin can. Nobody home, so I stuck my neck out, figured Harry would be home later—he was always home, wife and kids.

"Drive it in and we'll get to it," I says.

So Kos goes around through the office and in a minute I hear somethin' roarin' outside and I open the doors. I got a real sinkin' feeling when it come in. I would've figured it for a wreck. The fenders are all buckled up and there's cancer like you wouldn't believe. I got down on my knees and looked up the side, the way I seen auto-body workers, mud slingers, do. I'd read a whole bunch of books once about how you did bodywork and welding.

"So, Chief," Kos says. "Can you do it?"

I shouldn't get pissed off anymore when that happens, but my first reaction was to let him have it with the wrench I was holding. My second was to cut his car in half with the cutting torch. But what changed all that was his askin' *me*. I thought about it for a second.

"Come on in tomorrow noon," I says.

And he went out the garage, just like that. Didn't say a thing. I closed the door, stood there a few minutes wondering what the hell I'd gotten myself into, then threw the wrench against the wall. I went down to Burger King and had a Slopper, and thought about it. I go through these phases, see. It'll all come piling up on me out of nowhere and I'll get this urge to just pull out of this rattrap city, and then I'll go down to the lakes and swim. Sometimes I swim all night in Lake Calhoun, or Lake of the Isles. I just swim, and swim, on my back, looking up at the stars. It burns out of me and then I go on home, only that night I went back to the shop and took a look at Kosmoski's car.

What a rust bucket! I brought a light over so I could see better and got down on my knees. The rocker panels were totally gone. The doglegs, behind the wheels, were gone. Parts of the floor were gone. One of the doors had a hole punched in it, like a big knife had gone through. But I got to looking at that thing, and there was something about it.

It was like a yacht. Long and low, had a huge motor in it and a frame like you'd see on a tractor. It had fins like a headdress in back, standin' up all high like. This car was a goddamned chief, that's what it was all right.

I put the tractor stuff away. Heavy equipment. Got out the arc welder and went into the back for some light-gauge steel. I cleaned up the dogleg in back with a big hydrolic wire wheel, then went at it with a sanding disk. I poked and pulled and filed and shaped all those holes, smoothed them down and straightened them out. It was real quiet (even the drunks from Moby's had gone home) and I cut the first sheet for the doglegs and laid 'em in. I figured the gauge of the metal, done like I seen in the book. Clamped it down, set it in with the hammer, then lay a bead on her like you wouldn't believe. It looked right and I started on the other side, got a bit smaller rod and cut down on the heat. The beads put all that new metal into the old.

Seams. All of it. The new stuff going into the old. That car seemed to shake itself, the way you do tossing off a cold. I went like that until I had those doglegs done, then sanded down the beads all around.

I took a look at the rocker panels. Rockers are under the doors, and on new cars they're flat, and easy—I know that now—but the Chief, his were *round*. A special kind of round, and I thought to quit while I was ahead. I went over the shop, closing up, until there was only one light on right over the Chief.

"Well, Chief," I says. I was about to pull the light off when I figured. *Well, what the hell.*

I measured the rockers, or what was left of them, and scribed them out on flat stock. I cut them down, like I'd seen my mother, Martha, make moccasins. I got this electric feel in my hands and I just couldn't stop. I didn't think nothin', but just let it go, afraid I might lose it. I got on the floor on my back and tacked the rockers on, then heated them until I could wrap them over the old. The metal held, didn't warp or pucker, and then I laid a line on both top and bottom, did the other side in a lick, and stood back.

It was just getting to be morning, and a car roars up.

Harry come through the door and tosses his lunch pail on the desk.

"Don't say anything," he says. "I'm in a *very bad mood.*"

I'm in the office with a cup of coffee and he doesn't even ask what the hell I'm doin' in the shop at five in the morning.

"Did he bring the goddamned car in?"

I nodded.

Harry ripped a page off the calendar on the wall. "Fuckin' horse's ass," he says, and went charging out into the shop.

He was out there the longest time. I could hear the clock on the wall ticking.

"Eli," he finally says through the door. "Come on out here."

I guess that's all I got to say about Harry's. The Chief won first prize in that auto show. Kos got all the glory for the paint job he done on it—all flames and paint lookin' deeper than water, forty coats of hand-rubbed lacquer. But that old Kos is all right. I didn't get no credit, but he sends everything over here now and we got a business arrangement and my pay doubled. It'll do for now. It's hard to put into words what I'm learning in that place, but I got other things going too.

Wednesday nights, I go to AA.

There's some hard-luck stories you wouldn't want to hear down there, much less believe, and I suppose I wouldn't be goin' there if this thing hadn't happened.

There was this fat woman come in one night, and we were all sittin' around the table, coffees shakin' in a lot of dry hands.

Jesus, what a tub of lard, I'm thinking.

So I think to myself, right off, if Fats opens her mouth, I'm gonna space off, leave if I have to. I was half in the mood to leave already. I almost did leave. Went out into the hall for coffee, but come back in.

Around the table, checking in.

Hi, I'm Joe and I'm an alcoholic, and all that.

Hello, Joe, everybody says together and it reminds me of pow-wow. We get through all that stuff, and then there's the life stories. I've heard it all, but it helps sometimes to know you're not crazy, or if you are crazy, that you're not the only one. Well, it gets around to old Fats, and what does she do but go on a filibuster. I was looking right into her face, givin' her some real Indian treatment, of the silent, nasty type, when I started hearing what she was saying. She was talking about some goddamn old slippers.

"I looked all over the place," she says, "all over downtown. I said to myself, 'This time I'm gonna get Mom something she'll really like.' It was really cold, and my feet were freezing. And you know what?"

And I did know what. I sat there, couldn't believe it.

"I never once thought to get myself a pair of good shoes," she says.

I'd said the same thing myself.

"There I was," she says, "Salvation Army clothes, shoes with holes in the bottom, looking for slippers for my mother who was at home with her bottle. She always drank Dickle, and I never thought that a bottle of it would buy a pair of shoes. I just didn't think of it that way."

I got to lookin' in her face. She had a big, round, sad face, her eyes buried way in there. She pulled at her fingers, and as she went on I could see she was really workin' hard.

"—Christmas Eve," she says. "There was the tree, all the lights on it. It looked so pretty and warm and I thought about before Dad left. And I put my box there. A real nice pair of slippers. It was just the two of us, but I felt real lonely, and my mother was sipping at a glass as though it were pop, but I could tell. 'I'm sorry I forgot to get you something, Beck,' she said. 'I'll get you something tomorrow.' 'That's okay,' I said. 'Here,' I said. 'I got this just for you.' 'Oh,' she said, 'Not now. Let's just sit.' 'Come on, Mom,' I said, holding the box out. 'Open it.' Well, she made this face, and jerked the box out of my hand. 'Slippers,' she said, 'Real nice.' "

Funny, but I knew what the rest was too. She was trying not to cry and I leaned over against the table and held my stomach. She coughed a couple times, then finished her out.

"Next day, in the afternoon—" she says, takin' a deep breath. "Some company came over and after supper they sent me out with the trash. I'm standing there in the backyard, burning the trash, when I see the slippers in there, and I reached in and pulled them out."

She held up her hands. "Look," she said, and that's all the further it went. Got burns all over her hands.

Mine never went away neither.

I'm goin' there a year now.

Fridays I'm takin' night classes at the U.

I meet all kinds over there, spoiled kids, weak kids, smart kids, kids who I can tell are trouble already, kids who got as worse as I did but of a different kind, kids who don't care about nothin' and never will.

I'm studying anthropology. The only blood in the college. I'm a real case. Maybe I'll even get the degree—I got enough credits now—but what for? I could tell you all sorts of stuff about primitive community development and how to go about a dig. I can identify the age of an arrowhead by the way it's been cut and pottery by the glaze or lack of it.

But right down from the classrooms are the Projects, and it cuts me real deep to walk by there. It's like a war zone. The Projects got built about twenty years ago, when the Feds figured they owed the Anishinabe some for all the land they took; so they hired contractors, built this concrete jungle, the houses wall-to-wall. It's funny, cause they're always tryin' to show us how figured I was just about over and done for, and then I got the job at Harry's and quit the bottle.

I hadn't thought about it in years. But here it was, stronger than ever, and I was scared.

I had all kinds of crazy things runnin' through my head out there. That Na'mbiza might come up from under, all brassy scales and horns like buffalo, and devour me, that I should go back up north, only to do what I didn't know. I got this feelin' that what I'd learned at Harry's and at school was over, and I had to put it to use. I saw the whole city there, out in the lake, and the sky over it and the trees and the shore like someplace else, all broken into sky, city, and people. A loon called across the lake and it all come back to me, up at Turtle Lake, the reservation there, and I saw how it was all just breakin' apart. I saw myself with the welder in my hands, felt the surge of electricity, the arc as bright and hot as the sun. There was a power there in my hands, just the way Osada had said that time, and here it was, years and years later.

I got this vision. Felt my people under my hands, old metal, felt the new where it had to be. The power of God run through my hands, like electricity, buzzin' and poppin'.

It struck me like lightning, and out there in that lake the current run deep, right into my blood, into the land and my people behind me, and out of nowhere this thing come to me:

Those whom God chooses to love, he first destroys.

Blew us all to pieces, saw it right there on the lake.

I held up my hands and they were shakin'. My whole body was shakin'. I looked at those scars runnin' down the back of my hands.

I reached up into the sky and bawled, and for the first time I knew what I was—

A welder, that's what I was. Somebody to pull things together and lay down the seams.

stupid we are, how out of it—*The Indian Problem*, they call us—and they never so much as asked if we even wanted them houses built like that.

So we smash in the walls, break the windows, spend what welfare we get on new trucks, sittin' shiny out front—what we'd use if we were up north, fishin', but don't need down here. We're at each other's throats with misery, and everybody's mad.

"Goddamn Indians," everybody's sayin'.

Walking by the Projects gets me to thinkin'. Some nights I get to thinking so bad I can't sleep, and then I go on down to the lakes, like I said before.

In the winter I bundle up and walk out there on the ice and just stand until my feet can't take it. Summers I lay on my back, paddle in circles.

Water.

I can see myself, like in that picture Marty sent us, on this little bubble hangin' in space. Everything turns in me, grates away, the Projects, and the shit I take at Harry's, and all the stuff I learned in books. But this is what finally come to me one night out there, turning on my back.

It was a hot one, nearly ninety even after the sun gone down. I'd been in the shop all morning, then hiked up by the Projects and to the U for class, then down to the lakes. I had a night at the club comin' up, and I was feeling pretty lousy about the whole thing, couldn't get nothing funny out of what I'd seen lately and just turned around and around.

I felt like I was comin' apart in that water, like I had all these people floatin' out there with me.

"Quit the job at Harry's," one would say.

And no sooner'n it was out the other would come back, "Now what do you want to do that for?"

It got so I was feelin' like when I went through the DTs—my head on fire, my heart leaping like a fish in my chest, all these voices going around and around. I thought about welding, out there on the lake, and what my step-dad had said way back:

"It's in your hands."

I didn't pay much attention then—I mean, I was so sick I